THE BEAUTIFUL AND THE ABSURD

Stories for Our Times

THE BEAUTIFUL AND THE ABSURD

Stories for Our Times

Freeman J. Wong

 Bestview Scholars Publishing

Published in 2025 by
Bestview Scholars Publishing Ltd.
48 Leafield Dr., Unit B., Toronto, ON M1W 2T2 Canada
Email: bestviewscholars@gmail.com
Website: **www.bestviewscholars.com**

ISBN: 9781896848297
ISBN (epub): 9781896848303
Cover design: Dorothy Tsui
Proofreader: Doreen Martens

Library and Archives Canada Cataloguing in Publication

Title: The beautiful and the absurd: stories for our times / Freeman J. Wong.
Names: Wong, Freeman J., 1956- author
Identifiers: Canadiana (print) 20250192438 | Canadiana (ebook) 20250192446 | ISBN 9781896848297 (softcover) | ISBN 9781896848303 (PDF)
Subjects: LCGFT: Short stories.
Classification: LCC PS8595.O596 B43 2025 | DDC C813/.54—dc23

In this collection, "A Miracle Father Who Shines" is a true story using the subject's real name, Huang Qiao, while "Ray's Favorite Saying" and "Forgotten Favors" are also true stories but use fictitious English names — except that the real name of the main character appears once in each story. Also using fictitious names, "Miracle Reunion" is based on a Chinese self-narrative published in social media, which may be assumed as a true account of lost love regained. All other stories and characters are to be taken as fictional, in which case any resemblance to any person living or dead and to any event known or unknown should be considered purely coincidental. The author thanks Adriana Neil, Alice Huang, and Jeffrey Huang for their invaluable help.

The author's opinions do not necessarily reflect those of the publisher.

This is an original print edition of *The Beautiful and the Absurd: Stories for Our Times*.

Contents

Love and Romance
Miracle Reunion   7
Oh, Life!   13
Triangle Marriage   29
Lover's Shoelace   37

Heartwarming Anecdotes
A Father Who Shines   44
Ray's Favorite Saying   58
Forgotten Favors   68
Love and Joy   77
A Lovely Dental Patient   83

Crime and Punishment
Miracle Escape in Toronto   86
Unbelievable Therapist in the Morgue   93
Heroic Mother and Daughter   108
Surprise Arrests   116
Brutal Animal Cruelty   123
Telling the Truths in the Dark Room   132
Screaming Woman in the Clinic   137

Landlords and Tenants
May and Her Tenants   139
American Dream in the Making   146
Cause of Eric's Tragedy   150
A Landlord Speaks Out   159

Children under Protection
Perfect Candidate for a Bravery Medal   167
Foster Parents at Work   179
Fleeing Father   182
Christmas Gift for Chalway   185
A Fight Between Father and Son   189
Harvard University Boy   193

Parenting at Issue
Never Came Back   201
A Child in Pain   204
"My Daddy Touches Me"   206
A Daughter That Is Not   209
Parents' Meeting on LGBTQ2+ Issues   213

Love and Romance

Miracle Reunion

Accompanied by her daughter and son-in-law, Lady Rosen was patiently waiting in her wheelchair for an appointment with a pulmonologist in the crowded outpatient waiting room. The place lacked not only smiling faces but also space sufficient to move her wheelchair to the registration desk. Instead, her daughter went forward to book a consultation with a specialist, and then pushed her to a less crowded corner near the specialist's office. Rosen glanced at the name on the door, and instantly her heart trembled. The pulmonologist's name was Yeffrey Dunn.

"No, it can't be him," she murmured to herself. "He just happens to have the same name." She shook her head dejectedly. Yeffrey Dunn was an all too familiar name; one she had called out in her dreams at night and sometimes in the daytime, when no one was around. It had been hidden in her heart for more than forty years. She had cried for him often, her tears wetting her pillow at night. No matter how hard she tried, she couldn't suppress her sense of guilt or leave this sadness behind.

Tears came again as her mind wandered back to life forty years ago. Those were called the crazy years. Her parents, both educators, had been labeled "Rightist," one of five types of political enemies of the government. As Rightists, they had been forced to leave the capital, where life was stable and comfortable, and had been sent to the countryside in the Northeast, where hardship would, so it was said, eventually reform their ideology. As children of these political enemies, she and her brother also had to leave their easy life and go to the poor countryside to receive the kind of training that would turn them into better-educated youths, according to the propagated philosophy.

As assigned by the government, at the age of eighteen she arrived with five other high school graduates in a poor village approximately 1100 kilometers northwest of her home city. Her brother went to the Northeast to be closer to their parents, who might need his care. Now, Rosen, who had never done farming or other manual labor, not even cooking, was required to learn to make simple food, such as plain steamed cornmeal or sorghum buns, which she found tasteless. The first month, unable to swallow what she had cooked, she lost more than ten

7

pounds. She was required to carry pails of heavy manure and water on her shoulders, which caused swelling and pain from the first day. She had to dig up soil and spread it over the earthen floor of the stable, one layer of soil on top of a layer of horse manure. The mixture froze in winter but would make good fertilizer for the crops when it defrosted in spring. She had barely filled up the first cartload of dirt when she found her hands covered with blisters.

Seeing this poor girl suffering, her workmate, a twenty-year-old local villager named Darren Dunn, took over her heavy work, asking only that she clean the cart for him. She stood there admiringly as this muscular villager easily threw the heavy pickax that would land deep into the soil, which he would loosen easily. Then he would throw the soil onto the manure effortlessly. He bared his shoulders as he sweated despite the cold. His muscular strength struck a chord in Rosen's heart. How handsome and strong he was! From then on, they always worked together happily. Life began to improve for her, as he always took over her heavy work and did a double job himself. Before long she had integrated into the life of the village.

As the best-educated person among the graduates, Rosen was eventually given a job teaching in the village school. But she continued to have a special relationship with Darren, who also enjoyed being with her. She liked him for various reasons, one being that he often sent her delicious food, which was scarce in those days.

Then came this night when Darren visited her and said, "The township head's daughter has proposed to me. I don't know whether I should accept her or reject her." Rosen looked at him for a while. Their eyes met.

I can't let another woman take away a man I love! she told herself. Indeed, she had been struggling with the choice of whether to accept Darren and spend the rest of her life in this village. Life here could not be compared with that in the capital. But she wasn't sure if she would ever even have a chance to go back to her home city. Her heart pounded fast. Then she threw herself into his arms, caring about nothing in the world except their love. They stood wrapped in each other's arms for a long while, their youthful blood boiling. They made love that night, their first love.

She was a happy young woman now—enjoying true love and being loved. They married the next year. Two years later, their son Yeffrey Dunn was born, making her a happy mother. She felt she was the

8

happiest person in the world, being loved by a man she deeply loved, and with a lovely son to love day and night.

Then came an unexpected change in government policy. All educated young people who had been sent to the countryside to do hard labor could return to their home cities. Rosen's parents and her brother had returned to the capital. Like others, she was also eligible to take the national college examination and, if she passed, could go to university. Though her parents had heard about her marriage, they sent a letter recommending that she try the national exam. Otherwise, she might have to stay in the countryside and live this life of poverty forever.

She didn't know what to do. As a wife and mother in the countryside, her residence no longer belonged to the city. Besides, she couldn't pass the exam without sufficient preparation. Her husband, who had accidentally found the letter she had hidden under the bed sheet, noted her tossing and turning in bed and read her mind.

"I know the difficult decision you have to make," he told her. "I don't really want to force you to stay in this poor village. If you decide to return to the capital, we will just get a divorce."

She cried that whole night. Three days later, they got their divorce papers. She left the village before dawn the next day, without letting anyone know she was leaving. But first, she kissed her soundly sleeping son, tears gushing down her cheeks. "What a mother I am!" she berated herself, sobbing all the way back to her home city.

Back at her parents' home, she reviewed all the high school subjects and, as expected, passed the national college examination. She was admitted into Beijing Shifan University, or Beijing Normal University.

After graduation, she married one of her classmates. But he was not like her ex-husband, lacking his muscular strength. She missed the degree of understanding and intimacy she had enjoyed in her first marriage. Despite the gap between them, the couple had two girls together, and the marriage survived until the daughters graduated from university and became independent. Then she divorced him, at the age of fifty-two.

Single again, she missed her son and her first husband all the more. She thought of going back to see them and begging their forgiveness, perhaps even remarrying her first husband, if he happened to be single too, and bringing them to the city. But guilt and shame held her back. *I'll see them again in the next world instead,* she told herself.

The pulmonologist was wearing a mask that covered much of his face. He was clearly a knowledgeable specialist, who had a great manner with his elderly patient, full of love and compassion. She did not want to leave him, though she had no reason to stay any longer and he had so many other patients to see.

She thanked him again as she was wheeling herself out, but paused when she saw the name again on the door. Yeffrey Dunn. *It can't be my son,* she said to herself. *My husband was not a very well-educated man. He couldn't have educated my son so well and sent him to a famous university that trained him to be such a great pulmonologist.*

About to give up for the second time, she whispered to herself, "Nothing to be ashamed of, even if he is not my son! No shame can compare with what I have done to my son!" She felt a strong current running through her back and then all over her body. She raised her head, wheeled herself toward the doctor again, and looked into his eyes.

"Excuse me, Doctor," she said, "I'd like to talk with you for two or three minutes if I may. I hope you don't mind."

"It's all right. Anything else you need to clarify?"

She tried to calm herself and speak as serenely as she could. "I am a teacher in Ziujoeng District of this city. I settled in Tingawan Village in Simsai after graduating from high school many years ago. There I married a young man called Darren Dunn and I gave birth to a boy, called Yeffrey Dunn. Then, the government policy changed, and I came back to the capital city. Because of this, my son and I have been separated for more than forty years. I have missed him day and night for forty years! And I am missing him even more now as I am getting older and older. When I saw your name, I thought, could it be God's blessing for me? May I ask where you are from, Doctor, if you can forgive my liberty?"

The room fell utterly silent. Her daughter and son-in-law stared at her as if they were strangers, for they had never heard of this decades-old secret.

Dr. Yeffrey Dunn sat quietly, looking blank, saying not a word for at least half a minute. Deeply disappointed, Rosen was about to wheel away from him when she saw him slowly remove the mask from his face, tears welling in his eyes. He rose to his feet and said in a shaky voice, "I am no other Yeffrey Dunn. I am your very son Yeffrey Dunn! I am from Tingawan. My father is Darren Dunn. It is more than forty long years. Why didn't you even once come and see me? What held you back? My cruel mother!" He broke down and could not speak anymore.

Rosen felt her head spinning, her body collapsing. Her daughter caught her just in time to keep her from toppling from the chair onto the floor.

Recovering, Rosen burst into tears, overcome simultaneously by happiness and guilt. "It was not because Mom didn't want to see you, but because she felt too ashamed of herself to face you and your father, my child! How many days and nights I cried to myself! Mom was drowning in guilt. Mom let you both down. Mom did not dare ask for your forgiveness. Having this opportunity to see you and to know you have established yourself has brought me more joy than I could ever have expected."

Tears streaming down his cheeks, her son walked up to her and bent down to take her in his arms. She collapsed into his embrace, wailing. After forty years of separation, they clung to each other, and the others in the room shed happy tears at seeing this unexpected reunion.

When he finished his morning shift, her son joined the other three and they went to a quiet restaurant for lunch. They had so much to tell each other. After she left, Yeffrey explained, his father married another woman. He was ten at the time. His stepmother gave birth to a girl, giving him a sister, but because she often abused him, the marriage broke up. His father brought him up alone, giving him the best education he could, which ultimately helped him get into Beijing Medical University. "My father is living with us here," he told her.

"Will you really forgive me?" she asked him.

"Mom," her son said with tender love, "you are seventy-two now. Do you have time for me to hate you? You didn't care about any of that today, but fearlessly asked who I was and then accepted me. It's clear you never forgot me. This already makes me a very happy son, Mom."

Several days later, she visited her son's home and met her daughter-in-law and her grandson, who was already a university student. She also saw Darren, the man she had missed day and night for all these years. They greeted each other with a tight hug and, like his son, he told her he forgave her. Knowing that she had felt tremendous guilt all her life, he even comforted her. "Everything was caused by the government policies of those years," he said. "It's God's second blessing for us that we are reunited in our seventies. We should enjoy the remaining years of our lives and not waste any precious time."

A few days later, the old parents received their second marriage license and became a legally married couple again, after which Rosen told her friends, "For the rest of my life I shall do whatever I can to make up for whatever I have owed them and bring warmth and joy to the two men I love most in this world."

Oh, Life!

In this story, which begins forty years ago, I will call you Sunshine to protect your privacy. This name reflects much of your personality.

Dear Sunshine, it was good to be young, wasn't it? After I had suffered my embarrassing setback in dating another woman, I met you in your hometown, Tricapital. It was God's arrangement that we met while I was attending a conference at your university. Immediately I felt like a new man, believing that after all my setbacks in life, I had found the girl God had created for me! Happy events come in twos! I was equally delighted I spotted your friend Flora, who was the girl my good friend Yale was waiting for. I'll pause a second to thank you for introducing her to my friend. They got married later and have been a happy couple since. You and I did them a favor, and their happiness was a favor for me, too. So my trip to Tricapital turned out to be a double-happy event. Soaked in love, I thanked Heaven for having created a perfect girl for me.

As the old cliché says, it was love at first sight. The moment I met you, you felt like an old friend. You seemed to read my mind. You seemed to enter my soul. You seemed to know me inside out. You trusted me. You gave me hope. You instilled confidence in me. I felt secure. I felt appreciated. I felt blessed. You were the girl whom I would work for, fight for, and die for. That gave me the courage to approach you. Oh, that sweet smile on your face! Oh, those shy but brave giggles! Oh, those dignified chuckles!

Then we greeted each other. Then we chatted. Then we talked. Then a love story started—in your fourth year in university. I knew I loved you and you knew you loved me. I knew I was a good man who would make a good husband. You knew you were a decent girl who would make a loving wife, who would be loved in return. We were confident we could make a loving couple whom others would admire. My imagination was wild and boundless. Did you know all of this? Perhaps you did not. How could a man tell a young lady his feelings within such a short time? Would the average woman believe him? Would it be good to say these things in a relationship that had hardly started?

I have nothing to be ashamed of. I was a young man. A young man has feelings. A young man feels love when he is in love. A young man feels loved when he is loved. A young man who finds love wants it to develop into happiness—lifetime happiness. Joy was spilling out of my body. It was a feeling I had never had with any other girl. I was your first love, and you were my first love. You would have all my true love, as I would have yours.

That Afternoon

Soon came the afternoon when we met in my hotel room, next to your university. We were sitting on the edge of the bed, holding each other's hands. We were deep in conversation when we suddenly heard banging on the door. It sounded so urgent. I knew if we did not open it for them, they would kick it open. If it took us too long to open it, we could be detained by the police and accused of engaging in illegal activities— namely prostitution, a shameful crime at that time.

How long would be considered too long? The time it would take for a sleeping couple to get up from bed and quickly dress—that would be considered too long. That long would warrant any action they wanted to take. Thank heaven we did not do anything of that sort. We were not in bed, and we were fully dressed. I dashed to the door, realizing that I might look like an excited or roused young man, rather than someone walking on the street. The two rude men in the doorway stared first at you, then me. They evidently decided that we were in a dating relationship and ruled out the possibility of prostitution in the room. After checking our IDs, they finally left us alone.

Good heavens! I heaved a deep sigh of relief after they left, seriously displeased at their intrusion. Just imagine, Sunshine, if we were like some of those other young daters who got caught having sex before marriage—what consequences might we have faced? I shivered at the thought. You were still a student, and I was a university teacher. Society expected me to be a role model, not only for students, but for the general public. In the worst scenario, we might have ended up being paraded on the street or being dragged naked to the police station, with our crime being publicized through our two universities!

Then you invited me to meet your parents. I knew obtaining their consent could be a challenge, but I had full confidence in you. Finally, they gave us conditional consent, though young people in Canton were negatively labeled as liberal-minded, loose daters, like people in the

14

West. Today, when you look back and see how Yale and I behave, you know that it was unfair for your or Flora's parents to even question our personality or morality. Yale and I were, and still are, among the most traditional, decent men, the kind not easy to find anywhere. However, I fully understood your parents and would not blame them for being skeptical about me. After a happy stay in Tricapital, I returned to Canton.

Never had I been so happy in my life! I was so very proud of having found a good girlfriend. I beamed all day long. I thought of you all the time, even when I was teaching. Interestingly, this did not affect my work. In fact, I think it improved it. I could not see what I looked like when I smiled and chuckled, thinking of you, but I could feel that every cell in my body was filled with joy. I walked with confident steps, square shoulders, my head held high. I felt strength all over my body. I became nicer and kinder to my students, colleagues, friends, and even strangers.

Every morning I would go to see my old friend Yale, and then we would queue up in front of a snack cart to buy steamed rice-paste rolls for breakfast. While waiting to be served, Yale and I would talk about how you and Flora were doing. Those were always the happiest moments of our day. We were each waiting for our girlfriend to graduate and come to join us in Canton, or rather, marry us. In one of our last conversations, you lovingly joked that you had to listen to me regarding your employment arrangements upon graduation. I pointed out that our insistence on the move to Canton was not a matter of Yale and me being selfish or dominant, but rather the reality that it was simply the best choice. Yale and I had finished our graduate studies, and we each had a job that could support a family, but you and Flora still had to find work, and finding a good job was not easy. Needless to say, finding two jobs would be much more difficult, especially in Tricapital, where employment opportunities for foreign languages graduates were not plentiful. You agreed and assured me that you did not mean to complain about anything.

The most exciting event of this period was receiving a letter from you. We wrote to each other regularly. I knew I was bad at writing love letters, but every word I said was honest and sincere. Then, most exciting of all, you and your father came to visit me in Canton during the following vacation. I was so grateful to you for your visit, for being so close to me, for giving me such a happy time. For one thing, your visit confirmed that our relationship was developing, and for another, your father's coming with you in itself seemed to show his support for our relationship. Since it was vacation time, we enjoyed more private moments inside and outside of my residence, especially near the university pond when no one was around. We hugged and kissed like other lovers did. Your father had come to protect you, but we still found opportunities to hold each other intimately. Then, to my disbelief, he even permitted us to travel to a rural scenic spot by ourselves and stay there overnight.

That Night

It was a night I cannot forget. It was a night you cannot forget. That night, you cuddled in my arms; we were ready for our first holy intimacy, our first moment of pleasure—our first night. We had checked into two rooms in the hotel. Soon after we went to sleep, the hotel worker came to our rooms to check our IDs and other documents, just like the Tricapital workers did. Wasn't that annoying? Needless to say, as lovers we missed each other when we were alone in bed. I would be lying if I denied it. We were normal, healthy young lovers who yearned for each other. I don't think it was anything to be ashamed of.

The hotel was a simple building and there was no extra security door or gate anywhere. You felt scared after we went our separate ways to bed. I was afraid someone might break into your room and hurt you. A few moments later, I heard your door creaking and, to my happy surprise, you came to my room to join me. Of course, I hadn't locked my door, making it easy for you to enter.

"I'm scared," you told me.

"Come and lie here with me," I said.

So you got into my bed, but we kept our clothes on. I knew how cruel the justice system could be. Not that I was afraid of it, but it could ruin our long-term happiness. You can imagine what opportunity your coming to my room offered for a young man who loved a girl madly! At this moment we were ready to give our bodies to each other, to confirm our commitment to a permanent relationship—marriage and a family. When you asked if we should have some real intimacy, I was really grateful, but God! What kind of justice system were we living with?! In pain I shamefacedly said, "If we do it, we may not be able to go back to my university tomorrow." I really wanted to confirm my commitment to you, but it was a risk we could not afford—one that ultimately could ruin our relationship! At this torturous moment, I thought of the hotel worker who

16

had come to our rooms to check our documents. We had no marriage license to show them. I also thought of the two hostile hotel workers in Tricapital. All hotels were charged by the government with a duty to watch for "sex offenders," which in effect meant that unless a couple showed their marriage license, they were not allowed to be in the same bed. I was burning with fire—the pure fire of a devoted man who loved a wife-to-be. In fact, we were already running a significant risk simply by lying in the same bed. We could be arrested just for that.

To be caught naked in bed would be disastrous. I could be charged with seducing a student into a sexual relationship. I could even be detained for a few days, in which case to get out of detention would take my university administrators coming to take me back. Even a one-day detention would be too much for our relationship. Your father was staying at my home in the university residence by himself. If we got into trouble and could not return to him as scheduled, he would not even know what had happened to us. (There was no cellphone and no internet at that time.) He did not even know where to buy food for himself the next morning.

Worse still, if I was accused of such a disgraceful crime, I might even lose my job. If I lost my job, though we might not starve to death, transferring you to Canton would become a nightmare. In those days young people were shackled, morally and sometimes physically, by outdated ideology. Protecting you from harm and transferring you to Canton was the top priority, so we endured a night of anxiety and disappointment. Holding you against my body, I lay awake the whole night, waiting for the hotel worker to knock on our door again.

But I had no fear. We were not doing anything illegal. We were still dressed, and I knew if they caught us in bed, we could still defend ourselves—because you were too scared in the strange room and had to be with me.

To our relief, he did not come to bother us again that night. When day broke and we got up, I felt regret. If we had made love, we would have enjoyed ourselves and could still return to Canton without trouble. Oh, life! You never know!

This has been a life mystery for me: What did you think of me after that night? Were you happy for having a boyfriend like me, or were you disappointed? If you understood me, I would be grateful. If you thought I was a hesitant, indecisive man and were disappointed with me, I would not blame you.

After your visit, I began to look for connections to bring you to Canton upon your graduation. It was a great challenge to transfer anyone from another city to Canton, a more developed city. The personnel department of the provincial government controlled all the staff transfers. My university was under "double-layer" administration, namely, the national Ministry of Education and the Department of Higher Education of the province. As I mentioned to you previously, the mother of a young woman I had almost married happened to be the head of the Personnel Division of the provincial higher education department. She had the authority to block your transfer to Canton. As long as I worked for the university, whether or not you were coming to work for my university, any application for your transfer would require her approval. It was a cause for concern, but I did not believe she would have the ability to ruin our happy life. Definitely I would bring you to Canton, one way or another.

In a positive tone, a good friend told me that he had a friend working in that same personnel division, albeit at a lower position. I was not living at anyone's mercy. I was making a living by doing first-class work. For you, if necessary, I was ready to take up any other job that would enable you to come to Canton. I could even quit my teaching job and work in a foreign trade company in Canton, or even as a sales manager for a shoe factory. We could also move to another city, or even out of the country altogether. You were not a materialistic girl, I thought, so making a living was not an issue wherever we went.

Love, oh, love! The power of love! The power of hope! The waiting for the good to come! It was less than a year between our first meeting and your graduation, but every day seemed as long as a year for me. It was anxious waiting, painful waiting, and happy waiting.

That moment

It was a moment I cannot forget. It was a moment you cannot forget. Regrettably we did not have our first night at the beach hotel, but the time would come soon. Our long days of waiting would soon be over. I had learned from my good friend that Flora had just finished her last examination at university. She and you were in the same year, so her coursework completion meant yours as well. That was the day I had been waiting for. Happiness would no longer be just a possibility for us, but soon a reality. I rushed to a phone booth to call and congratulate you on the completion of your coursework and to discuss your transfer to Canton, where we would live happily forever. I knew it wouldn't be immediate, because you had to find a job in Canton and have the new employer send a transfer letter to Tricapital, but I wanted to arrange a temporary visit first: either for you to come to see me, or vice versa. This time when we met, things would be different. We would not worry about being caught sleeping in the same bed anymore, because we loved each other and wanted to get married. We could also have a baby, if you became pregnant.

Then, as in a tragic love story in a movie or novel, came the crushing blow. You told me you had decided not to come to Canton. When I asked you if you meant to end our relationship, you said yes, and that you were firm on the decision. This thunderbolt struck me dumb. At that moment, my mind went blank, and later I was unable to remember anything you told me or I told you or what happened to me after that. The happiest man in the world instantly seemed dead and gone. A furnace of molten steel suddenly turned into a cold lump. The only thing I remember now is that I went to tell my good friend about the sad news: "Sunshine does not want to come to Canton. She is not mine anymore."

You had graduated, and you had matured. You were my first love. You were my only love. You were what I had been waiting for and dreaming of. Now you had made the decision, and I had to respect it.

I do not remember how I survived the fatal blow. There remains a blank period in my memory during which I cannot recall what I did or what happened to me or around me.

Wasn't it ironic? You and I had been reading stories and novels. And what had happened to us was just like something we had read. Look how we met, developed our relationship, lay in bed together, preparing for a reunion that was to last for a lifetime—and then came the sudden end! When I finally recovered from my mental meltdown, I realized that in matters of love I was an unfortunate man. But I did not blame you. I knew there must be reasons why you made this decision.

Though our courtship seemed short, it brought me joy and happiness that I would cherish forever. I treasure all the sweet memories. By the same token, I am writing this story lest my memory fail me in the future. Forty years later, instead of talking love, we may talk about the meaning of love.

I have tasted firsthand the sweetness and bitterness of love. I started dating at a late age, and I had little experience. I had missed opportunities. Your cruel blow not only struck me dumb but also woke me up. I realized it was like karma for me. There were girls who liked me and waited for me for a long time, but I did not know or did not share their feelings, so I had let them down. In this case, I deserved some punishment. There were girls I liked and wanted to develop a relationship with, but they did not like me due to my second-class rural resident-ship and because I had a mother to support, whom many girls considered a financial burden. There were other good girls and good families who liked me, but I did not accept them for various reasons, including bad ones. It was after I had experienced all these setbacks that I met you, fell in love with you, and eventually lost you. I took losing you as karmic punishment for everything I did not handle well in the past—I deserved it.

Your final decision left me a broken man, but since evidently you were happier with another man, I should be satisfied. Strange to say, my love for you had previously overflowed to several special groups of people in my life. After I met you, I liked anything and anybody that had something to do with the places where we had spent time together or with your name. *Chuan*, part of your province's name, became a special word for me. Before our breakup, I had thought that if *Chuan* was part of a student's name, I wouldn't mind giving that student a ten percent bonus mark for a reasonably good assignment. If they had your surname, they could receive another ten percent bonus. If someone looked like you and came from Tricapital, she should receive a bonus of up to thirty percent, and if her entire name happened to be the same as yours, a bonus of up to fifty percent could be considered.

Was there any logic to this? Unknown. Did it violate academic integrity? Definitely. Was any bonus ever given to any student? No. Yet, you can see the power of love—it can cause a lover to become irrational and do unethical things.

But now, my mind froze, my heart froze, my blood froze. I had become a different person. I became indifferent, dejected, depressed.

Your second surprise decision came too late. A girl who had endured the pressure of her family and friends picked up your deserted man for her life partner. I was equally surprised that she thought I was a worthy choice, but in the absence of love and hope, I enjoyed being liked and found it consoling. I liked her because I thought she had a unique ability to judge that I was not bad husband material, unlike the previous girls who complained about my family openly even while we were dating. The irony is that my mother, whom many girls worried about, does not even want to live with me. She prefers living in the countryside. She came to live with us in Canton for a month after my first child was born, but she was very unhappy and cried a lot until she went back home. She cried again when she came to stay with us in Toronto, so she went back home and became a happy mother again, living in her native village. She dislikes the cities as much as city women dislike mothers-in-law from the countryside.

The sad truth is that when you called me about your new trip to Canton I had committed myself to the new girlfriend. She was a good person, and I could not betray her. Worst of all, unlike the days when I was yearning for you, my blood had stopped boiling and my body had become cold. That was the reason we could not restart our relationship. Thus, this all became a lifetime regret for you and me.

Unfortunately, our love relationship ended, and we each ended up in an imperfect marriage. You think of your first love, who will think of you, especially during unhappy moments in your new life, especially when either is misunderstood or mistreated by the new spouse.

Forty years later, we still miss each other, as very special friends. We still want to know about each other's life. I know you have a lovely daughter who has grown up and become independent. I am sure Yale and Flora have told you that I also have children, who are all good, talented, and independent. If I do not look in the mirror, I feel as young as I was when we were dating. If I do, I know I am old and ugly, with gray hair and even sun spots. If age has taught me anything, it is that love is one thing and marriage is another. Love keeps you young forever, but marriage makes you old quickly. Nonetheless, even if you are not the happiest person in the world, if you are married but still have a man or woman to think about when you are alone, you are a fortunate person.

That Email

It was an email I can't forget; it was an email you can't forget. It was an email I dared not answer; it was an email you dared not answer. Your life remains a secret to me, and mine remains a mystery to you. I am embarrassed to say that a love story that has taken forty years to write is only as good as this.

That day in 2008, your university friend from Montreal emailed me and mentioned your name. He was unknown to me, so I thought perhaps a scammer was attempting to take advantage of our old relationship. Therefore, I told him that the owner of the email account was not available. In his second email he provided details about you that convinced me he was a decent person. Using your own words, he asked if I had forgotten you, "a floating cloud in the sky, one of the many girls you had met." It sounded quite offensive to me, but I did not mind. Forget you? How could I!

"She had almost become my wife," I said to him. "How could I ever forget her!" Then, he and I chatted on the phone. At his request, I authorized him to pass on my email address to you. The following day I received a long-awaited email, telling me about your marriage and life. I felt so happy for you for having a promising daughter who was studying in the United States. This email confirmed that you still missed me, as much as I missed you, even after marriage. We should have become a couple, but fate first teased us and then separated us. Feelings are not suppressible. It is normal to regret something you have not done right. This just happened to be such an important thing that we had not done right. It is a lifetime regret that will cling to our souls until death.

When we lose something valuable, we miss it. When we lose someone special, we miss them. The more we love a person, the more we miss them. Such feelings may be so strong that we are not even afraid of letting husbands and wives know about them. The best way for them to deal with us is to leave us alone, so they will be less frustrated. If they complain and fight over such issues, that will only bring more trouble.

For childless couples, the solution is easier. Divorce is their answer. For couples with children, things are different. A broken relationship brings great harm to the offspring. Children whose parents do not love each other often lack self-confidence and self-esteem, and many suffer. That is why many loveless couples remain married—just for the sake of their children. The common saying goes, "Mothers are the greatest people in the world." But fathers can be equally great. We both have children. Fortunately, they are all well-behaved, great children who make us proud. A divorce for me is unthinkable. Like many other couples, it is for our children that we choose to stay married and try to live happily.

That day when your email finally came, I was thrilled at seeing your name. I was shocked and disappointed that you were not one hundred percent happy with your second man, but it also consoled me that you still loved me, as I did you. If only I had known this early enough! My immediate response to your email was a long sigh—"Oh, life!"

You did not reply to me anymore. Not long after, my Yahoo email account was hacked and all the emails, including yours, disappeared. Again, we were lost in the dark.

I have tried to find your email address through several friends and acquaintances, but in vain. It is January 2025, and this is the 40th year since our first date, and I am still waiting. If I cannot find you and if you happen to read this story, could you please send me a line to the same Yahoo email address?

That Conversation

Despite all challenges, time still flies. Every day, the sun rises in the morning and sets in the evening. Our dates remain fresh in my mind as if they just happened recently. When you are busy, you get old without knowing it.

But why did you end our relationship? I've continued to wonder why over the past forty years. On my last birthday, I thought, "If I don't find the answer to this lifetime mystery, I will have to find it in the next world." After Chinese New Year, I decided to make one more attempt.

As luck would have it, a happy surprise appeared in my Yahoo email last Saturday. An internet friend of mine from your neighboring city shared with me stories of her recent success at work and in life. I was thrilled and wrote back to congratulate her. Hoping against hope, at the end of my email I gave her your name and your year of graduation and asked if she could find your contact information for me. To my disbelief, the next morning she sent me your details. I trembled at seeing your name and phone number. It was more precious than a winning Lotto ticket for $100 million. I knew that the life mystery would be solved and my life would change soon.

Because of the time difference, I waited until evening to contact you. IPhones can do video calls, so I tried to call you, but it failed to connect. I tried twice more but still could not reach you. I knew the two communication systems were not compatible, so I decided to try my landline in my other house the next day. That is the line I use to call my mother and other friends in Asia, and the connection is guaranteed.

Knowing there was a 12-hour time difference, I planned to call you in the morning.

After breakfast I went back to the smaller house, but the traffic was really slow, for the streets were covered with piles and piles of snow. By the time I sat by the old phone, it was already 10:10 p.m. in your city. If it were any other friend, I would not call at this hour, but you were no ordinary friend and I knew you would not mind. I decided to call you right away, for I did not want to wait another day.

My heart pounded fast when I heard the first ring and then the second. Thank heaven! I heard you pick up the phone, but I heard no voice. I knew you were at the other end, so I called out, "Sunshine."

You responded, and I melted into happiness, trembling.

"Why is your voice so hoarse?" you asked.

"I may have caught a cold," I said, but the real reason was my lack of sleep with the excitement at being reconnected with you. I wanted an answer to the mystery. This was the moment I had been waiting for for forty years.

"Sunshine, I don't know whether we should cry or laugh. And I don't even know how to begin our conversation. It has been so many years, and there is so much I want to talk about. But I will just ask you this question first: "Why did you decide to end our relationship that day, forty years ago?"

"What?" you screamed. "It was you who broke up our relationship!"

"I was dumbfounded when you abruptly ended our relationship," I said, but with this strange counter-accusation my excitement immediately became nervousness and then sadness. I knew something very bad must have happened between you and me, something that led to this separation. I not only got no answer to my simple, straightforward question, but now I was somehow having to defend myself.

"Let's be fair, Sunshine," I said, "Upon your graduation from university, I called you to congratulate you and wanted to discuss your transfer to Canton, but you said you did not want to come. When I asked if you meant to end our relationship, you said yes."

"That was not the case," you said. "You betrayed me. You were dating another girl from your hometown, introduced to you by an acquaintance from your hometown, all the while we were dating."

"Oh, God, Sunshine," I said, "that's not true. You know me well. None of the three facts you mentioned is true. First, I was not dating any other girl while we were dating. You were the only girl I dated and loved. I did

24

not even know any other girl. Second, there was no girl from my hometown. Third, no one from my hometown had ever introduced a girl to me."

"Isn't that girl your wife?" you asked.

"You must trust me on this. If I have done something, I will admit it, but you can't accuse me of dating another girl while I was dating you. It is a matter of principle. The fact of the matter is that it was some time after you decided to end our relationship that I got to know her, in a night class. She was not introduced to me by anyone, and she is not from my hometown."

"She is from Canton, then?" you said.

"She's from a neighboring city," I said. "You deserted me. Your decision paralyzed me. Another man would have committed suicide. We almost got married that night when we were at the hotel in—what city was it?"

You named the city, and I was so happy to hear it. At this moment I realized I had lost memory of some events after I was struck by the sudden ending of our relationship.

"I just thought that you must have found a better man than me, and if that was the case, I just had to respect your decision," I said. "I stood in front of the phone for a long time, not knowing what had happened and why. Then I thought, if we had made love that night, could it have saved our relationship?"

"It could have made things even more complicated," you said hesitantly.

"I was worried about that possibility too," I said. "If we did it and if you changed your mind, I would have felt really guilty."

"Why did you send all my letters back to me?" you accused. "Do you know I threw up when I received that package? It's a normal reaction to such an act."

"Oh, my!" I was speechless for a moment. "I am sorry. It was my fault." In fact, I hadn't even remembered doing that. It didn't register in my memory, just as I had forgotten the city's name. Now I realized that I might really have had a mental meltdown due to the emotional blow of losing you. I was similarly confused about certain details, such as the sequence of events, as Yale pointed out afterward.

Then you made me really uneasy. "In those days, we relied on letter mail for communication and I would have had to take a bus to call you long distance," you said. "I don't remember saying I had decided to end our relationship."

"Oh, life!" I screamed helplessly. "What an unfortunate man I was. It was like you put me in a garage sale, sold me off cheap. I was sure you had found a much better man than me, someone from a government official's family maybe. I know I was from a rural place, and as I realize now, I also presented you with an unfair condition—that we would live with my mother. I know I had plenty of faults that your parents and friends could find."

"They conducted an investigation to check your background," you said.

"Oh, my God!" I said dejectedly. "That was why! I did not marry this young woman whose mother happened to be the head of the personnel division, which at the time controlled which people from outside the province would be permitted to join their spouses working in the universities and colleges in Canton. She was the person who would most likely conduct the investigation against me. In fact, I was expecting such an investigation, but I was still shocked at hearing about it. I would not be surprised if that woman and her mother tried to ruin my reputation and my life. I was even prepared to quit my teaching job and go work for a private business if they blocked your transfer. The pay would be five or six times as much as what a university lecturer earned. We would make a living one way or another. I had told you about everything, including that woman."

"My parents said they would break my legs if I married you," you said.

"Oh my God, but why didn't you tell me about that?" I said, feeling really hurt, but you did not answer.

"Why didn't you reply to my friend in Montreal who emailed you?" you asked another question.

"My youngest child was only six or seven years old," I said. "If we got together, that would only mean two broken families. That would be devastating to the children of two families. That is why I only answered your email in two words: 'Oh, life!' I wanted to write more to you later, but all the Yahoo email accounts were hacked not long after. As a result, every account holder had lost their email contacts. My old emails were all lost, including yours and your friend's. After that, there was no way I could get in touch with you anymore. Even your university friend Flora in America didn't have your contact information."

"How could she not have it?" you said.

"I have no idea," said I.

"I know I was like a princess," you said. "I could not take care of people. I was not a good cook."

"Come on! Those things were never a problem. They were never in my mind. We could always learn together," I said.

"I was told that men from the region were dominant," you said.

"Now I know what was going on and why our relationship ended," I said. "There were people who tried to break us up. They might have been love rivals, parents, relatives, friends, acquaintances—and more likely, retaliation by the woman I had dated previously. Collectively or individually, all of them may have contributed to ending our relationship. In classic love tragedies, the worst cases involve killing a rival, or ruining their reputation, until the young couple is separated for good. It happens all the time, everywhere, in every country."

"Everything was chaotic," you said. "Everything was crazy. But anyway, in a way, you were like my mentor," you said.

"Come on, your mentor!" I scoffed. "I wasn't even qualified to be your boyfriend or husband!"

"It was you who brought me to the more developed cities, where I eventually grew to be the person I am today."

"I just want to let you know that I have no hard feelings, and that I enjoyed every moment when we were together."

Then, you also told me about your deep feelings for the places we had visited and things we had done together. You appeared to have answered the forty-year-old question, but some things still remained a mystery to me.

We wanted to ask about each other's work, but it was already midnight in your city. We decided to end our conversation, but I abruptly asked, "Is it better that we have talked?"

"Yes," you said, "It's like a movie."

"It is indeed!" I said.

Reunion

Logically, as soon as we could, we met, hugged, kissed, and made love for the first time, in the same beach hotel in the same city where we slept with our clothes on forty years ago. There we became as young as four decades ago and enjoyed every moment of our reunion, free of fear. Oh, love! Pure love! True love!

Alternatively, at the earliest time possible, we met in a luxurious hotel where we spent another unforgettable night together. We hugged, kissed, and lay in the same bed with you cuddling in my arms, but again we kept our clothes on, sleeping together without making love. That is called love without sex. Oh, love! Pure love! True love!

The reader is free to choose whichever reunion they prefer for us.

Today, I understand that everything has been prearranged by heaven, and that there is a pattern in the arrangements. As I see it, no marriage is perfect. If perfect lovers were ever to exist, they could not marry each other without suffering. Imperfection is the nature of marriage. If you don't accept that, you will have to stay in love forever without marriage.

I thank heaven that you and I are now reunited, albeit late. We still feel blessed that after forty years of separation we have returned to each other's arms. Does our reunion rank above the average marriage? Being a man of gratitude, I am thankful for all these arrangements.

After all, we are just like actors in a movie.

Triangle Marriage

A trial that was scheduled to start in the B.C. Supreme Court abruptly ended. The jurors were immediately dismissed without knowing what had happened.

Lane, an attractive woman, married Huchard, a talented programmer, in their hometown on the edge of the Pacific. The next year, she gave birth to their first child, after which, for a better life, Huchard immigrated to Richmond, B.C., Canada. After he received permanent residence in Canada, Huchard sponsored Lane and their child to come join him. They reunited with him in Richmond in 2005.

Lane, who had attended a trade school in her native country, could barely speak English, so finding a high-paying job was nearly impossible for her. Besides, hiring a good babysitter would cost even more than she might earn in a minimum-wage job. She chose to be a full-time mother and homemaker instead. IT professionals were in demand and Huchard's income was good, sufficient to guarantee the family a comfortable life, even with a mortgage. The following year, their second child was born.

Lane, who became much busier now, sought help from her parents, asking them to come to Canada to help with household chores. They agreed, and so the young couple invited them on a visitor visa. Needless to say, covering the needs of a second child and parents who were now living with them required a significant amount of money. To add to the already heavy burden, Huchard unexpectedly had to switch jobs, which resulted in a large reduction in income.

Lane felt she had to go out to work to help support the family, but a foreign trade-school certificate was not enough for her to land a good job. Even a college diploma might not be sufficient in the job market, and besides, her English was so limited. She could not apply to any job that required any level of English proficiency, so she only applied to jobs that required her mother tongue.

Nonetheless, Lane had her own advantage. She was still young and attractive and spoke her mother tongue fluently. She had a slim figure and a temperament that impressed every employer who interviewed her. After trying several companies, she was hired by an immigration consultant agency.

Lane soon discovered that her company was engaged in illegal activities. The owner helped clients from his home country forge documents for the purpose of immigrating to Canada. He had succeeded in many cases, charging a huge sum for each. He became filthy rich but was unable to cover up his illegal activities for long. Before she knew it, he was arrested, tried, and sentenced to seven years' imprisonment, with a $900,000 fine. All those who came to Canada with forged documents were deprived of their status. When the company disappeared, Lane lost her job and returned home.

That this company had become so notorious made it impossible for her to mention this first work experience to any new employer. Lane became, once again, a newcomer with no Canadian work experience. She thought about what sort of suitable work she could do, such as being a restaurant waitress, a tourist guide, and a cleaner, but those were the lowest-paying jobs. If she could find other opportunities, she would rather stay away from such jobs.

Then she thought of the job she had been doing: helping her boss bring in illegal immigrants through fake marriages. She was very familiar with the process. It would not be difficult, if she wanted to do it herself. Each person paid tens of thousands of dollars, which had promoted her boss to the ranks of the wealthy. It would mean at least securing middle-class status. The more she thought about it, the more tempting it became.

Why not create an immigration consultant company and just work at home? she asked herself. *I will be the boss and also the employee. I don't have to hire anyone else. I will earn the consultation fees and keep it all for myself. It is absolutely safe. No one will know what I am doing.*

She talked with her husband, who thought it was a feasible plan. A home business was easy to set up and operate. The setup cost and monthly fees would be minimal. Each client would bring in $70,000 or $80,000, which equaled the after-tax income of a $120,000 annual salary.

The next day, they cleaned up a room on the main floor and turned it into an office. Immediately they were ready for business—immigration consultation, specializing in family reunions. To her surprise, she learned that all immigration agencies needed a license from the College of Immigration and Citizenship Consultants. Every immigration consultant must have a license to practice and is regulated accordingly. It would take several months to apply for a license, and even if she tried, she might not pass the required tests.

30

Lane could not wait. She wanted to make money quickly, so she decided to operate her business without registering the company. She thought of working in partnership with a licensed company. For every case, she could get everything done and then just pay the partner a fee to complete the legal procedure, which would inevitably reduce her profits. For a small business like hers, that could be a big challenge. Finally, with her husband's support, she decided to wade into the unknown gray zone anyway. Her favorite saying became, "You can't be rich without a dirty windfall."

Lane lost no time advertising her business on the internet, but for five months she received only inquiry calls without securing a single client. Finally, a caller named Chuck Whale expressed serious interest in hiring her.

"My wife and I are a middle-aged couple," Whale said. "We have no postsecondary education and no special skills needed in Canada, but we want to immigrate to Canada. We know Canada will not accept us if we apply ourselves. We can afford and are willing to pay $50,000, if you can bring us into Canada. That's the only money we have."

"I will think about how to help you," said Lane. She did the numbers, discovering that if she had to pay a fee to a licensed company to finish the work she could not do, her profits would be meager. After several sleepless nights, a great idea struck her.

"I can help them by faking a marriage with the man," she told her husband.

"Oh, no," he said. "What a disgrace if our relatives and friends learned about it!" But she repeatedly told him how safe it was, and how easy it would be, and that before anyone knew it, the couple would be in Canada and they could be remarried. Her husband could tolerate a lot, but not the idea of divorcing and remarrying.

"Look," she continued, "it's just two papers: a divorce paper and then another marriage license when we have the money. Isn't it easy! Two worthless papers for $50,000!"

"No. That's a terrible idea." He repeated his objection, but she kept whining, "I can't even find a labor job that pays $9 an hour. Look at all these bills we have to pay. The two children also cost a lot of money." For an entire week, from morning till night, day after day, she kept annoying him with the same issue, until he found it difficult to work or sleep. Finally, he gave in.

31

The next week, Lane and Huchard officially divorced in B.C. Then Lane instructed Whale to divorce his wife. When he got his divorce papers, she flew to his home city, where they applied for a marriage license and received it on the same day. Everything was completed perfectly within three days, including a wedding that no relatives or friends attended. Legally, they had become a married couple. Lane immediately submitted her sponsorship application to the Canadian Consulate General in Whale's home city.

After that, she flew back to Canada and began to arrange a wedding chamber. She knew how strict the Canadian government was about verifying spouses immigrating to Canada through the family reunion category. Immigration officers would ask very specific questions about small details, like: "What color is your wife's/husband's underwear?" "Do you sleep on the left or right side of the bed?" "What kind of toothpaste/bath soap do you use?" "Does your husband/wife take a shower or a bath every day, and when does he/she do it?" The application would be rejected if the husband and wife gave conflicting answers.

Lane had helped clients prepare for such interviews, and she knew what to do. Her preparation was thorough, and both passed the interviews after being asked the same questions simultaneously by immigration officers in two separate offices. Her fake husband was interviewed at the Consulate General in his home city and she in Vancouver. They performed so well that their fake marriage was deemed a real one by the immigration officers. Four weeks later, Whale received a visitor visa to enter Canada to join his newlywed wife. By the following Sunday, he was with Lane at her Richmond home.

According to their agreement, Whale paid Lane $30,000 after he landed at the Vancouver international airport, but he had yet to get his official permanent resident (PR) card. Only when he had received the card would he pay Lane the balance of $20,000, and only then could they divorce, freeing Whale to remarry his real wife and then sponsor her to come to Canada to reunite with him.

Lane had thought the scheme perfect, but to her mounting concern, Whale's visitor visa soon expired without the appearance of the card. He had no trouble renewing the visa, but still his PR card just would not come. Her client kept asking when he could expect to get it. She kept comforting him while harboring secret anxiety that the immigration officers might have discovered something wrong with their application.

For the sake of his $20,000, Lane decided to let Whale stay in her home so he would be familiar with the details of her house—just to make sure he would smoothly pass any upcoming immigration interviews, tricky ones that often took fake couples by surprise. To prepare him for questions regarding sexual activities, she went to bed with him and ended up sleeping with two men under the same roof—the ex- but real husband, and the legal but fake husband. She had asked her real husband to move out of their bedroom and gave it to Whale, keeping his belongings there in what she called their master bedroom. She hoped Whale would familiarize himself with everything in it, so that when the immigration officers came to verify the existence of their marriage he would be able to provide any evidence they wanted.

With Whale to all appearances becoming the master of this house, Huchard became a tenant, though he maintained his relationship with Lane. Meanwhile, Lane's parents continued to live there as well, looking after the two grandchildren. Regarding what really went on in the relationship between the two men and Lane, no one knows for sure except themselves.

True or not, according to Whale's confession, "Lane not only had a marriage license with me, but she slept with me too. She slept with her ex-husband and me in turn. She was the queen in the house." Yet her friend was positive that "everything Lane did was to help her fake husband get his PR card as soon as he could."

What a meticulous woman she was! But now her real husband truly regretted what he had reluctantly agreed to. He was less and less sure about whether Lane was acting as she did to get Whale his PR card, or to get the $20,000, or other reasons.

To complicate matters, there was another surprise during Whale's year-long stay in Lane's house. Her belly kept growing, and she gave birth to her third child. She told her real husband that it was his, but in the long form, the baby's father was recorded as Chuck Whale, her fake husband. She told her real husband that she had named Whale the baby's biological father to help him speed up the immigration process and, more importantly, to finally secure his $20,000. If she did not do so, she argued, wouldn't it be self-incriminating? No DNA test was ever done, so no one except Lane knows who the real father was.

As flawless as Lane's scheme appeared to be, contrary to everyone's expectations it had led to having a strange man living in the house for nearly two years. As much as Lane wanted to help Whale's real wife and bring her to Canada as soon as possible, the woman was causing problems herself. Over the past two years, she had experienced great hardship. She and Whale had spent all their savings on their hope of immigrating but had seen no progress. Besides assuming the roles of both father and mother, she had little money to buy food and pay bills. Whale not only seldom sent money to support her but seemed to have betrayed her. She reached the breaking point when she learned he had fathered a child who took his last name. She threatened to divorce him and tell her children never to recognize their father, whom she described as a shameless bastard.

Whale was under tremendous pressure. According to Lane, he should have received his PR card within a few months after they submitted their immigration application, but he never did. Since he was legally married to Lane, if she had no objection, he didn't mind sleeping with her either. He thought it was understandable that, like other men, he had sexual desire. But he knew that the child was not his and that his name was put on the birth certificate just to further legalize his status in Canada. So what happened afterward really took him off guard.

Lane began to ask him to pay for the baby's diapers, formula, and toys, among other things. Whale was still a visitor without a work permit, and his only way to earn money was to work illegally. If he had money, his priority was to support his own family and to save for the $20,000 payable when he received his PR card. Unsurprisingly, he refused to pay for anything. He felt bitterly disappointed that he had come to Canada hoping for a better life for his family but could end up losing his real wife. Lane kept pressing for money, so he contemplated returning home instead of continuing to wait.

Despite pressure and threats from Lane, Whale would not give her any money. "Our original written agreement never says I need to pay you anything else except the money for my PR card," he insisted.

Lane's real husband also grew anxious and restless. Knowing their long-time visitor would not pay for anything, not even rent, he came to Lane's defense, ganging up against him.

Before the young child turned a year old, the three got into a fight that brought the police to their house. Whale was arrested and had to go to court, where Lane accused him of assaulting her. That accusation was supported by visible injuries on her body. The judge therefore issued a one-year restraining order against Whale, which meant he could not be in contact with either Lane or her baby. Whale had to rent a room for himself elsewhere. Life became even harder for him. Finally, he decided to go back home to join his own family.

Since Lane had not delivered on her promise of a PR card, Whale asked her for a full refund. If she agreed, they would divorce and he would return home to be reunited with his real wife. Lane rejected the request, saying that she had spent it all and had no money to return to him. She told him that she had not only wasted a great deal of time on his case, she had missed other business opportunities as a result. Besides, he had been living in her house for nearly two years without paying rent—which alone, she insisted, was worth about $30,000, not to mention the tremendous amount of work she had done and the anxiety she had experienced. Instead of giving him a refund, she wanted him to pay the $20,000 balance.

Whale's restraining order finally ended on August 27, 2009, but on August 26, Lane told him, "Your name is on my child's birth certificate, so you are responsible for giving him a living allowance. You'll need to pay $2,000 every month until he becomes an adult."

"Two thousand a month means $24,000 a year! Eighteen years means $432,000!" Whale was aghast. He had little education and had no special skills. There was no way he could pay her $2,000 every month. "But you told me the child is not mine and my name was put there just to speed up my immigration process," he said. "For what reason do I have to pay you $2,000 every month?"

"As long as your name appears on a child's birth certificate, you are the father," she told him coldly. "If you are the father, you have to pay. That is the law in Canada. Don't ask why!"

The next day, with the restraining order officially at an end, he could see Lane and her child again. He asked Lane and Huchard for a meeting at a McDonald's near their home to talk things over and see if they could find a solution. They agreed, and the three met late in the afternoon. Their conversation started with casual chatting but soon turned into a thunderous dispute that shocked other patrons.

The fight turned physical, the three tangling fiercely. Huchard pushed Whale to the floor as Lane threw a kick at him in her high-heeled shoes. Whale rose to his feet in silence and pulled an object from the bag he was carrying—a long steak knife. Instantly, he charged at Huchard and stabbed him repeatedly. Terrified, Lane came to Huchard's defense, but Whale turned on her, plunging the knife into her several times. Patrons fled the restaurant in panic, jumping over bodies on the floor blocking

35

their way. Warm blood flowed across the floor. Whale's hands and feet, his shirt and pants, were covered with blood. He dropped his knife to the floor and sat down next to the lifeless couple, waiting to be arrested. At long last, what he felt was relief. He need not worry about money, food, and rent anymore. He need not worry about being divorced or staying married.

Fully armed police arrived en masse, with a dozen police cruisers and emergency vehicles gathering outside the restaurant. The officers carried long rifles, a frightening sight in a normally peaceful restaurant, but it was an easy arrest. As ordered, Whale raised his hands over his head and walked backward until the police could grab him. Then, they abruptly pushed him facedown and handcuffed him.

On February 21, 37-year-old Chuck Whale, the man behind a vicious double murder at the McDonald's in Richmond, B.C., was sentenced to life imprisonment with no chance of parole for fifteen years. In court, Whale said that Lane had married him in his Pacific coastal home city and then sponsored him to come to Canada, but she continued to live with her former husband, which frustrated him. His account was about as true as his new marriage, but it hardly mattered. He had shown remorse, entered a guilty plea, and accepted life imprisonment, which he said he deserved.

Before sentencing, he told the judge, "In the past I thought I was being manipulated by Lane, but now I realize she truly loved me."

Lover's Shoelace

Rayhan left Bridle Mall with a dozen roses beautifully wrapped in glossy plastic. He sniffed their aroma and blew them a kiss, as if kissing Lilly. His heart pounded fast as he imagined holding her in his arms. He strode rapidly toward the bus- stop on Finch Avenue. *The bus is too slow*, he told himself. *Dating without a car won't do!*

Bus 39 arrived five minutes later. It was crowded and he could not find a seat. He would rather have waited for the next bus, but he could not afford to miss their lunch appointment at 11:30. He boarded the bus, holding the roses close to his nose, smiling to himself. *Smells as sweet as Lilly.*

The bus started moving and was soon at full speed. Shortly before the next stop, the driver suddenly braked so hard that Rayhan tumbled, nearly crushing his flowers. Instinctively he sprang back to his feet and regained his position. Thank goodness, he had not damaged any of his roses. He breathed out a sigh of relief but was embarrassed to realize his pants had dropped to the floor.

"Oh my God!" the girl next to him screamed. Everyone looked in his direction and saw him there in his underpants, his long trousers lying over his shoes. His face reddening, Rayhan pulled them back up quickly.

"What are you doing?" a middle-aged man asked sternly. He turned on his cellphone, evidently ready to call the police.

"I am so sorry," Rayhan apologized, realizing the cause of the mishap. "My belt has broken."

The man moved closer to verify his claim. Indeed, the buckle had separated from the strap. The nosy passenger burst out laughing and put the phone back into his shirt pocket, wondering how Rayhan would fix his belt, with flowers in one hand and the pants in the other.

Rayhan cleverly thrust the flower stems under his left armpit. After that, he lowered his left shoulder to permit his elbow to hold the pants against his abdomen, thus freeing both hands. Then he tried to put the buckle back onto the strap, but a pin or something was missing and he failed. Finally, he tried to see if he could wear the belt without the buckle, but it was too short. Sweat beaded on his forehead and then streamed down his cheeks.

Lilly will understand, he comforted himself. It was her parents he was worried about. His real anxiety was about whether they would accept him.

Lilly's parents were bankers, one working for TD Canada Trust and the other for Scotiabank; he was from a much less affluent family.

His options narrowing, Rayhan thrust the broken belt into his pocket. Then he bent down and untied the shoelace on his right shoe.

Would it be long enough? He pulled the lace out with his right hand. It looked strong except for two worn points. He put it through his belt loops. "Thank God! It's longer than the belt!" he said, as he tightened it. "It's even better than the belt!" Fellow passengers, watching this, chuckled with relief, impressed by his cleverness.

"Congratulations!" shouted one onlooker. With his pants secure again, Rayhan straightened up, grinning. The whole bus burst into warm applause.

"Unbelievable!" he said to himself.

Finally, Rayhan arrived at the Rose-and-Rose Restaurant on Bloor Street. He looked at the time on his cellphone: 11:00 a.m. He walked in and was greeted by the hostess, who showed him to Room 3, a private space off the main dining room, where Lilly was waiting for him. She was wearing an elegant dress he had never seen before and gazing at an oil painting in which a handsome young boy was staring at a beautiful girl. With her back to the door, she had not noticed his arrival. Rayhan decided to have a little fun with her.

"Surprise!" he announced as he charged at her from behind, blindfolding her with his hands. "Here are my roses for you, sweetheart!"

"What are you doing? Hands off me!" she shouted as she struggled to break free of his hands. Rayhan was shocked by this reaction, for Lilly had never rejected his touch. In her struggle, she broke Rayhan's shoelace, which made his pants drop to the floor. Other diners, hearing the commotion, looked through the door of Room 3 and saw a pantless man hugging a struggling woman. They started screaming and called for help. Someone pulled out a phone and took pictures.

At this moment, a middle-aged man in a suit, who was returning from the restroom, dashed over and separated Rayhan from the lady.

"You?! Humph!" she snorted.

"Oh, God! I am really sorry," screamed Rayhan, as he pulled up his pants and tightened the shoelace around his waist, several inches of which had broken off. He desperately wanted to sink through the floor. The woman wasn't Lilly!

Could she be? Oh, God! He dared not guess. But no guessing was needed. Rayhan had reserved this room for lunch with Lilly and her parents. Apparently her parents had arrived ahead of her.

Neither did Lilly's mother need to ask who he was. She was now looking him over from head to foot, her eyes passing over his jacket, pants, shoes, and then back to his haircut. None seemed attractive or acceptable to her. One of his shoes was missing a shoelace—she had never seen anyone wearing a shoe that way. Then she stared straight into his eyes with a glare that seemed to pierce his skin and flesh, right into his heart and soul. Rayhan endured this nervously, not knowing what to say or how to behave.

"Where is Lilly?" he finally asked, flushing. "I am really sorry."

He heard no answer but saw the muscles on Lilly's mother's mouth twist to the right corner, giving out a chilly message. She rose and left the room with Lilly's father in tow, leaving Rayhan alone.

In less than three minutes, two police officers arrived at Room 3. They asked Rayhan to show his ID, followed by a few questions. Then, they announced he was being arrested and charged with sexual assault. Lilly, running late, finally ran into the restaurant looking for Room 3, only to bump into Rayhan being walked away by the police in handcuffs. The entire restaurant was watching this spectacle, wondering who the young man was and what he had done.

"Rayhan! What happened? Why?" Lilly cried, instantly bursting into tears.

"Please call a lawyer!" Rayhan said, hanging his head in indescribable embarrassment.

Lilly did so immediately, and a lawyer arrived at the police station with Lilly not long after the police cruiser. Lilly was clueless about what had happened but had a bad feeling her parents might be involved.

"God, what's going on?" she asked the lawyer. "Did they get into a fight or something?"

Rayhan, with the lawyer sitting next to him in an interrogation room, told the police what had happened to his belt and what he did in Room 3 in the restaurant, and why. "I am so sorry, sir. It was a pure misunderstanding. Lilly's mother really looked like my girlfriend."

At hearing his tale of the broken belt and the shoelace, the officers broke into laughter. But his hugging of Lilly's mother was still a matter to be clarified. They would release him without charge, they said, if Lilly's mother agreed to withdraw her accusation of sexual assault. If not, the case would have to go through the process. Rayhan would have to appear in court the next day, and a judge would decide whether the case would be dropped or he would be tried.

While waiting for the lawyer to emerge from the police room, Lilly called her mother.

Rayhan began to pray. If he was unable return to work on Monday, his boss would find out what had happened and might decide to fire him. Having the charges dropped immediately would be the best scenario, but if he had to go on trial, his name would be published and he would never be able to clear his reputation. Not only would he lose his job, but he would not be able to find new work. Worse, he might even lose his girlfriend. The more he thought about it, the more frightened he became.

Lilly knew her mother held the key. She loved Rayhan, the most honest and decent man she had ever known. He would never intentionally have assaulted her mother; in fact, he wouldn't ever touch a woman except herself. Lilly rushed home to talk with her mother.

"Mom," she told her, "I know this is just a serious misunderstanding between you and Rayhan. Rayhan just had a bad day. His belt broke on his way to the restaurant, so he had to use one of his shoelaces as a belt, which unfortunately broke when he was giving the roses to me in the restaurant—or that's what he thought. It turned out to be you, of course. He mistook you for me because he couldn't see your face. His shoelace broke by accident. None of this was intentional. He did not mean to do it. Even if it was me he was hugging, he would not intentionally pull off his pants! Mom, you must believe me. Don't wrong a good man. Putting him on trial could ruin his entire life. Mom, please ask the police to drop all the charges against him and set him free immediately. Mom, I beg you, please!" Lilly was sobbing now.

"I could ask the police to drop all charges against him and let him go home today, but I would rather you reconsider your relationship with him," her mother said coldly.

"Mom," Lilly continued, "I know you love me and want me to find the best man in the world so that I can live a happy life. I truly appreciate it. But I must tell you that Rayhan is just a candidate I am trying to get to know. We don't have a true dating relationship yet. He is like a good friend, one of the many friends I have. We haven't committed to each other, so there is no real relationship yet. So you don't need to worry about our meeting from time to time. I will never decide on a relationship with any man without your consent—and Dad's."

The muscles on her mother's face relaxed and she said, "I am pleased you understand me. I never had any doubt that you would choose the most suitable partner. Honestly, you have to know that hugging a woman in public in his underwear is unacceptable. Any woman in my position would have called the police. I hope you understand that."

"Of course I do," Lilly said, making sure to sound obedient, knowing that her mother would change her mind soon. "Mom, how about this? Since we're not sure about Rayhan yet, I may as well stop meeting him altogether. There is no rush getting to know him anyway. I won't meet him again unless you and Dad like him and permit me to do so."

"Do you really mean that?" she said, more relaxed now.

"Definitely," Lilly assured her.

"If that is your decision, I have no objection," said her mother, rising to her feet to give Lilly a warm hug.

"But Mom, I would really feel bad if Rayhan has to go on trial for such a mistake," said Lilly. "It was because of me. Even if he were a stranger, I would feel bad for him."

"I will call the police immediately to withdraw my accusation and ask them to release him," said her mother. "Cheer up!"

"Thank you, Mom!" Lilly smiled through her tears.

Fortunately for Rayhan, it all worked out as Lilly had hoped. She waited for Rayhan outside the police station, without her parents' consent. Rayhan was released and the charges dropped. The incident would not affect him in any way. Except for the police, the lawyer, Lilly, and her parents, no one else knew about the incident.

Lilly whispered into Rayhan's ear what she had told her mother and her strategy to develop their relationship without further complications. Rayhan nodded, they kissed, and left the police station.

It was 5:00 p.m. Rayhan, hungry and listless after this ordeal, started walking toward the mall west of the police station. Ten minutes later, he was standing in front of a newly opened buffet restaurant offering "Lunch $25—All you can eat." It looked quite luxurious, with well-dressed patrons waiting in the reception area.

I need a celebration—for my regained freedom, Rayhan was thinking when he heard a commotion some distance away.

At the southeast corner of the parking lot, four men were dragging a driver out of his seat. Rayhan immediately recognized it as a carjacking in progress. Since more than 12,000 vehicles were stolen in the city

41

every year, this was not as unusual as it should have been, and unlikely to garner a quick response from the police. Rayhan had experienced his own car theft and felt his blood boiling.

He ran straight toward the scene, jumping on top of one of the men and kicking him to the ground. A second thief charged at Rayhan with a knife, managing to cut his left arm before Rayhan raised a leg and kicked hard at the armed robber's wrist, sending his knife flying some fifteen meters away. Another kick to the man's private parts left him rolling on the ground in agonizing pain. A third, robber armed with a cleaver, charged at Rayhan with it like a hungry wolf. Rayhan took a step backward, neatly avoiding the blade, and was about to kick at the carjacker's wrist to disarm him when he heard a shot. What he saw next was his attacker falling toward the car door—an unexpected fourth robber armed with a handgun had apparently shot one of his own gang members by mistake while aiming at Rayhan. But another bullet hit Rayhan's left shoulder and, glancing down, he saw blood gush from the wound.

While the armed carjacker paused to reload, a loud siren announced the arrival of three police cruisers, which were soon followed by an ambulance. The robbers instantly vanished into a hidden lane to the north as the police entered from the south and east.

Paramedics took Rayhan to the emergency room at the Central General Hospital, and soon afterward he was undergoing surgery to the shredded muscle in his shoulder. Doctors said he should recover in the next two or three weeks and told him he was lucky: the bullet could have hit his heart if his body had been exposed at another angle.

Rayhan was patched up and recovering in a hospital room when a tearful Lilly unexpectedly appeared beside his bed. He was in pain but grateful to see her and glad for her kisses and embraces, which felt more effective than the painkillers.

"I want to thank you, Rayhan. My father wants to thank you, my mother wants to thank you, too," she said, sobbing.

"Why?"

"You saved my father's car, and probably his life," she said. He looked at her quizzically. "Rayhan, did you not see the driver of the BMW? That was my father. He could have been killed or died of a heart attack if you had not come to his rescue. You not only saved his car, you saved his life! The police said those guys were part of the worst gang in the city. They run the biggest car theft racket there is, and they're willing to kill.

42

Even the police are having a hard time rounding them up. The courts, too. You're my hero."

Lilly's parents, who had been lingering in the hallway, slipped into the room and approached the bed.

"Rayhan, our family is truly grateful to you for risking your life to save ours," said the mother. "It's God's blessing that Lilly has you as her boyfriend. Whatever important decision you both make for your lives, you have our full support and blessing."

Rayhan smiled as Lilly sobbed in his arms.

Heartwarming Anecdotes

A Father Who Shines[1]

The commotion in the hall caught Huang Qiao by surprise. "Freeze, or I will beat the heck out of you!" His third wife was shouting at their young son, whom she'd been chasing with a whip in hand. Quickly taking refuge behind his father, the boy stuck out his head and said, "I was just chasing the rooster for fun. Why don't you just mind your own business?"

The mother was in a fury. "You damn little bastard—"

"You damn old woman!" the fearless boy cut her short.

"How dare you!" shouted the father, seizing the boy's hand. "How dare you talk to your mother like that? What will become of you when you grow up!"

Wrenching his hand out of his father's, the boy threw himself on the hall floor, doing his utmost to make a scene. He was a spoiled child who not only cared little that he was misbehaving but wanted his parents to accept it.

The father, blood rising to his face, stomped on the floor. "Stop it! And kneel before your mother at once!" Kneeling was a severe form of punishment in those days.

"I was just playing with my rooster. What have I done wrong?" the boy protested. "I won't kneel."

"So you even disobey me!" the infuriated father roared, reflexively raising his hand, intending to teach him a lesson. Seeing the furious father's fist in the air, the soft-hearted mother suddenly feared he might harm the boy, which he could do easily with just one blow.

"Please," she begged the father, "it's my fault. I haven't trained him well. Will you let me take him into my room and discipline him myself?"

"No, my dear wife, I'm afraid he cannot get away with this today. He deserves severe punishment."

"All right," she agreed, thinking that perhaps this was best anyway.

---

[1] This story is based on several sources in Chinese made available in the public domain by Huang Zhangfa and Huang Yonghui, among others. All descendants of the Huang family can use this story for noncommercial purposes as long as due credit is given to the author.

"Now, won't you kneel before your mother!" the father ordered the boy again.

"All right, since you want me to kneel, I will obey you," said the boy, who was about to comply when his grandfather, supported by a cane, appeared in the hall. "Oh, my! Why such a commotion? What does a little boy really know at such a young age? Why resort to corporal punishment?"

Seeing his rescuer had arrived, the boy ran over to him and hid behind his back. He knew he was the favorite grandson. Grandpa had often given him candies and taken him out to go fishing, catch grasshoppers, and other fun activities. "I just won't kneel before her. Just see what you can do about it!"

The furious father was deeply embarrassed that the little boy had disobeyed him by taking advantage of his grandfather, who was the number one authority in the family. If he punished the boy, he would offend his own father. If he did not, the child would get away with his misbehaviour, which could get even worse.

In shock and pain, Huang Qiao realized that it was the father's fault if he raised a child without training him properly. He had three wives, and they had many children. He suddenly recognized that his children needed family rules.

After the grandfather took the boy with him, Huang Qiao asked his wife what had been going on when he arrived home. She told him the boy had bumped into a crowd engaged in cockfighting on the threshing ground next to the paddy fields. He became curious and wanted to catch the big rooster and join them in cockfighting, but the rooster was hard to catch. The moment he touched the rooster, it simply flapped into the air, jumping and flying ahead of him. The boy chased it all the way into the hall and then into the bed chamber, where it jumped onto the dresser and even flew into the bed. The scared rooster created a terrible mess in the chamber, soiling the bedding and the mosquito net, kicking over the candle stands, and smashing the fine blue vase painted with beautiful flowers. The boy's mother had followed him into the chamber and blamed him for all the mess caused by the rooster. Now as frightened as the rooster, the boy shot out into the hall. With great effort, his mother caught him there, but before she could give him a beating, he had freed himself from her, at the point where Huang Qiao himself entered the scene.

The whole incident reminded the father of another episode. Huang Qiao's first wife had paid her parents a visit the previous fall. Her elder son accompanied her on the trip. On the trip, he met a female cousin and apparently fell in love with her at first sight. He invited her to the orchard, where they ate pears, and with that began their courtship. When the mother found out about this, she gave her son a stern warning, prohibiting him from dating his cousin, but he ignored her, rejecting her poking into what he thought of as his private affairs. She could not tolerate this bold disobedience and as a result cut her visit short and brought him back home without delay.

The more Huang Qiao thought about these incidents, the more uncomfortable he became with what was happening in the family. He gathered together his three wives, and all agreed that they should create a set of behaviour guidelines for the seven sons (which eventually became twenty-one, as each wife would give birth to seven), who were studying in the private school the father had founded. Immediately following their conversation, Huang started writing his *Family Behavior Guidelines*, which consisted of seventeen rules composed in prose form. Each began with "Father says," followed by an ordinal number from "first" to "seventeenth." Each rule began with a summary three-character headline, followed by details.

The sons were taught the rules, and each was told they must memorize them. Then came the day when they were asked to recite them to the father. None was able to recite the lengthy rules accurately from start to finish. The first son managed to recite the first eight rules. Another son, who was told to continue from the ninth, went on until he finished the fourteenth. When he stumbled with the next rule, he was stopped. Another son then started to recite Rules 15, 16, and 17. The father was not satisfied, noting that they all had struggled through their recitation. He was moved to discipline them but held back, feeling it might be unfair. After all, the rules were written in prose, which was by no means easy to memorize. The longer rules each exceeded thirty lines.

Though they had found it a challenge to recite them fluently, the rules nevertheless seemed to have been improving the sons' behavior. None had misbehaved after the introduction of the family rules. This comforted the father greatly. He then decided to revise the rules and make them easier to memorize, and he began converting them into rhyming poetic lines. After more than a year of revising, based on his careful observation of his sons' response to the rules, he presented them as twenty-one

46

guidelines, including an introductory stanza and a concluding one. He read them aloud to himself numerous times until he was satisfied with them. Then, he announced the new *Huang Family Behavior Guidelines*[2] to his sons, an approximate translation of which is as follows.

1

First, cherish well the nature of our bond;
Read "Lu E,"[3] the fine poem that'll respond.
Dad toiled with strength, his life as hard as stone;
Mom nursed you till her energy was blown.
Yu's Shun[4] tilled land, yet was praised as the best;
Zhong You's[5] care for his mom surpassed the rest.
E'en young lambs to their mothers kneel[6] in grace;

---

[2] This translation by Harry J. Huang (Freeman J. Wong, 黄俊雄, 1956 –) was based on the Shaowu's edition of the twenty-one behavior guidelines originally written in Chinese by HUANG Qiao (黄峭, 872 – 953). Due to the limited syllables of the English line, summary translation and other similar techniques were adapted in the rendering of the source text. Close rhymes appear in a number of couplets in the English translation, and the metrical pattern is not highly regular. This English translation may be republished independently or posted in social media for noncommercial purposes, as long as due credit is given to the author and translator in the following format.

The Huang Family Behavior Guidelines （黄氏家训）
Original Chinese by HUANG Qiao (黄峭, 872 – 953)
English Translation by Harry J. HUANG (黄俊雄, 1956 –)

[3] This poem expresses children's gratitude to parents for their upbringing.
[4] Emperor Shun of Yu State was extremely poor during his childhood, but he was such a good son that his filiality impressed Heaven, and then a celestial elephant and a celestial bird came to help him with his farming.
[5] The original line may also be rendered as follows if space permits: Zhong You (also known as Zi Lu, one of Confucius' disciples), who ate coarse food but often carried rice home for his mother from more than 100 li (0.5 kilometer) away, is a role model for you and your brothers.
[6] Translator's notes: (1) That young lambs kneel when being fed by their mother is interpreted in the Chinese culture as a gesture of gratitude. (2) The translator regrets that the limited space of this line does not accommodate the words of the second half of the source line that says wild ducks also feed back their old mothers, and therefore a summary translation approach has been taken,

Above all, strive to be a good son's place.

2
Next, always hold the ethics of mankind;
Be joyful, striving brothers of the kind.
Observe the ranks—eldest first and youngest last,
Create a bond where respect is steadfast.
Rich brother shan't despise a needy one;
Remember your bond if one needs a bun.
The dodder and pine grow into one tree;
Greet siblings on the road and do not flee.

3
Third, keep your self-image in the best light;
Be lively, neat and cheerful day and night.
Sit straight and stand with grace, respect wise friends;
Refinement helps you make amends, not bends.
Snakes coil and stretch, then straighten in their time;
Small insects change from slush to form in rhyme.
When you become a father on some date,
Serve gladly as a bowl, a pot, a plate.

4
Fourth, remember that in your years of prime
You must not be a weak man anytime.
Show both your strength and softness as you need;
Then you will be a man that all will heed.
Embrace the wisdom of the past with zest;
Pursue the ancient sages who are best.
Outdated ways and low moods are your foe;
Keep striving hard to put on your best show.

5
Fifth, you must manage well the cash you spend;
There'll be many events you need attend.
Be frugal and watch closely what you buy;

---

resulting in the loss of some details; this may also be found elsewhere in the English translation of the twenty-one behavior guidelines.

An overjoyed guest'll have the last reply.
We toil each day for food and clothes we wear;
A lazy man will find no place to share.
Don't waste your funds on things you do not need;
If you are poor, then seeking help is freed.

6
Sixth, do not be a pedant anywhere;
For any pedant finds no thoroughfare.
Study hard with high ambitions in mind;
Leave ignorance and folly both behind.
A life of ease is hard to keep in sight;
But precious knowledge gained will bring you light.
Though poor, Li Mi and Mai Chen[7] reached great goal:
They read books from ox horn and shoulder pole.

7
Seventh, keep all bad habits far away;
Work hard, avoid waste, and happy you'll stay.
Drink in small sips if you have wine in store;
Don't shop on credit when funds are no more.
Gambling is never the right path to choose;
Sleeping in will cause your marriage to lose.
Time flies just like a shooting star in sky;
Don't be a flower that blooms just to die.

8
Eighth, take charge of your home and have your say,
Knowing the roles both man and woman play.
Prevent quarrels like those from neighbor B;
Do the same kind deeds done by neighbor C.
Heaven showers on *liyi*[8] homes joy and health;

---

[7] If space were not limited, this couplet could be translated as follows: If Li Mi of the Sui Dynasty (581 – 618) and Zhu Mai Chen of the Western Han Dynasty (206 BC – AD 24), who were born into poor farmers' families, had simply accepted their fate instead of studying hard, they would never have reached their status of nobility! Li Mi was seen reading books hanging on an ox's horn while he was herding cattle. Zhu Mai Chen was reading his books hanging on the shoulder pole while he was carrying large loads of wood.

A harmonious home brings bliss and wealth.
A gentle voice can ease your home of strife;
A good son'll raise fine children full of life.

9

Ninth's about family chores in a chain:
Home's easy to start, yet hard to sustain.
Watch every lamp and candle that gives light;
Secure each gate and lock the door at night.
Fix roof leaks promptly when they come in sight;
All fallen fences should be mended right.
Assign each child their tasks when skies are bright;
Gather your cows and sheep, sleep free of fright.

10

Tenth, read Ten Poems together, line by line;
Some may seem unpolished, yet they all shine.
Enjoy the subtle beauty that they yield;
Learn hidden meanings from each verse revealed.
Care for your mother when she's growing old;
Officials should have bigger hearts of gold.
This yet does not express all I would say;
May you come to understand me one day!

11

Elev'nth, don't be an overbearing man,
But serve the people kindly as you can.
Condemned officials find no place to hide;
A great name lives forever, far and wide.
Do not abuse your best and noble days;
Hot-headedness will only lead to strays.
Earth has seen many heroes live and die;
What you loathe is gossip fly'ng in the sky.

---

[8] *Liyi* (礼仪) in *pinyin*, which means etiquette and rituals, is used to accommodate the number of syllables of the line.

12

Twelfth, I would love to see the Huang clan grow;
My brothers, sons, and grandsons make us glow.
Branch rivers flow forth from the same clear source;
Trees spread from the same roots by nature's force.
Don't offend Emperors where'er you are;
Be humble to others, both near and far.
A home with peace and harmony will thrive;
Pass on forebears' morals—keep them alive

13

Thirteenth, always be an honest, good man;
Be fair with everyone, make each a fan.
Help relatives and friends who are in need;
Don't shun a neighbor who has eaten seed.
Harmony's a wonderful thing in life;
Endurance and patience are pride's true wife.
Teachings from ancestors are worth their gold;
Take right path, and you'll face no woe or scold.

14

Fourteenth, when you do business outside,
Don't mistreat partners; don't fight and don't chide.
Share profits fairly in your hawking trade;
Don't cheat the old and the young who need aid.
Birds rest in trees before the last sun ray;
Rise at cockcrow to begin each new day.
Read classic lines of poetry all your life;
They guard you from risks better than a knife.

15

Fifteenth, don't indulge in a life of ease;
Tolerate others for the sake of peace.
Entertain guests with wine that you have stored;
Shun officials if you have no gold hoard.
Humble yourself to neighbors—no hauteur;
Accept kin and friends, be they rich or poor.
Embrace what Heaven has arranged for you;
The Three Precepts can be followed as due.

16

Sixteenth, don't fight for whatever appeals;
Endurance and honesty are great deals.
Land passed to young generation holds weight,
But etiquette also makes a fine estate.
Most important, always obey the law;
Make me proud and never commit a flaw.
I ponder on my past and find my life
A lawful, diligent one without strife.

17

Seventeenth, know that in life, wisdom leads;
Precaution and caution prevent misdeeds.
A man's heart is like a dagger in dark;
Crises arise, like chess games you would mark.
Great ambition seeks advice from wise friends;
Guard against bandits and devilish ends.
You may be all right if you have some cash;
If you've spent it all, quickly they will dash.

18

Eighteenth, always watch what you do and say;
In this cold world, we play the minion's way.
With good friends, you enjoy toast after toast;
In unwanted talk, one word matters most.
If blessed, you will find life a joyful feast;
If unblessed, you'll find it worse than a beast.
Trouble often starts from unneeded talk;
Once mishaps befall you, you'll be in shock.

19

Nineteenth, nurture fine traits as best you can;
Always strive to be an outstanding man.
In cold winter, wear warm fur and no tat;
In hot summer, sleep on a bamboo mat.
Preserve filial piety you can vaunt;
Smart children and grandkids are what you want.

Be a Confucian, steadfast and renowned;
We, father and son, are forever bound.

20

Twentieth, here's advice that may make you bored:
Don't do a thing that you cannot applaud.
Careful second thoughts'll keep you safe and sound,
But you'll gain from pain when mistakes are found.
Live a leisurely life, resentment freed;
Loyalty's foe is ignorance and greed.
Nothing from harming others will you gain;
Honest men survive tough times without pain.

21

Twenty-first, out my last advice will stand;
I hope none of my sons will ruin my land.
Prioritize the needed cash and grain;
Pay all your taxes early, free of pain.
Children owe parents a mountain of thanks;
Husband and wife's love fills oceans and banks.
I cannot write down all I wish to say;
I'll leave all this here for you to relay.

Huang Qiao thought the rhyming rules should be easy to memorize. After sufficient practice, he called the same elder sons to the hall to recite the revised family rules. As expected, they did quite well this time. When the recitations were about to start, two of the sons looked nervous, while the mischievous rooster-chaser appeared absent-minded. He did not even seem to care, which offended the father, who then told him to do his recitation first.

To the father's surprise, this naughty boy did his recitation fluently and effortlessly. His two elder brothers tried after him. They both managed to recite all twenty-one advisories, albeit less fluently. The father was impressed by the naughty boy's talents and still took comfort in hearing the other two sons finishing their recitations.

With the family rules in place, the sons knew what was expected of them and they all behaved accordingly. The father grew older as the sons grew up, one after another. "What a great family you have!" their neighbors would flatter when they met the parents.

Indeed, the brothers all studied hard, respected their teachers, loved the old and the young, were kind to neighbors and friendly to strangers. They became model children in the village. Huang Qiao's extended family duly became a rich and reputable one that was known far and wide. Life was peaceful for the Huang family until the father's eightieth birthday. Dressed in their holiday best, all the children and grandchildren, among other relatives, had gathered for this joyful occasion. While everyone was enjoying their festive feast, Huang Qiao surprised them by calling for their attention.

"The swallows here look like they're having an easy life," he sighed, pointing at the birds in the courtyard outside the hall. "Yet, unlike those living in the mountain forests, they may not be able to survive in the wild, because they lack the survival ability." He paused to let them digest his meaning and then continued, "An easy, comfortable life makes people complacent and unmotivated to accept challenges in order to find success and achievements in life. For a brighter future and a better life, you have to be independent." Then he paused again before abruptly announcing, "I want all my twenty-one sons to leave me and find a new place to build your new home."

"Father," said the eldest son, "you are getting old and need care. If we all leave you, won't it seem as if you have no sons? Then, what's the use of having so many sons if none of us can look after you when you are old?"

Indeed, the old man's words had shocked everyone present.

"But you are getting on in years," said his three wives, knowing that he would soon need care. "May we beg you to keep at least some of the sons to look after you?"

He looked at his anxious sons and said, with deep emotion, "I would love to have all my sons living with me until my death, but these are uncertain times. It's more risky to live together here than to go out and find your own homes in other places. I have fought for the Emperor for many years and have traveled to many places. There is good land everywhere that has not been cultivated. Take your family with you and settle wherever you see fit." His sons understood his concern and felt his profound love. They fell silent, warm tears welling up in their eyes.

Huang Qiao then swept his loving eyes over his three wives, knowing they were not getting younger, either.

"All right, then," he said, "each of you will keep your eldest son. The eldest son will stay to look after your own mother in her old age. The rest of you will leave home and build your own home in a new land."

Immediately, the father divided his family wealth of 80,000 *guan* (a unit of 1000) of copper coins and 800 *chen* (a unit of approximately 400 grams) of gold and silver into twenty-one equal shares and gave each son one share. He also gave each of the eighteen departing sons a fine, strong horse to help with moving to their new home, yet to be found.

In addition, he gave every son a copy of their family tree so that they would remember their roots. Everyone present had a heavy heart. His wives and daughters were especially emotional, but they had faith in him and believed this must be the best option for the family. Otherwise, the father would not have done it.

The loving father meticulously attended to practically every detail in every son's life, financially, physically, and spiritually. The last words he said to them were in the form of a poem, now known among his descendants as "Farewell to Sons"[9].

Your strong horses will take you to new land;
Settle in any fine place you'd demand.
Stay in the new land as if it's your own;
It will be just like the old home you've known.
Remember my farewell words day and night;
Burn incense for ancestors each twilight.
May Heaven bless my sons, twenty and one;
You shall all thrive and shine like the bright sun.

---

[9] This translation by Harry J. Huang is based on the version from Jieyang, China. As mentioned in the story, the original Chinese by Huang Qiao was an oral farewell that was believed to have been transcribed by the twenty-one sons afterward and then passed onto their own children and grandchildren, generation after generation, which appears to have resulted in the different versions that exist today. This English translation may be republished independently or posted in social media for noncommercial purposes, as long as due credit is given to the author and translator in the following format.

Farewell to Sons

Original Chinese by HUANG Qiao (黄峭, 872 – 953; Jieyang Version)
English Translation by Harry J. HUANG (黄俊雄, 1956 –)

This poem was to serve as an identity key or code for the extended Huang family. The eighteen sons bravely explored new places in all directions, each settling in his favorite land with his family. Huang Qiao was very pleased when they returned for a family reunion two years later. As he had expected, every one of them had not only survived but started to thrive and prosper in the new settlement. Not long after their reunion, Huang Qiao died a natural, peaceful death in his sleep.

During the funeral process, while his coffin was being carried to the graveyard, the bright, sunny sky suddenly darkened, followed by thunderbolts and pouring rain. The pallbearers had to leave the coffin on the mountain slope to take shelter from the downpour. Then it stopped abruptly and a bright sun appeared in the sky again. When the pallbearers came back, they could not find the coffin.

"Good heavens! Where is the coffin?" they uttered in fear. "Could someone have stolen it?" But they knew this was impossible, for they were the only people around. Besides, locally a coffin and funeral was thought to bode ill for a thief. No one would even think of stealing it. After a period of frantic searching, to their shocked disbelief, they found a deep crack had opened in the mountain slope, and it had somehow swallowed up the coffin. They were still some distance from the pre-dug grave. Anxiously, the nervous sons urged the pallbearers to find some way to rescue the coffin, but the Taoist who was accompanying them asked them to stop.

"No. Don't do it," he said. "This is Heaven's will. It is a Heavenly burial." The sons obeyed him, which made them very proud afterwards. They acted in accordance with the Taoist's instructions by filling up the crack with soil until the coffin was properly buried. They also filled up the pre-dug grave at the original site, moved the tombstone over and built a new graveyard at the Heavenly site. Everything was meticulously done under the instructions of the Taoist. The locals believed the mountain crack was such an unbelievable event it could only have happened to an Emperor on his day of passing. News of this incident surprised everyone who heard about it, far and near. "Was he a Heavenly man?" the villagers would ask. No one knew.

As outstanding as they could be, more than half of Huang Qiao's sons became Imperial officials, while the rest worked at other government jobs. Any of their positions represented great achievements in those days. His sons were all highly reputed scholars and officials respected by the populace.

Time surely flies. In case you are curious about the size of Huang Qiao's extended family, in 2025, 1072 years after his passing, "Farewell to Sons" is recited by about 17 million of his descendants living in mainland China, Taiwan, Hong Kong, Macao, and many other countries in Asia and other continents.

They carry on the tradition of teaching their offspring the same family rules and farewell poem, one generation after another. This poem, in particular, has more than 100 versions, with minor differences that have become the identity code of the different branches or regions. Whichever version is read aloud to the descendants, they would immediately identify from it their ancestry. Every year, numerous descendants from all walks of life come to Huang Qiao's graveyard, which lies on a peaceful, picturesque evergreen mountain in Shaowu, China, to connect their life with him and pay their respects. Huang Qiao wanted a big family, and today's Huang family would surely make him happy.

What a miracle father! What a miracle family!

Ray's Favorite Saying

Green paddy fields stretched from the ferry dock on the south bank of the Banyan River toward the horizon, where they appeared to merge with the sky. Hot summer air rustled the luxuriant rice seedlings, stirring wave after wave in the boundless green patch, carrying refreshing country air to passersby. The thick green plants and the water underneath formed a natural coolant for the midsummer heat in this region, which often reached 39 degrees Celsius. In the inch-deep water, a frog would start croaking, instantly triggering more croaking from far and near. The soothing southern breeze rippled throughout the vast fields, which were visibly divided by irrigation streams that ran alongside earthen roads lined with willows swaying in the scorching sun. On the trees, cicadas chirped rhythmically. How lively and happy they sounded in the quiet fields, when the farmers had gone home for their two-hour lunch break!

Situated 200 meters away from the southern riverbank was Plum Village. On its outskirts lived a famous farmer, Shining Ray, locally known as Shaohui Huang (黄绍辉). Ray was a fulltime herbal specialist and a one-man hospital, doing the jobs of a dermatologist, cardiologist, gastroenterologist, gynecologist, pediatrician, and ENT specialist, among others. He treated practically every disease the local farmers had, including some those other doctors and hospitals failed to cure.

Out of gratitude and respect, patients far and wide called him Half-Celestial (Half-God). Patients from other villages called him Doctor Huang, Doctor Ray; but in Plum Village, those of his generation would call him Brother Ray, while the younger generation would address him as Uncle Ray. He humbly called himself Farmer, a title as unique as himself. He had never attended a medical school or received a medical degree. No one knew exactly how much education he had or where he had acquired it. All they knew was that he was a learned man who had read many books, including classics. Most notably, he authored the "Herbal Rhymes"[10] that summarizes the nature of each category of herbs. It is an invaluable guide for herbalist trainees. It is a guide like no other TCM practitioners or TCM university professors had ever produced.

---

[10] See Huang, H. J. (2015). *My Father and His Herbal-Remedy Stories*, 26–31.

Living conditions were not very good in his time. Ray's home was also his clinic. There he lived, treated patients, ground herbal powder, and made herbal pills for patients. He did not charge his patients a fixed fee. They could pay him with a nickel or a dime, or a fresh fish or a live chicken they had raised—according to their ability or what they had. He accepted whatever they were able or willing to pay him. He did not mind if the poorest patients did not pay him at all. His joy lay in curing patients and making them happy. His pet saying was, "When the patient is happy, the doctor is happy."

One early spring day, an anxious young couple appeared at his door with their crying baby.

"Uncle Ray," the young mother said, "our baby has not pooped for several days and his face is full of bumps now."

Ray immediately examined the baby's skin, checked his eyes, and looked into his mouth. Then he said to the young father, "Go and find some earthworms and bring them back to me, along with your baby."

"Earthworms?" the young father repeated, frowning.

"Yes. You need seven to nine," Ray said.

The father quickly went back home, got a hoe, turned over some dirt at a corner outside his house, and instantly caught seven earthworms. Immediately, he brought them to Ray, with his wife carrying the baby in her arms. Ray skillfully put three of them over the baby's navel and placed a cup over them to keep them there.

"There you go. You can take the baby back home now," he said to the parents.

"But Uncle Ray, doesn't he need some medications as well?"

"No. He doesn't. He will start pooping no later than tonight," he assured them. Only then did they leave, reluctantly.

"Will this really work?" the wife said to the husband on their way back home.

"Uncle Ray has all those rare remedies for so many rare diseases. He has been practicing medicine for many years. Don't forget, he is called Half-God. We must trust him," the husband said with confidence.

Two days later, the mother smiled all the way back to Ray.

"My baby started pooping just one hour after the treatment," she said to Ray, looking relaxed. "He is normal now. Thank you so much, Uncle Ray!"

Ray smiled. He did not have a habit of saying, "You are welcome" when patients thanked him. He would just smile, and when he smiled every patient knew he was happy.

"Uncle Ray," a beautiful girl of sixteen burst out just as the young mother was about to leave.

"What can I do for you?" Ray asked.

"Uncle Ray, I am in big trouble." The girl was weeping. She wiped her tears on her sleeve, but they continued to run down her cheeks. "Look at my ugly eye! I have this terrible pimple on the eyelid! No one will marry me if I have a scar here. My eyelid will be deformed. I will look like an ugly monster! Please save me."

"Relax. I will fix it for you," he said confidently.

"Fix it?" she repeated, suddenly afraid of what he meant. "Are you going to cut it off?" She looked nervous and worried. "Something like this happened to my cousin. She ended up with a terrible scar on her eyelid. It ruined her life. She used to be the prettiest girl in the school, but the scar makes her look like a monster. She is thirty-five now, and no man wants to marry her because of her eye." She started crying again. "Uncle Ray, I would rather lose a hand or a foot." She kept talking while Ray went over to his wife's sewing basket.

"Now raise your hands and show me your fingers," Ray said after he returned with a length of thread. The patient cooperated, and he made an ox tie on a knuckle of one of her middle fingers. "Done," he said, meaning that she could go home now.

"What's this?" she said, frowning at the little thread tie on her finger. She felt it was pretty tight, somewhat uncomfortable. "But will this really work, Uncle Ray? Aren't you going to give me some medications? At least, I need some medicine to put on the pimple."

"No. You don't. Just relax and go home now," he said, as he got up to see her off.

Reluctantly she left, wondering, *What could it really do? Won't it delay my treatment and make it worse? I saw him going to the sewing basket and coming back with the thread. He did not even put any medicine on the thread. How could it have any medicinal effect?*

She was ten steps away when she suddenly stopped, turned about, and said, "But Uncle Ray, would this really work? Don't you want to give me some medications?" She looked really confused. "If it is doesn't work, and if it turns into a runny pimple, my life would be ruined."

"You must trust me," he said. "If you cry, it will make it even worse. You are not the first patient I am treating. At this stage, my treatment success rate is one hundred percent. This thread is used to expel the swelling and prevent it from developing into something worse. Don't remove the thread, but keep it as tight as it is now. Several days later, you will be fine."

"Oh, thank you," she said, feeling relieved now, albeit still worried. Since Ray seemed so sure that she did not need any medications, she decided she had to trust him. Finally, she left in hesitation, almost wanting to beg him for some medications again.

Two days later, she came to tell him that the red pimple had started shrinking and that she was only feeling a bit of discomfort and itching on the eyelid. She was confident that she would recover soon. Another three days later, she smiled sweetly all the way to his home to announce her recovery. She had brought him a large carp fish, a token of appreciation for the painless, perfect cure. The girl kept wondering how the thread had cured her scary pimple.

"If you really want a name for your treatment," said Ray, "you can call it thread-cupuncture. It is just like acupuncture, but you may not understand. Anyway, I am glad you are fine now."

No wonder people call him Half-God, she said to herself, passing a middle-aged woman who had just appeared at Uncle Ray's door.

"Please save my son, Dr. Ray. Please," the woman cried. "He is getting worse and worse in the hospital. His hands are stiff and curling backward now and he can't raise them anymore. You are the Half-God. Only you can save him. Please."

"Calm down. Tell me what has happened," he said kindly.

"He was as strong as an ox, but last month, when he was working under the pines with another young man in the mountains, pine caterpillars dropped onto their bodies, or something. They first had painful rashes, and soon their trouble was out of control. They both have been hospitalized in the county hospital since. Now my son cannot even use his hands. If you don't save him, he will d—" She broke down, but Ray had not seen him, so he was not sure if it was curable.

"Well, I can't promise you anything right now," he said, "but if you like, you can take me to the hospital. I can take a look at him and see if I can help."

"Yes, of course. I thank you from the bottom of my heart," she said. She thought she should really kneel before him to show her gratitude, but she felt the urgency of the moment. Immediately they got onto the backseat of two bicycles and were taken straight to the hospital.

"I cannot do anything for your son," Ray told her and her husband, after his visit to the son's bedside in the ward, "because he is under the care of the doctors in the hospital."

"But he is not improving here. He is getting worse and worse every hour! You need to help us. Please! Otherwise, he will die," they begged tearfully.

"If you really trust me and want me to treat him, he has to leave the hospital. And he can only receive my own treatment, without other doctors' medications."

"Of course, of course, of course," the desperate couple said with relief. "We will take him out right away, and he will be under your care from this moment on. Thank you! Thank you! Thank you, so, so, so much! You are our savior!"

After the diagnosis, the bicycle rider took Ray back home. Shortly after, the twenty-year-old patient appeared in front of his house, on the back of someone's bicycle. Ray went out to meet him, seeing the pain in the young man's eyes. He was trembling, unable to control his hands, which had curled backward with the palms facing skyward. Ray knew what had caused his sickness and why the university-trained doctors had failed to cure him.

He did a more thorough examination, checking his pulse, looking at his tongue, and asking some questions. Then, he prescribed oral medications for him and prepared some herbal cream for external application. At the time he told no one exactly what medicine was used, but about ten days later, the young man had fully recovered.

The patient and his parents were overjoyed at first but immediately saddened when they got the heartbreaking news that the other young man, who had remained in the hospital, had died of the pine caterpillar infection.

How miserable the dead boy's parents were that they had not heard earlier about the "Half-God"! It was too late for their son, but Ray felt it was his duty to educate other doctors so such tragedies could be prevented in the future. He shared with other medical practitioners his clinical experience, including the crucial ingredients he used in the herbal cream.

"It is the nature of the pine caterpillar venom that determines the type of medicine to use," Ray told other medical workers. "Pine caterpillar venom is acidic, and so is that of other insects. If you use the right type of medicine that neutralizes its acid, you may cure it. Otherwise, the condition may deteriorate." Ray also educated the general public on the issue. After that, no other such deaths were reported in the region.

Ray was like a busy hospital, working seven days a week. He was always on call and never took a holiday. On Chinese New Year's Eve, he was about to eat his most important dinner of the year when he heard a panic-stricken neighbor calling outside his door.

"My daughter-in-law had an accident! Her pressure cooker exploded and her face is all burned," she cried. "She is dying of pain. She needs your help!"

"Where is she now?"

"I left her lying on the floor. My son is bringing her over," she said. "There! There she comes."

She was a frightening sight! The beautiful bride, who had been married less than a month, was mutilated beyond recognition. Her face was covered with blisters, some as big as eggs and others as small as beans. Her forehead and eyelids were badly burned.

Fortunately, Ray had emergency medications on hand for practically all ailments. He immediately brought out the Emergency Rescue Cream for Explosion and Fire Burns, his own invention and recognized as the best of all burn creams by his patients. He gently pricked open the blisters before applying the medicine, after which he bandaged up her face. Her burns were so severe and the area so large that the first application used up his supply of burn cream. He had to go to a large pharmacy to purchase additional ingredients to prepare a much larger amount for the patient. But under his meticulous care, the patient was spared of any skin infections. Eight days later, she was able to go to visit her parents, free of infection and with no bandages. The only difference was that her face appeared dark brown now, different from the original fair color. Her flesh had been affected quite literally by the extremely high temperature. If she had not received timely, effective treatment, she would have suffered severe infection that could have left ugly scars all over her face, especially her eyelids.

"Your color will recover slowly," Ray told the patient. "It will take months or even longer, but it will recover eventually." She was very happy and grateful that he had saved her face.

"How much should we pay you for all the medications and treatment?" she asked Ray.

"Just pay me thirty *yuan* [worth about four dollars]," he said. It was a large sum for the patient.

The neighbors paid him, but they complained about the high cost.

"Uncle Ray charged my daughter-in-law an unbelievable sum of thirty *yuan* for treating her burns!" said the mother-in-law, speaking loudly deliberately so as to be heard by Ray's wife, who was passing by her door.

This displeased Ray's wife. "How could you have charged the neighbors so much money for treating her burns?" she lectured him. "Thirty *yuan* is far too much for them!"

"I know thirty *yuan* is a lot of money," said Ray, "but it didn't even cover the cost of the ingredients I had to buy. I did not charge them for the other ingredients, my time making the cream, or the many hours of labor I put into her treatment. If she had gone to the hospital, it could easily cost her two or three thousand *yuan*, and she might still end up with scars all over her face."

His wife did not know who was right, but she was upset that the neighbors were not happy. Ray didn't know what to say, and he never explained anything to them either. He continued with his life and work.

The next day, a young worker from the Farm Machinery Factory limped to his house for similar treatment. He had been burned by red hot iron while trying to pour it into a cast mould. His right leg was covered with black, sticky tar. He said he had used tar because the burning happened so suddenly and he could not find anything to ease the excruciating pain. His coworkers had first poured cold water over it to cool it down, but this did not work. Then, someone went to the drugstore next to their factory to buy some over-the-counter burn cream for him, while several other workers tried to fan the burns for him, but, as hard as they worked at this, the fanning didn't work either. When the coworker returned with the burn cream, they immediately squeezed out all the cream from every tube, spreading it evenly over his burns. But nothing eased his unbearable pain. Then, desperate for anything that might help, they covered his leg with tar. It was literally burnt, as *burn* implies. Had he not been such a strong man, he would have passed out more than once. When the lathe operator told them about the miracle doctor, he came without delay.

After a careful examination, Ray started removing the sticky black substance from the man's leg, and then applied his miracle burn cream on the large wounds that covered nearly half of his leg and his foot. The young man felt immediate relief as Ray's medicinal cream was being applied. Then Ray bandaged it up for him, so he was able to wear pants to keep his leg warm. The young man returned for a new coat of burn cream every day until he was fully recovered. No infection occurred, so he had no scars.

"I am so grateful to you for this miraculous recovery. My unbearable pain eased the moment you applied the cream on my burns," the young man said sincerely. "How much should I pay you for the medications and treatment, Dr. Ray?"

"Just pay me sixty *yuan*," Ray said with a smile.

"Are you sure that's enough to cover the cost of your medicine? And you have been taking such meticulous care of me for so many days!" The young man felt rather guilty, though truly grateful.

"It's all right. Just pay me sixty *yuan*," Ray repeated. "When you are happy, I am happy." Ray felt thankful the young man hadn't accused him of being greedy. For Ray, a good reputation was more important than life itself.

When the happy young man, after paying Ray, passed by the previous burn patient's house, the old lady appeared at her door and asked him, "So you have fully recovered from your burns?"

"Yes. I am so grateful to Dr. Ray," he said.

"How much did he charge you?"

"Just sixty *yuan*."

"Just sixty *yuan*! Isn't he a greedy man! He rakes in so much from you and thirty *yuan* from us. In less than two months!" she grumbled.

"What are you talking about?" the young man said, feeling offended. "Don't make me sound like an ungrateful man. I owe my entire leg to Dr. Ray! Don't you drag me into your unfair complaints! Yes, I know you have been complaining to everyone. I think it's mean and unfair to complain about such a great doctor for charging you far less than the cost of the ingredients he bought from the drugstore. Did you pay for his bandages and labor?"

"You have such nice words for him. Have you been bribed? The medicine didn't even weigh a pound!"

"A bucket of your smelly poop weighs a hundred pounds, but can you eat it? Is it worth more than a bowl of your rice?" he counterattacked. "You are talking about the *weight* of his medicine? Humph!"

"Young man, you are so rude! How could you talk to your elder like this?"

"I did not intend to be rude, but your rudeness and meanness toward my beloved doctor forced me to talk this way. I have never spoken to anyone like this in my life. I will tell you what: the day I got burned, my coworkers bought twenty tubes of the best burn cream for me from the drugstore. They cost me eighty *yuan*, but they could not even cover my burns, and they did not ease my unbearable pain. I was burned by red hot iron! The medicine from the drugstore was utterly useless for me. For me, sixty *yuan* for saving my leg is nothing. Even if he charged 600 *yuan*, it would still be a great deal for me!"

"You sound filthy rich!" she said, slamming her door shut.

"It is not a matter of rich or poor," the young man shouted to ensure she would hear him. "It is about fairness. It is about morality, it is one's conscience!" The old woman did not respond.

Every day, patients with rare diseases visited Ray. There was a woman who had a tongue so swollen that it filled her entire mouth so tightly that she could not eat, drink, or speak. Ray was called for late at night and used a flashlight to find his way to the patient's home. On the way, he picked a big bunch of herbs from the roadside, which he pounded to make juice once he got to the patient's home. He fed the juice into her mouth drop by drop while her husband pried it open with a metal spoon. Miraculously, her condition began to improve, and she was able to eat the following day. He did not finish her treatment until the following evening.

No sooner had he returned home that night than a young man who had suddenly found himself unable to urinate came to seek his help. Ray recognized this as a potentially life-threatening emergency. Carrying a flashlight, he dug up the roots of a small banana tree and smashed them into a paste, which he mixed it with a bit of salt. He covered the patient's groin with a thick layer of this mixture. The young man's condition improved instantly, and in less than five minutes, he was able to urinate again.

Patients called Ray "Miracle Doctor," "Half-God," "Half-Celestial," and so on, out of respect and gratitude. It was their way of acknowledging his outstanding medical expertise and to express their true appreciation of his miraculous treatment and his high ethical standards. He always put his patients before himself, often forgoing meals to provide timely emergency treatment for them.

Thirty years later, after the passing of her mother-in-law, Ray's first burn patient in this story felt a desire to apologize to him for her lack of appreciation for his treatment, though it seemed too late to do so. She now owned a hardware store and did not lack for money. But being unable to confess her guilty feelings to Ray in person weighed her down, especially when she thought of the way her mother-in-law had complained. Every morning, when she washed her beautiful face and looked in the mirror, she could not help but think of Ray. "Thirty *yuan* for this pretty face!" she would murmur to herself, and uncontrollable tears would well up in her eyes.

During the day, she would forget these thoughts, but at night she would dream of confronting her mother-in-law and scolding herself. One night she dreamed of seeing Ray in the mountains, collecting the same herbs needed to treat her burns. She went up to him crying, "Uncle Ray, I am so sorry my mother-in-law and I treated you unfairly. I know we did not even pay you enough for the ingredients you used in my medicine. I am really sorry. I beg your forgiveness!"

Ray raised his warm hands to wipe away her tears, saying, "You don't have to apologize. It's such a small thing. I have long forgotten about it. You did not owe me anything. I was even happier than you when you recovered from your burns without a scar."

"You are so kind!" she said.

"When you are happy, I am happy," he repeated his favorite saying. "Will you forget about it and be a happy person from now on?"

She nodded. When she woke up, she was a new, happy woman.

Forgotten Favors[11]

It was the fourth day after the Chinese New Year, and 95-year-old Veda heard noises outside her country house, somewhere out by the dirt road. She peered out from the partially open door and, to her surprise, caught sight of a small crowd. Security had been good in the village for many decades, and she had never worried about intruders in her home. She had a habit of keeping her door open for her elder son and granddaughter-in-law, who would bring her groceries every day. An open door made it easier for them to enter and created a sense of closeness with the young people.

But who are these strangers? she wondered, dragging her heavy feet toward the door. *Should I close the door?*

"Grand-aunt," a young man called out as he ran toward her door.

The rest of the crowd caught up with him. Though Veda had cataracts and her hearing was not very sharp, she immediately realized that they were friendly visitors. Quickly, she opened the door wider for them. She counted heads—there were five of them.

"Hi, Aunt Veda," a familiar voice called out.

"Oh, dear! Please do come in," said Veda, still unaware who the visitors were. Almost every middle-aged person in the village called her Aunt Veda; those closer to her age called her Sister Veda, and the younger people would call her Grand-aunt.

"You are?" Veda said, waiting for the old lady to introduce herself.

"I am Suna," she said. "Have you forgotten me? Here are our gifts for you." Tears involuntarily rolled down Suna's cheeks. Veda was surprised and uneasy, saying, "Why did you bring me gifts? I am delighted you have come, but I don't want any gifts. Everything costs money. Now, make yourselves at home and have some tea."

The visitors took their seats around the tea table, where she served them *gongfu* tea. A soothing breeze carrying the fragrance of magnolias from the tree outside floated into her hall. Suna and Veda sat on opposite sides of the tea table, while the younger people sat facing them in a

---

[11] Note: This story is based on a few of the numerous good needs done by **Huang** Huiying (黄惠英) (1931–) of Meipan Village, Jieyang, China, named Veda in the story,.

semicircle. Veda first poured boiling water into the small, elegant clay teapot, the size of an apple. Then she poured out the water immediately into tiny white porcelain teacups the size of a ping-pong ball. After that, she filled the teapot with *Tieguanyin* tea, poured boiling water into the tea leaves, and put back the lid. Most local people would pour out this first water quickly, saying that doing so was like washing the tea leaves, as if washing vegetables, but Veda's younger son did not think this was necessary. He would say, "If you folks don't like the first serving, just give it to me. That's the first and best tea I always enjoy."

"High water and low tea" was the proper way of pouring boiling water into the teapot and then pouring tea out of it. This meant raising the kettle high—about four or five inches above the teapot—when pouring in the boiling water, but keeping the spout as low as possible when pouring the tea out of the teapot into the small teacups, of which there were usually two to five in a set. "Let me do it," said Suna's son, who offered to serve tea to everyone present. It was local etiquette for young men to serve tea to the elders and others.

The other young people, who were carrying gifts, got up and carefully placed them on the table. These gifts consisted of two large vacuum-sealed packages of *Tieguanyin* tea, each weighing 500 grams, two fine boxes of fresh cookies, and other expensive dry food.

"Suna, but why did you bring all these things here?" Veda said, puzzled, as she looked at the pile on the table. "I don't deserve any of these, and I won't take any. I hope you don't mind, but thank you for your kindness. You must take everything back and enjoy them yourself. The young people would love the cookies." She started putting everything back into the bags in which they'd been carried.

"You have not changed a bit, Aunt Veda! Every time I want to give you something, you always say no. All you say is no," protested Suna. "You don't care about my feelings. I mean it. I feel sad if you don't take my gifts. They are not worth much. They are just meant for you. No matter what you say, we will not take anything back today. We have come all this way just to bring these small gifts to you." The more Suna talked, the more emotional she became.

"But why, Suna?" said Veda. "I have not done anything for you."

"You haven't done anything for me!" cried Suna. "You don't know how grateful I have been to you all my life. This is just a small token of heartfelt thanks for your kindness. It has been buried in my heart for fifty years. You would be torturing me not to take my gifts," Suna sobbed.

"Now relax, Suna," Veda comforted her. "But I still don't understand."

Suna took a deep breath and said, "As you know, in the 1970s, life was hard for all of us. You were not much better off than us, but that spring day, you gave me fifty cents. It was money your daughters had earned from embroidery. From time to time, when you knew I was running out of food, you would give me a dime or a nickel that allowed me to buy rice. In the worst year of famine, we might not have survived without you. My family and I owe you a big debt of gratitude! I have been telling my children and grandchildren how kind you were to us and that they must never forget your kindness. Today, they have come with me to thank you for everything you did for us."

"Suna, that was fifty years ago," Veda said. "If you add it all up, it was less than a buck. It is not worth mentioning. I am so glad that everyone's life is so much better today. Honestly, I always felt bad I could not do more for you."

"But you were poor yourself, and we all knew it. You spared some grain for the needy seniors by adding more water into your own porridge. Everybody knew it. When I wanted to give you something in return later, like some fruit or vegetables, you would say no. You would push it back to me, and I always gave in and took it back. Today, I have come with my children and grandchildren. You cannot do that anymore. We won't go back home if you don't take them. They aren't worth anything. Just a token of our heartfelt thanks. I have thought of giving you some money, but I knew you would not like it. That is why we brought these few common things for you instead. Just some tea, cookies, and food items. It's all cheap stuff."

"Oh, no. No, no, no!" Veda shook her head. "No, not even the cookies. I really appreciate it, but you know, I am old, and I don't eat sweet stuff anymore. Take them back and let your grandchildren enjoy them. Children love sweet things. I also have tea here. So you should take it back and enjoy it yourself. This is very expensive tea. Everything costs money. I won't take it."

"You know what, Aunt Veda," said Suna. "To tell you the truth, I did not buy the tea. My son-in-law gave it to me. So it didn't cost me any money."

"No, I still cannot take it," said Veda. "Your son-in-law had to pay for it too. Everything costs money. It is very expensive tea. Please take it back and enjoy it yourself. And all these other good things too, everything is expensive. Everything costs money. I just won't take any."

Suna became very anxious now. She had come to make Veda happy by giving her the best gifts she could buy, but again, Veda wanted her to take everything back. Her face reddened and she started to sweat.

Knock! Knock! Knock!

Veda and her visitors raised their heads, looked toward the door, and saw a middle-aged man at the door: Loyal Lad, from the village.

"Come on in!" Veda greeted him. "The door is open."

Loyal Lad stepped into the hall and hugged Veda. "How wonderful it is to see you again," said Veda.

"Here is a gift for you, Aunt Veda," said Loyal Lad. "I hope you like it."

Veda looked into the large, heavy gift bag and said, "Why? Why did you bring such delicacies to me? I am delighted you have come, but I don't want you to bring gifts. Gifts cost money. Everything costs money. I don't want you to spend money on any gifts for me. I don't need anything."

"Aunt Veda," said Loyal Lad, "life is not the same as twenty years ago. Now we are not poor anymore. We don't need to worry about money, food, clothing, and lodging anymore. This is just a token of appreciation—just to show my years of gratitude to you."

"I don't know what you mean," said Veda. "I haven't done anything for you to deserve these expensive gifts."

Loyal Lad then reminded Veda of a day he could never forget. "That cold spring day," he began, looking at her kindly, "I was working in the fields when it suddenly started to pour. I had no rain gear, and soon I was soaked to the skin. I was cold and hungry, so I stopped working and decided to go back home, but then I started shivering uncontrollably. When I was about to pass your home I felt I could not take it any longer. I saw you sitting by your stove, cooking. You greeted me and asked me to come into your house and wait until the rain stopped. So I came in, and I was still shivering. When I saw your porridge in the pot was ready, I asked you, 'Aunt Veda, can I have a bowl of your porridge?' You quickly said, "Of course, you are most welcome.' You even said, 'I am sorry I forgot to invite you.' You immediately offered me a bowl of hot porridge. It stopped my hunger and warmed me up, but I felt really embarrassed that I had asked for food from you. When I returned home, I told my mother about the porridge and how embarrassed I was, but she assured me, 'Don't take it to heart. Aunt Veda is no ordinary person. She's different from others. She is generous, kind-hearted, and she did not mind.'" Tears welled up in his eyes.

71

Loyal Lad did not really want to retell the story, especially in front of so many other people, but he knew if he did not give a good reason, Aunt Veda would not accept his gifts. For that reason alone, he retold his embarrassing story.

Veda remembered this incident and stopped his narration at once. "Now, sit down and tell me how you have been doing all these years," she said. "Help yourself to some tea."

"Aunt Veda, you must take my gifts today," he begged.

"Okay, okay, I will happily accept all your gifts," said Veda, taking the heavy bag from his hand. This was the first time she had ever accepted someone's gifts without a fight. This surprised Suna and her family.

"Now look, Aunt Veda," said Suna, "that's unfair! Why did you accept his gifts but refuse mine?" Veda was about to answer the question when she saw a car pulling up in front of her house. Out came seven people, led by a hunchbacked lady who cried out, "Sister Veda!"

"Oh, dear!" said Veda.

Supported by her son, the unexpected visitor came in without being invited and threw herself into Veda's arms. She was an old neighbor who had lived in the old village compound forty or fifty years ago. In their village, a married woman who came from outside the village would be called Mrs. plus her husband's given name. Depending on their seniority, women born in their village, married or unmarried, would be called Sister, Aunt, or Grand-aunt plus their own given names, to simultaneously show intimacy and respect.

"You are Do—?" Veda said slowly, waiting for her to confirm her own name.

"Donna, your old neighbor!" she said. Then she swept her eyes across the young companions still standing outside the door and said, "Now, say hello to Grand-aunt Veda." Her son, daughter-in-law, and her three grandchildren greeted Veda in chorus.

"Come on in and have some tea, all of you!" Veda said to the young couple and their three children, who were still standing outside the door. Every one of them was carrying something in a gift bag. They quickly put their bags on the side table.

"These are our gifts for you, Sister Veda." Donna pointed at them.

Veda went over to see what gifts they had brought her: name-brand tea, a bag of fresh *longan*, a huge box of fine assorted cookies, among other expensive things that the villagers would customarily send to important friends and relatives.

72

"Why all this?" Veda was puzzled. She could not recall doing Donna any favors. All she remembered was that fifty years ago, like others, Donna's family was not rich and life was hard for them. "I am so glad you have come, but you must not bring any gifts. Gifts cost money. Everything costs money."

"My son sent me the tea. I did not buy anything. He owns a tea shop," said Donna, who knew well that Veda would not accept a gift from anyone who'd had to buy it. Even if their gifts were fruits or vegetables they had grown, she still did not want to accept them.

"Donna, you know, I don't really drink tea. I mostly drink plain water," said Veda.

Donna became upset at hearing this. Her son had driven her all the way to pay Veda this visit with the gifts that were sincerely meant for her. She knew that in the past, when everyone around them was poor, Veda would give money and food to neighbors, especially childless seniors or elders neglected by their children. On several occasions in the past when Donna had tried to return favors to her, she had simply thrust her gifts back into her hands. It was well known that once Veda decided to return or refuse a gift, no one could bend her will or change her mind.

"The tea is free," Donna continued to explain to Veda. "I did not spend any money on it. I didn't buy it."

"I am so happy you have come, but you have to take everything back when you leave," insisted Veda. "Now, everyone, make yourself at home and have some tea. How have you and your family been doing all these years? I suppose we haven't seen each other for at least thirty or forty years!"

"Indeed," said Donna. They all started telling stories of the years when Veda had left the village and lived in a nearby city. Veda had also lived with her younger son in Toronto for two months and with her daughter in Paris for some time, but she eventually chose to move back to the village. While she was away, Donna's life had improved day by day. Her children had grown up and gone into business instead of farming. They had all become wealthy, and each owned a new four-storey house. Her grandchildren had their own happy families, too.

"Sister Veda." Donna suddenly became emotional, tears spilling from her eyes, surprising her host and everyone present. Veda did not know the reason for the tears and dared not interrupt her. She knew Donna must have something to say and that it was best to let her finish whatever she wanted to say.

"I have been feeling so grateful to you all my life," Donna continued, "throughout the past fifty or sixty years." Veda was a little relieved. At least it didn't sound like anything bad. There was silence for a moment.

"Well, Donna?" Veda frowned at her.

"Do you remember? Fifty or sixty years ago, my family had nowhere to cook our meals. It was you who offered part of your burnt-down house for us to put our straw-burning stove and cook our meals."

Veda was relaxed now. "Don't even mention that," she said, dismissively. "The pleasure was mine." Though her short-term memory was fading, Veda did not confuse past events. She had inherited two houses from her mother and rented them to a neighbor for two dollars a year until one burned down in a fire that had started in the chimney. The house was completely ruined, except the four walls built of red mountain earth, sand, and limestone. Veda knew the renter was not rich and could not afford to rebuild the house for her, so she didn't even bother to ask if they wanted to install a new roof for the house and continue to live in it. Nor did she sue them for the loss. Needless to say, a house without a roof was not livable.

Without asking her permission, the renter's neighbor began to use the roofless house as a chicken coop, occupying half of the floor. Donna had five children who were growing up and required more space, but all they had was a tiny house about four meters wide by seven meters deep. The parents' bed occupied almost half of the floor space, and a dining table took up a quarter. A stove took up more space, leaving hardly enough room for the children to sleep. Since the neighbor was using Veda's burnt-down house as a chicken coop, Donna, who lived next door, moved her stove to one corner of the ruined house and started doing her cooking there.

The chicken coop owner was not pleased and said to her, "You should not be cooking here. My chickens are here. They run around. It is unsafe for them. Besides, it's not a clean place. It's not suitable for cooking."

Donna knew it was not an ideal place for preparing food. Neither did she really want to be cooking next to a chicken coop, but she had no real choice. If she had permission to cook there, she would do it. She negotiated with the original occupier, but it didn't work out well. To avoid further offense, she talked to Veda, who was known throughout the village for her golden heart, and asked permission to cook there.

Veda happily permitted Donna's family to use a corner of her roofless house for cooking. She also talked with the original occupier and asked him not to drive Donna away. He agreed, and the problem was solved without complications. Donna's husband put up a plastic sheet over the stove as a simple roof. This place then served as their kitchen for many years.

Veda had long forgotten the event. It was just one of numerous favors she had done for needy neighbors. During the years when everyone was poor, though she was short of money for her own family, she always managed to spare a few dimes to help others. Sometimes she would give them some rice and sweet potatoes. When she was young, she also helped carry fresh water to the needy senior ladies' homes, even if doing so placed an additional burden on her and her own family. She always took pride in doing her best for them.

"I am glad I did something for you during those challenging days," she said, finally realizing the purpose of Donna's visit. "All this said," she added, "I won't accept your expensive gifts. I want you to take everything back, and I hope you don't mind. I am now living by myself. I don't eat a lot. I don't drink tea, I don't eat sweet stuff, and I don't need more food than I have. You have so many young people at home. They would enjoy these things more than I do."

On hearing this, Donna quickly wrapped her arms around Veda, while her young people began to put the tea into Veda's drawer, the cookies and other fine foods into her refrigerator. Veda tried to free herself to return the gifts to them, but in vain, for Donna was much stronger than her. Then, abruptly, Donna freed Veda and dashed out of the house, leaving Veda standing there helplessly. Donna felt a sense of melancholy, realizing that, because of her age, Veda could not move as freely as she once did.

"Bye!" Donna shouted from a distance, smiling at Veda and relieved that she had successfully left the gifts at her house.

"Bye," said Veda, unwillingly.

When Veda turned about, the first family who had arrived at her door was nowhere to be found. Loyal Lad had also disappeared. All she saw was the gifts they had brought for her.

Though she had never intended to accept any gifts from others, Veda ended up accepting all of them.

"Why send me all these gifts? There are so many of them!" she murmured. "Just come visit me. Don't bring any gifts. Everything is expensive. Everything costs money."

But no one heard her. They were all overjoyed that they had managed to leave their gifts at her house. They congratulated each other on having had the good fortune to come at the same hour on the same day.

Weren't they lucky!

Love and Joy

Shockfact is an Asian immigrant who came to Canada two years ago, eager to enjoy the country's freedom of speech. He scolded his wife when the food was too hot or too cold. He openly criticized the two or three city councilors and MPPs whose names were known to him, as if he had a solution to every problem in Toronto and the rest of Ontario. His favorite target, however, was the unpopular Prime Minister, whom he blamed for every single crime in Canada. He was no less aggressive in attacking people of other walks of life. His last attack, one I read, was targeting TCM (Traditional Chinese Medicine) practitioners: "You TCM practitioners are all liars and cheaters. You use trickery to steal money from patients. Get the f--k back to China!" Everyone complained that this man spilled out shit whenever he opened his mouth, but he would counterattack: Don't we have freedom of speech in Canada? But Shockfact's happy, free life did not last forever.

On Father's Day last year, he and his wife suddenly realized they had a problem. They had always wanted to have a child, but his wife just could not become pregnant. All his elementary school and high school friends, cousins, and coworkers of his age had become fathers and mothers, some with three children already.

At the age of thirty-nine, the couple were still struggling to get pregnant. The more he wanted a child, the more frustrated he became. And the more frustrated he was, the more scared his wife was and, thus, the harder it became for her to conceive. They had seen Dr. Smith, an obstetrician, many times and had taken all his advice wholeheartedly, including lovemaking skills and postures, until the doctor said, "Would you consider seeing a TCM practitioner?"

"Oh, no," he said. "The last healthcare worker I want to see is a TCM practitioner. TCM is simply witchcraft. It has no scientific theory. No one knows how it really works." His wife tugged on his sleeve, wanting him to stop.

"Well," Dr. Smith said, "we may disagree on this point, but many of my patients who were deemed incapable of conceiving in fact became pregnant after they saw a good TCM practitioner."

"If I can find a good one, I don't mind seeing one," his wife said.

"But Dr. Smith, do you know any good TCM practitioner in Toronto?" he cut in.

"Dr. Wise on Victoria Park, north of Finch Avenue, is a very good one. He has a PhD in TCM and acupuncture." With this, he gave Dr. Wise's phone number to his wife.

Dr. Smith could see that Shockfact was blinking nonstop. Evidently he was not pleased. Lowering his head and looking away from Dr. Smith, Shockfact grumbled, mostly to himself, "I can't believe it. Western medicine is so much superior to outdated Chinese herbal medicine. And herbal medicine is, at least, something you can see and feel, even though it is not good. But acupuncture! Dr. Smith, you must be kidding! You are such a great doctor, and yet you believe acupuncture may help my wife get pregnant. What has that little needle got to do with pregnancy?! Believe me, it won't work. You claim some of your patients successfully became pregnant after receiving acupuncture treatment, but could you tell me how all this really happened? It's just bullshit! I just don't believe it! Before I came to Canada, I was a member of the United Coalition Against Traditional Chinese Medicine, based in Shanghai. Members of our coalition did not believe in Traditional Chinese Medicine. And that includes herbal medicine and acupuncture. We worked relentlessly to wipe it out in China! I came to Canada to enjoy modern Western medicine, and now I've got a Canadian doctor telling my wife to see an acupuncturist who came from China. What an irony that is, and what an insult it is to me!"

Dr. Smith had been expecting such a response and remained silent. Finally, Shockfact pulled himself up, loosened his tight jaw and squeezed out a begrudging thank-you to the doctor.

This grumpy man grew even more anxious and agitated as they left the doctor's office. Something, he thought, must be wrong, though he didn't know what. Possible or impossible, he wanted a child badly, and the sooner the better.

"If you really want to see Wise, you can go," he told his wife. "I don't care."

His wife immediately called Dr. Wise and went to see him late in the afternoon. He examined her and checked her pulse, then gave her acupuncture treatment and prescribed some herbal medicinal powder for her. After two weeks of treatment, she felt something changing in her body. Her period did not come at the usual time of the lunar month. *Is there any chance I'm pregnant?* she wondered.

Indeed, she was. Shockfact was overjoyed! He became a happy man for the first time in his life. But to save money, he asked his wife to stop seeing Dr. Wise. He was sure he could find other ways to protect her pregnancy. His wife's belly bulged rapidly after the third month. Shockfact was so happy that just glancing at her expanding belly made him grin every time.

He prided himself in his potency, imagining the glorious day when he would become a father. He already had two lists of names, one for a girl and the other for a boy. He had told his wife to buy baby clothes and plan a "twelve-day-old" celebration and a "one-month-old" celebration.

To his dismay, his wife suddenly started to bleed profusely from her uterus on the fourth Sunday of her third month of pregnancy, and he had to take her to the hospital for emergency treatment. He'd acted as quickly as he could to save the baby, but after they had spent five hours in the emergency room, the hospital obstetrician made it official: she had had a miscarriage.

Shockfact, who had always acted tough in front of his wife and others, was not so tough this time. Devastated by the news, he went to the washroom intending to splash his face with cold water. When he looked in the mirror, he couldn't believe his eyes: the face in the mirror was that of a stranger, wan and sallow.

He burst into tears, questioning himself in front of the mirror: Had he committed some sin against any immortals? Had his parents or ancestors done something wrong that brought on the loss of this baby? Was this trouble predestined? His wife stayed in the hospital for a day and was released the following afternoon.

When she came home, she felt even more devastated. With no strangers around to witness it, she cried and cried and cried. Shockfact became annoyed with her and turned rude again, blaming her for being too excited after becoming pregnant, for eating the wrong food recommended by Dr. Wise—for everything she had done. That was what he had done all his life anyway: blaming her for anything that went wrong.

Two months later, the unfortunate wife went back to Dr. Wise to tell him about the good news of being pregnant and the bad news of losing the fetus. She sought further acupuncture treatment from him, determined to have a baby. This time, she also told Dr. Wise about the pressure she faced at home. Dr. Wise asked her to bring along her husband on her next visit.

When she asked him to come with her, he refused. But she insisted that he could be the cause of their problem and that he must come if he really wanted a baby. Reluctantly, he came with her the following morning.

Oh, it's you! Dr. Wise said to himself, recognizing the man. At a community lecture once, Shockfact, sitting in the front row, had heckled him, repeatedly interrupting and insulting him when he spoke about how to maintain a healthy lifestyle. "Your way of life is not the best way," he had shouted. "It's out of date. It's based on beliefs, not science. You don't even know the physics theory or exactly how each herb and the acupuncture needle work inside the body, and you call yourself a TCM doctor and an acupuncturist! What a joke!" The audience booed him down, but soon he started up again. "The only criteria to judge if TCM works is by looking at the life span of the population. Do people in China live longer than Western people? No! That means Chinese medicine is inferior. TCM is just like the stinking outhouse people used in the old days. Western medicine is the modern toilet we have today. We shouldn't cling to the old outhouse. We should embrace the clean new toilet."

Instantly, Dr. Wise realized that the verbally abusive man in front of him was the problem. He looked him over from head to foot, without betraying the fact that he recognized the aggressive man from his lecture. "Welcome to my clinic," he said to Shockfact.

Shockfact lowered his head, his face reddening. Unmistakably, Dr. Wise was the speaker he had once insulted.

"I know you may not be a TCM fan," said Dr. Wise, breaking the silence. "But if you really want to have a baby, you need to cooperate."

"I will," he said, unwillingly.

Dr. Wise told him he should be more caring, loving, understanding, and a more considerate and kinder husband. He must free his wife of any pressure and make her happy, if he could. He also told him about healthy vegetables and fruit, especially asparagus and broccoli, which he said were good for the baby's nerve development. Finally, Dr. Wise suggested that they each receive a round of acupuncture treatment to regulate their hormones and improve their energy levels and ultimately their overall health condition. Strangely, Shockfact had no objection. Thus, they had their first treatment before returning home.

Shockfact left Dr. Wise's clinic with an uneasy feeling but also a premonition that his wife would soon become pregnant again—and that this time she would have a live birth. He and his wife fully cooperated with Dr. Wise. As expected, his wife became pregnant again the following month.

Her new pregnancy went smoothly until she entered the fifth month, when she suddenly felt pressure in her abdomen with abnormal discomfort. Panic-stricken, Shockfact dared not delay. He took his wife directly to Dr. Wise, who immediately gave her acupuncture treatment to regulate her system and calm the fetus. Her discomfort disappeared thirty minutes into her treatment. Then, everything returned to normal. Shockfact gave a sigh of relief when he saw her smiling after getting off the acupuncture bed.

On their way home, the formerly abusive husband did not utter a word. His mind was blank; his eyes were blank; he still looked anxious and restless. Before they reached home, something flashed across his mind. He suddenly suspected that he might have a problem himself— and it could be the way he lived. It was a strange feeling he had never experienced before.

To his wife's disbelief, Shockfact's priorities changed that evening. He posted no comments on the news website. Instead, he did some house chores, even helped with cooking and dishwashing. Once a week he would take his wife to Dr. Wise for maintenance treatments. He also took her to the obstetrician once a month for routine checkups. He knew that another miscarriage would drive him to desperation, which he just could not afford. These changes gradually transformed him into a new person.

In his wife's last month of pregnancy, he had become a tolerant, patient, and caring man, looking after his wife happily. The tight muscles on his face were replaced with a smile, especially when he thought of the joy of being a father. Unknowingly, he had also started to show respect for Dr. Wise and other alternative medical practitioners. In the thirty-eighth week of pregnancy, his wife's water broke and the experienced obstetrician, Dr. Smith, managed to deliver their baby boy just in time. Without Dr. Smith, they might have lost the baby again.

Hearing the baby's first cry in the delivery room, Shockfact was overwhelmed with emotion and practically drowning himself in happy tears. Nervous and excited all at once, he could hardly believe what had happened. Grinning at the bundle of joy his wife was holding, Shockfact realized that he owed the live birth of his son to Dr Wise as well.

At last, Shockfact surfaced from a turbulent ocean of emotions and feelings. On the twelfth day after his son's birth, he decided to send a special gift to Dr. Wise that could be displayed in his clinic. He made a trip downtown and hired an artist in Chinatown Center to create a red silk banner with the following words embroidered on it:

Your great needles bring us a boy;
Your boundless love revives our joy.

A Lovely Dental Patient

He lurched into the dental clinic groaning in pain. It was an elegantly designed clinic that featured two Roman-style pillars at the entrance to the treatment rooms from the waiting area. The waiting room was decorated with beautiful flowers and potted plants. The dentist had bought none of them—they were all gifts from patients who appreciated his care and service. Pot lights in the ceiling radiated warm light. The electric fireplace in the middle of the wall opposite the front desk was decorated with a handful of smooth oval pebbles the size of a quail eggs, adding an artistic look to the otherwise modern equipment. Three patients sat in leather armchairs waiting for their appointments. Everyone was taken by surprise by the groaning intruder.

"F--k!" he muttered, a sharp contrast to the beautifully decorated place and civilized-looking clientele. "I am dying here. I need to see the dentist right away," he told the dentist's assistant, Susanna.

"If it's an emergency, you should go to Emergency at the hospital," she said.

"F--k the hospital!" he shouted, taking Susanna by surprise. She had received rude patients before, but this was the first time someone had begun scolding everyone and everything the moment he entered the clinic. "I can't wait until I see a doctor in the f--king hospital. I need to see the dentist at once."

"Do have you have an appointment with us?" she asked politely.

He said no and continued his four-letter rant. Dr. Edward, hearing the ruckus, came out to see what was going on. He spoke with Stephanie and then returned to his current patient. "If you can wait until Dr. Edward has seen his patients, we will try to work out an emergency appointment for you," she explained

He asked how long it would take, and when he was told there were three others before him, he shouted a string of abusive words before leaving, slamming the door behind him. Noting his eyes flaring with fury, three patients rose to their feet and curiously followed him out of the waiting room area, standing in a line in front of the plate-glass front of the office that faced the man's car in the parking lot. Fortunately, he did not, as they might have feared, drive through the windows into the clinic. He got back into his vehicle and left in peace.

Three hours later, to Susanna's disbelief, the grumpy man returned. He looked like a wounded soldier fresh off the battlefield and was now sporting a four-inch white bandage on his forehead, a smaller square one on his chin and one on each cheek. His right hand was also bandaged. It was clear that his injuries were quite serious. He reminded Susanna that the dentist had promised to see him early in the afternoon.

Susanna immediately informed Dr. Edward of the man's unexpected return. Dr. Edward told her to bring him in after he finished work on his last patient.

Despite the man's abusive language and rude behavior, Dr. Edward treated him professionally. He asked where he had got all the bandages, and the man told him he had just seen a doctor in the hospital. He kept cursing the hospital for making him wait in Emergency for hours and hours without treatment, medication, food, or water. Dr. Edward had heard of the long waiting hours there, but he didn't comment.

"The f--king emergency doctor suggested I should see you to check if the nerve of this damn front tooth is damaged. Half of it was broken when I fell."

Dr. Edward examined the broken tooth, touching it gently with a small hook. The man screamed in pain. Dr. Edward asked him to open his mouth wider so he could see his molars, but the patient found it too painful to open wide. Believing there was no immediate danger or threat to his health, Dr. Edward asked him to rest for two or three weeks until the pain had subsided and then come back. Dr. Edward would find out if other treatment was needed. Meanwhile, he offered to prescribe some antibiotics and painkillers to reduce his pain and prevent infection. But the man said the hospital had already given him both. The examination took thirty minutes.

The man left the treatment room and made straight for the door. Susanna called to him from the front desk.

"What is it?" he said, sounding annoyed.

"You haven't paid for your visit."

He drew out his provincial health card and said, "Here."

"We don't accept OHIP cards. The government doesn't cover dental care," she said.

"What the hell is this?" He was upset all over again. "I went to the hospital, and they didn't charge me a penny. They even gave me free medications. Why do I have to pay for emergency dental care?"

"I know you get everything that is covered by OHIP for free, but not dental care from us," she explained.

"The hospital sent me here. You can call them if you like. Since they sent me here, I shouldn't have to pay. You can ask them to pay for my emergency dental care."

"Here's your invoice, anyway," she said. "It's just $50, as Dr. Edward gave you a fifty percent discount. If you don't have the money or don't want to pay today, you can pay later."

It was the best Susanna could do in such a situation. The man took the invoice and left without saying another word. Susanna watched this "wounded soldier" leave and nearly laughed.

Work at Dr. Edward's clinic went on as usual, until December 21, three years later. A shy man dressed in a suit came in, carrying a large potted poinsettia.

"Is Dr. Edward in today?" he asked Susanna.

"Yes, but he is with a patient at the moment. What can we do for you?"

"Oh, nothing. Nothing really important," he said hesitantly. "I have this gift for him." He placed on the counter the huge red poinsettia, which immediately enhanced the holiday atmosphere in the clinic. Just then, Dr. Edward stepped out to give some instructions to Susanna, who told him about the gift the man was dropping off.

"Oh, thank you." He smiled at the stranger.

"Dr. Edward, I have come to apologize to you," the man said, lowering his head as he drew something from his pocket. "And here is my late payment for my emergency visit that day—three years ago."

Only then did the dentist and Susanna recognize him. "Never mind," said Dr. Edward. "How are you doing?"

"Life could not be better, Dr. Edward. But please forgive me for my rude behavior that day. I was in such pain. I had been waiting in Emergency for so many hours without food and water and, worst of all, without seeing a doctor or even a good nurse that day. When I left the first time, I was so angry at the world I was tempted to drive my car through your front window. What a crime I could have committed! Whenever I think of it, I shiver. I really feel ashamed of myself. Please forgive me."

Their conversation continued another five minutes. Dr. Edward assured him of his forgiveness and congratulated him upon his successful career and happy life. Susanna, who felt proud of her expertise in dealing with challenging patients, laughed in surprise as he left. "What a lovely patient he is!"

Crime and Punishment

Miracle Escape in Toronto

Chokan and Sam shared a two-bedroom basement apartment in a detached house in North York. Chokan was a 43-year-old divorcee of few words who had no friends. Sam was a 29-year-old sociable college graduate who had an attractive girlfriend. Whenever Sam's girlfriend visited him, Chokan felt rising irritation and jealousy. He imagined what Sam was doing with his girlfriend behind the locked door of his bedroom. Then, he would think about the intimate times he had shared with his ex-wife during their six-month-long marriage.

It was just another Sunday; Sam's girlfriend had stayed overnight, and her visit left him smiling long after she had gone. It was April 14, 2014. After breakfast, Sam was on the sofa in the living room, chatting with the girl on his cellphone, when an agitated Chokan stepped out his room.

"Won't you shut up!" he shouted.

"Mind your own business," Sam snapped. He wasn't proud of that response, but he'd been taken by surprise and in the moment he had nothing nicer to say.

"You've been disturbing my life ever since I moved here. For six months!" Chokan screamed, his voice sounding choked.

"Have I done something wrong?" Sam said, trying to de-escalate the situation.

But Chokan kept scolding him, and Sam decided silence was the best response. That only infuriated Chokan more, and after shouting some more he found himself out of control.

He ran into the kitchen and returned with a meat cleaver, which he plunged into Sam's abdomen. Stupefied, Sam tried to fend off the weapon but was too weak to defend himself. He begged Chokan to stop, but the roommate continued to stab him. The landlord, living upstairs, heard the commotion and ran down to check, only to see blood all over the sofa, the floor, and on Chokan's hands and clothes.

Chokan was sitting beside Sam's motionless body. He did not resist when the police came and arrested him. He was taken directly to a hospital for a mental health assessment. Forensic reports issued a month later stated that he had been suffering from severe depression.

At the end of a two-week trial, as instructed by the judge, the jurors found Chokan guilty of killing Sam by stabbing him to death, but not criminally responsible because of severe mental illness. Instead of going to jail, he was detained in a forensic psychiatric hospital for treatment, which would last indefinitely until it could be determined that he posed no threat to the safety of the public. After that, he would be set free.

A treatment team composed of psychiatrists, psychologists, social workers, nurses, and security guards in the secure forensic ward of the hospital offered him the best treatment possible. Unlike other killers found guilty of murder, Chokan was treated like a king. His detention maintained jobs for a raft of medical professionals. A wild guess is that it cost at least $1 million a year, or $2740 per day, to keep him in the psychiatric hospital. Normal patients might have to wait months for an appointment with a specialist, but Chokan had free access to any doctor on his treatment team. Besides first-class medical treatment, he enjoyed a cozy room and ate healthy food prescribed by a nutritionist. No one working on his health team uttered an unfriendly word; nobody ever raised their voice when talking with him—not even the police or the prosecutor. Four years of psychiatric treatment, slightly longer than the average 1100 days in such cases, cost Canadian taxpayers at least $4 million.

Chokan's mental state was assessed once a year. To everyone's relief, he behaved satisfactorily throughout the first year. He never attacked another patient or hospital worker. Then came the second assessment, and the third. He was a miracle patient in the hospital. Finally, his case was submitted to the provincial parole review board to determine if he could be released into the community through a gradual integration approach. The final decision stated the team's opinion that he would pose no threat to the safety of the public. Accordingly, arrangements were made and he was allowed to go out into the community for short periods unaccompanied.

Then, an unbelievable miracle happened. On July 17, 2019, four years after his detention, this mentally ill killer left the hospital on a temporary pass and secretly flew out of Canada. No one on the treatment team or other hospital staff or the police knew where he had gone. His disappearance shocked the mayor and everyone else in the city, except perhaps the psychiatrists, psychologists, lawyers, nurses and others whom he had repeatedly told about his intention to escape to his home country.

That day, while Toronto police were looking for him all over the city, Chokan was knocking on his mother's door in another country.

"Mom, it's me, Chokan," he said after three gentle knocks. It was 2:00 a.m., exactly twelve hours ahead of Toronto. His mother, who'd been asleep, heard his voice and got up, thinking she must have been dreaming. She opened the door anyway.

"Oh, Chokan! Is it you?" she cried. "Is it a dream?"

He slipped into the living room quietly and closed the door behind him, saying, "Mom, it's me. It's not a dream!"

"Oh, my child! I missed you day and night." She hugged him tightly.

"Mom, I cannot stay home. I must find another safe place to hide myself," he said calmly.

"Why? What has happened?" she said, terrified.

"I killed my roommate in Canada," he said, sounding guilty. "I have let you down. I am sorry, Mom."

"How did you escape from them, then?" She looked into his eyes.

"I will tell you about everything when I have found a safe place," he assured her. "I have to find a safe place immediately, or it will be too late. They will find me and have me deported back to Canada. Then I can't see you again."

"May God bless my son! What place is safe for you, then?"

"The deserted Tea Farm Village on the mountaintop in the neighboring county has some small old houses for rent. They cost only a hundred bucks a month." With this, he showed her some pictures on his cellphone.

"How did you know about these rental places?" said his mother. "Are you sure they are available?"

"I found them as soon as I got off the airplane. I called and reserved one house already. They know I am coming, and they are expecting me."

"My dear child, no wonder our friends always said your IQ beats everybody else's!"

Three hours later, Chokan and his mother were settled in a hundred-year-old thatched hut with no electricity or running water. They had to use an oil lamp for lighting and fetch water from a pond behind the house. He knew life would be different here, but it would be better than the imprisoned life of a psychiatric inmate. He could enjoy freedom and fresh air in this beautiful mountain village. It was so clean and quiet.

"Now, Chokan, have some food first. I have brought this from the fridge back home. And tell me exactly what happened. Why did you kill your roommate? Was he a bad man?"

"No, Mom. He was a good man. He was a happy man." He sighed.

"If he was a good, happy man, why did you kill him?" She frowned. "Was it an accident?"

"No, not an accident. I killed him because he was a happy man. He had many friends. He had a beautiful girlfriend who was so nice and kind to him, totally different from my ex-wife."

"So, that was the reason?" She sounded scared.

"I was just jealous of him. I had no friends. No women. I was lonely and sad," he said, as tears began to run down his cheeks. "I could even hear them making love in bed."

"Oh, my Lord!" she sobbed, shivering. "So you killed him yesterday and escaped from Canada before they could catch you?"

"No." He shook his head.

"If the police catch you here, they may even put you to death according to the law in our country." She sounded terrified now.

"Mom, it is not like what you said," he said calmly. "I was arrested by the Toronto police. I was then legally released. Even if the police here catch me, they cannot put me to death because I have been tried in Canada already."

The mother looked relieved, but she was still puzzled. "You said you were arrested and tried and released. How can you kill someone in Canada without going to jail? I have never heard of such a thing in any country."

"Mom, in Canada, everything is possible. I really killed my roommate. I was really arrested and then tried and then released into the community. When I tell you the details, you will believe me," he said confidently.

"I am dying to know the details." She looked at him lovingly.

"Mom, it's getting late, so I will just tell you a summary tonight." His eyes met hers. She nodded.

"Mom, that morning, I got up from a sleepless night. I was upset with my roommate, who'd had a great time with his girlfriend the previous day. When I saw the beautiful photo of his sexy girlfriend on his cellphone, I just lost control of myself. So I started a quarrel with him. He did not want to argue with me and remained quiet. If he talked back, it might have released some of my pressure, but he kept quiet and that made me even madder. Then, I just ran into the kitchen and got a meat cleaver and started stabbing him. I must have stabbed him over a hundred times.

"When the landlord came down to find out what was happening, I suddenly woke up, knowing I had committed the worst crime in the world. I knew I had ruined my own life and would have to spend the rest of my life behind bars. At that moment, I knew only mental illness could save me, so immediately I began to act like a madman. I did all kinds of disgusting things that only an insane man would do. I did so many, but they were all so disgusting that I don't even want to tell you about any of it. All I want to tell you is that the so-called psychologists and psychiatrists assessed my mental health and finally told the court that I was suffering mental illness at the time I was killing my roommate. Believe it or not, in Canada, if they think you are mentally ill when you are killing someone, you don't need to go to jail. In fact, even if you kill a whole city or commit treason that results in a million deaths in Canada, you might still go free of punishment. You don't go to jail. You go to a mental hospital instead. For a long time, I was locked up there and couldn't leave that place. But otherwise, they treat you like a king, I guess because you help create jobs for a whole team of people. They're all well paid. They never said anything bad to me. They treated me like a baby who knows nothing and who deserves the best parental care.

"I was never mentally ill in the first place. I just continued to live my life in the mental hospital, and they were all so happy that I never attacked any person there. Mind you, some of those detained in the hospital really are crazy people who do crazy things, but I think more than half of them just pretend to be insane, like me. The psychiatrists and the psychologists find out all about this before long, but they don't care. Why would they care anyway? The more patients they have, the more money they make. The healthier the patients are, the easier their treatment is. For a person like me, they didn't really need to give me any treatment. I just recovered and became a normal person myself. They could claim that the treatment team did a miraculous job with world-class results.

"Mom, you still look confused. Let me tell you more about what happened later on. I hear it costs $3,000 to $6,000 to keep someone like me in the mental hospital. Hospital care in Canada is really expensive. Even if it just costs $4,000 a day, it could have cost about $5 million in my case. If I did not cause more trouble, and if the doctors thought they had made enough money from me, they would set me free. Why would

90

the government keep me longer in the hospital anyway? They would be broke if they kept me for another four years. It is the same situation with other patients, sane or insane. Some of them are really crazy guys and they will continue to kill people no matter how long their treatment is, but to save money, they just release them. Then, after some time, they will begin to kill innocent people again. I think they just don't care.

"It's like a joke, Mom. Like a joke created by the law, a serious joke played by the psychiatrists, psychologists, lawyers, judge, and jurors. All of us mentally ill killers should be locked up in a jail instead of a psychiatric hospital, and for a longer time than the mentally healthy killers. A hospital isn't for murderers. It's for patients who are insane but haven't committed crimes. They put me and other murderers in this expensive mental hospital.

"I think it's irrational to believe insane murderers can be cured. Even I know there is no cure for folly and lunacy. If they built a mental jail in Nunavut and locked me and other mentally ill murderers up there for life, I would not mind. I think it's fair, and we'd all deserve it. Personally, I feel sad for the victims' families whose relatives have been killed by us so-called mentally ill murderers, who are above the law or protected by the law that guarantees us an easy life we don't really deserve. I never once got beaten, and I never spent a day in an actual prison, but that is the Canadian law. As I said before, it's stupid. I just don't have other words to describe it. I don't know who ever created it. The funniest thing is that even though most Canadians are mad about this law, their government never does anything about it.

"Stupid or not, I don't care. At least, it protected me. I killed someone. And I ended up staying in a room that was much more comfortable than my basement room. I ate much better food than what I had had on my own. Just imagine: four years of free rent and free food. In fact, I gained more than twenty pounds. See how strong I am now. I was underweight before I killed my roommate, because I could not afford the nutrition my body needed.

"Believe it or not, I was dealing with a team of idiots the whole time. To prepare for my escape, starting from day one in the mental hospital, I kept telling them that I wanted to go back to join my mother in my home country. I told them more than three times a day, every day, until they did not believe me. Then I just did it. I had kept my passport and some money in a secret place for those four years I was locked up in the hospital, and once they allowed me to leave it for a day I just booked my own ticket and flew home. Mom, that's how I escaped."

Chokan paused to hear his mother's thoughts. She cleared her throat.

"Canada is such a great country," she said, relaxed. "What a miracle! They did not lock you up for killing your roommate. You were treated like a king. No wonder every violent criminal in the world wants to go to Canada. I hear the government doesn't even check the criminals' backgrounds when they apply to go to Canada. Honestly, I don't care how weak their criminal justice system is. I thank God that you are back. If you had murdered someone in China, you would have been put to death long ago. Here, let me look at you again. My child, I am so very proud of you!" She paused and then shouted all of a sudden, "Oh Canada! I love Canada!"

Unbelievable Therapist in the Morgue

Steels, a convicted rapist, had done his time in prison. At 10:00 a.m. on June 29, two prison guards walked him out of the heavily guarded Doer Jail. Hesitantly, he left this now familiar structure and wandered into a fast-food restaurant down the road, as if he had walked into Doer Jail's cafeteria for his free lunch. Only when he saw the menu hanging on the wall behind the cashier did he realize his worry-free prison life was over. Even the cheapest lunch cost $7.99. But he wasn't hungry and did not need any food yet.

He left the restaurant and entered a small fashion store, thinking that he might as well get himself a new jacket and a new pair of pants. He had $1000 in his pocket and could easily afford both. "Some new clothes might make me look handsomer; maybe change me to a new man." Thinking about that, he started looking for his new clothes in earnest. Finally, as recommended by the shop owner, he settled on a black suit that cost $89.99. It came with a free tie and a free white shirt. He tried it on and thought he really had changed into a new person. "Can I just keep the suit on?" he asked the shop owner.

"Of course, as you please," he replied, suggesting that Steels buy a pair of new shoes to match. "You can have a pair of leather shoes or sneakers just for $30," he said. "I usually sell them for $40."

"Okay, I will take a pair of black sneakers too." He tried size 11 and kept them on as well. Then, he paid and disappeared into the crowds on the sidewalk.

The sun was bright and the air refreshing. Flowering trees were blooming, their fragrance tickling his nostrils. Small, colorful birds were singing sweetly in the treetops, fluttering from branch to branch. *How wonderful it is to be free,* he thought, inhaling the fresh fragrance. Glancing down at his new clothes and shoes, he was proud of the decision he had made in the fashion store. *Looking like a professional! If I don't tell anyone, no one would ever know I just got out of jail.* He reflected more on this. *Why would I tell anyone about it anyway?*

Steels was not the most handsome man in the world. He was five feet tall with small eyes, thick lips, and a flat nose, but he was a healthy man attracted to every woman, even the least pretty ones. He had never been loved and never had an opportunity to love any woman, and he resented it. He broke the law more than two years ago primarily because he was starved of love, or so he told himself. It was a reason few women would accept for rape.

He was fundamentally an honest man who believed in fairness, and therefore had never complained about his two-year imprisonment. In fact, except for the harsh treatment he got from the prison bullies, he thought the jail time was too short. For the harm he had caused to the girl, he thought even a 15- to 20-year sentence would be fair. After all, his rape had caused her depression, which led to her suicide. Not only was his sentence short, life had been relatively easy in prison. Before going into custody he'd had to work several part-time jobs to pay rent and buy food, but in prison, except for going to bed and getting up according to the prison schedule, he had little to worry about. He didn't need to buy food or cook. He didn't need to buy detergent and wash clothes. Everything was done for him. It felt a bit like staying in a free hotel. The food was tasteless but nutritious enough to add twenty pounds to his body weight.

But Steels had no wish to go back, because he realized it was the one place in Canada where real justice was served. If an inmate was judged not to have received the appropriate punishment for their crimes, the other inmates would increase it with torture to the extent deserved, especially if it was a sex crime. That could include breaking a hand or foot, smashing your head against the wall and forcing you to drink your own urine or eat your own feces. It could be painful and horrific at times. Still, Steels figured such additional punishment was fair. In fact, he felt happier being merely forced to drink his own urine after the tyrant inmates broke his nose during his first month of imprisonment.

The sun was moving toward the west. It looked like three or four o'clock in the afternoon. Suddenly, Steels realized he had no place to stay for the night. In jail, he hadn't needed to think about that. But out in the free world, he had to find somewhere to sleep. He knew that if he really had nowhere to go, he could go to a homeless shelter. The Scott Mission was one such place, but he hated the thought of the bedbugs, fleas, ants, and cockroaches he'd been told were there. It was said the bathrooms, especially the toilets, were repulsive and that people stole each other's stuff. *I have some money and new clothes and shoes,* he said to himself, standing in the shade of a purple maple outside Bedford Park. *I don't belong there. I would rather go back to jail, though I don't really want to."*

While he stood there, lost in thought, an attractive young woman of his height, with brownish skin, dressed in a silky cream-colored blouse and an orange skirt, brushed past him. Her perfume tickled his nostrils, striking a chord in his heart. Suddenly, he felt a fire burning inside him, and his heart started pounding rapidly. If this had been a private setting, he would go after her, but he could not do it with so many pedestrians around. *No, I can't do that*, he murmured to himself. *I can't commit that crime for the second time.*

He followed her closely, but casually, as if she had not attracted his attention. After the second block, he slowed down to increase the distance between them. She went into a takeout restaurant and bought a sub sandwich, and so did he. He enjoyed every bite of the delicious meal as if he were eating it with the girl. Then she went into a convenience store, and he followed her there, too. Back on the street, she was about to enter an old high-rise building. He quickened his pace and caught up with her at the moment she was opening the door with her electronic key.

"Oh, thank you!" He squeezed out a smile at her before the door closed behind them. She smiled back at him, heading straight to the elevator. Steels looked around and saw nurses and other hospital workers dressed in scrubs. He realized he had followed her into a hospital by means of a staff door. By now he had calmed down and asked himself why exactly he had followed her here. She pushed the UP button while he waited on the other side of the elevator door, keeping a safe distance.

The elevator door opened. He raised his hand and beckoned her to go in first, and so she did. He went in behind her. They stood face to face, alone in the elevator car.

No, you can't do that, he said to himself. *No. You can't!*

"Which floor are you going to?" she said after she had pushed her button.

"Oh, in fact, I am trying to find HR. I'm looking for a job. Do you know which floor it's on?" he said, feeling pretty proud of himself for coming up with such a witty reason. He was pleased that the sweet girl had been so kind to him.

"Come with me," she said with a smile. "It's on the top floor."

What a sweet girl! He felt himself becoming nervous, his limbs trembling gently. Then he caught sight of the ring on her left hand. *Oh, gosh!* He sighed to himself.

"Here we are," she said sweetly when the elevator door opened. "Human Resources is at the end of the corridor."

She walked straight to the end of the corridor and then entered a reception area. Steels followed at her heels.

95

"Hi Sue," she said to a pretty woman sitting at the front desk of the HR office. "This gentleman is looking for a job. I've brought him here." Then, bidding Steels "good luck," she disappeared into an office.

"Many thanks!" he responded, relieved that he had not given in to his temptation to break the law again. He was still a good man with a bright future. *That was scary! Just cannot ever do it again. Must never, never do it again!* he swore to himself.

"What kind of job are you looking for?" the receptionist asked.

"Anything. I am willing to do anything."

"Well, we do have an opening in the morgue for an orderly. It involves taking patients who have died to the morgue, washing the body and placing it in a body bag for storage until it's claimed. Is that something you could see yourself doing?"

"Yes," he said nervously.

"Does that make you nervous?" she asked.

"No. I'm just excited about the possibility of working here. I'm happy," he said. "I would be grateful for the job. No matter how hard it is."

"If you don't mind," she said respectfully, "what weight can you lift? We have bodies that weigh 200 pounds or more. We usually have two or even three people working in a team, but currently we have only one worker on each shift. It's not a terribly popular job, for obvious reasons I guess. Could you manage it if you worked by yourself?"

"Yes. I can," he said confidently. "My name is Steels. I am as strong as steel. In fact, I prefer working by myself. I am a conscientious person. I need very little supervision. Just tell me what to do and I will do everything as well as I am expected to, or even better. I could lift and toss a weight of 200 pounds without problems. I might need help only when it's heavier than 500 pounds."

"It won't be a problem if you need help with anything of that size," she said, taken aback.

"Thank you," he said, waiting for her to offer him the job.

"You're welcome. But I am not the boss. I cannot give you the job, but I will tell my manager what you have told me," she said. "Wait a moment while I tell him you're out here."

She collected the notes she'd made and went into the room in the right corner. Ten minutes later, she emerged smiling.

"I am delighted to tell you that my manager is interested in offering the position to you after you pass the required security checks and meet other requirements," she said.

"That sounds scary," he said. "What security checks? And what are the requirements?"

"It's just a formality," she said. Everyone working here has to pass a Vulnerable Sector police check. If you're a good person and are able to do the job, you will get it."

"When can I start working?" he asked.

"Tomorrow is possible, but you'll need to get that check done quickly."

"Great," he said. "'I'll start tomorrow."

"Hold on. We haven't even discussed pay. What were you expecting?"

"Anything," he said.

"The job pays $1100 a week before deductions—that works out to be nearly $60,000 a year. Is that acceptable?"

"Oh, good. Just good. Good for me." He was so happy and nervous he didn't know what to say. *Unbelievable! Just unbelievable!* he murmured to himself. He filled out all the forms. He had no home address, so he put down a fake one, which he figured he would correct as soon as he rented a place. He used an old phone number that was not in service, which he would edit after he bought his phone and opened an account the next day. After checking all his information, the assistant called the manager, who looked over the forms, asked Steels as few questions and told him he could start work the next morning. "Just get that police check done and bring the document to us as soon as you get it. It usually takes a couple of weeks."

The HR manager and his assistant breathed a sigh of relief. They had advertised this position for three months, but no one was interested in it. The difficulty of getting deceased patients off the wards promptly, especially in a time of bed shortages, had put pressure on the CEO, and they were willing to take some shortcuts to get the situation resolved. The police check requirement—which would have revealed his conviction record—was soon forgotten.

Steels turned thirty-five on the day he started his job. What a happy coincidence! He arrived at the hospital half an hour early. Under the 40-by 20-foot sign making the building as the Central Women's Hospital, the short man looked even shorter and smaller, but he was indeed strong for his size. He had carried heavy loads on construction projects before he went to prison. And inside, he had more than once carried heavy ill or injured inmates on his shoulders to the clinic. He had been nicknamed Steelman, though he was still no match for the heavyweight bullies.

Staring at the sign and logo, he thought of the unforgivable crime he had committed and made up his mind to be a useful citizen from that day on. He felt grateful to the hospital for giving him a new life. He raised his head, shrugged his shoulders and strode confidently into the building.

After dealing with his first three corpses, Steels got over his initial squeamishness and started to actually enjoy his job. In fact, it was quite easy, and since he always wore a mask and disposable gloves, it was not dirty. The female bodies were mostly slim and short, easy to wash. Few people were willing to touch them, but he enjoyed his job. The best part of the role was that he was his own boss. Once a body was brought into the morgue, he would lock the door, remove the clothes and everything else on the body, and then wash it. He imagined trying to revive the women he held. He felt he was the luckiest man to enjoy eyefuls of bodily beauty of the fair sex in its primitive form, something not even kings or presidents could see for free.

Everyone in the hospital was busy doing their own job, and no one cared about what he was up to. Steels liked it that way. He didn't care about their work either. All his colleagues liked him, knowing he would arrive within three minutes of being called. He was diligent about his work, about washing the bodies and making sure they were accurately tagged. Families and funeral homes were satisfied with his work. The director of the morgue inspected his efforts in the first week and again on the following Friday. He was impressed by how clean and well organized the morgue had become since he came.

After lunch the next Monday, Steels found he was getting a strange reaction. When he stopped by the nursing station in the emergency department, the nurses suddenly stopped gossiping about something to stare and smile at him.

"Do you know what just happened, Steels?" said the head nurse.

He shook his head.

"Twenty minutes ago," she said, "one of the richest pharmaceutical executives in the country came to our hospital out of the blue to announce a donation of $100 million for the hospital's Heart Research Center. It's all in appreciation of his daughter's coming back to life yesterday. Some kind of miracle. The coroner found her alive and conscious just after you washed her body."

"Wow!" uttered Steels, shivering. The hospital CEO himself came walking down the hallway toward him. "Congratulations, Steels. A great job well done!" he said, smiling. Steels had heard the woman whose body he collected the previous day had died of a heart attack, devastating the father. But now, the father was grateful to the hospital for something no one imagined possible. His daughter, revived in the morgue!

News reporters swarmed the CEO in the waiting area, asking many questions and finally turning to Steels for permission to interview him. But the humble employee shyly turned down the requests, saying the morgue was short of staff and he was too busy to talk to them. "All I can tell you is that it was God's will. God's blessing. I don't know how it happened," he said. The reporters were satisfied with his brief response. The headline, "God Brought Brown's Daughter Back to Life" dominated the news the next day. In appreciation of his good work, the CEO asked Steels if he might like to work in the office of the research center instead. It would be a promotion, but Steels replied, "Labor work is good for me. I can't do anything in the office. But thank you anyway." The CEO was impressed and grateful to have such an honest, hard-working employee. He wished everyone doing menial jobs at the hospital was as selfless and hardworking as Steels.

The following Thursday, Steels continued work as usual. Though he could simply wait for a call, he usually pushed his gurney back and forth between Emergency and ICU. If someone died, it would most likely be in one of these two places. The emergency room was crowded as usual. From the nurses' station Steels spotted a young woman sitting with an older woman, evidently ill, at the back of the waiting area.

Steels recognized her immediately. He had met Joyce the day before, when she first brought her mother here. He had helped them with directions and Joyce told him her name, which kept him awake the whole night.

An ER nurse came by with her kit to take the older woman's temperature, blood pressure, and pulse, and examined her eyes. Joyce refrained at first from revealing details of her mother's condition and medical history, feeling it was a matter of respect for the nurse's authority, but became uneasy when she realized the nurse was only collecting basic data to help prioritize who would be treated first. Her mother did not appear to be dying or suffering a traumatic injury, but Joyce worried that her condition could be more dire than it looked.

"My mother has this condition that causes the kidneys to chronically produce stones," Joyce told the nurse. "It's an old condition that can turn deadly rapidly. In fact, on Tuesday, the day before yesterday, her lab report showed that she had an infection. Her family doctor prescribed her antibiotics, but it doesn't seem to be working. She is nauseous and has vomited several times. She doesn't need another test. She is very sick. She just needs treatment. I'm worried she's already suffering from sepsis. She needs to see the doctor immediately."

The nurse did not respond to this plea immediately, making the daughter feel helpless and desperate. Noting the woman's distress, the nurse said, "A doctor will see her as soon as he can." Joyce felt relieved at hearing the word "soon." The crowd in the ER felt overwhelming, and if the doctor promised to see her mother *soon*, she felt she could not complain, even if they had to wait a little while. Every fifteen minutes or so, the nurse would repeat to them "as soon as possible," not "soon."

The doctor did not see her mother in the first hour, or in the second hour. Joyce grew more and more frustrated and anxious with each passing hour. Finally she confronted the triage nurse and demanded, "When can a doctor see my mother? She is very sick. She is in great pain. You can see it for yourself."

"I don't know," the nurse admitted. Joyce's jaw dropped. She wanted to complain but could not find the words.

Her mother's condition was deteriorating. She could not find a comfortable position on the hard chair and told her daughter that she felt like she could pass out at any time, or just fall dead. Joyce asked the nurse for a special seat or bed for her mother, so she could lie down to ease her pain. The helpful nurse pushed over a cot within a couple of minutes. That helped a little.

Joyce was unpleasantly surprised by the lengthy wait. They had come here many times before and received treatment promptly. Why not today? It looked like some sort of administrative change had happened at the hospital.

Every ten or fifteen minutes, Joyce went back to the nurses' station to ask when her mother would be seen by a doctor and the nurses, who often appeared to be chatting about personal affairs, would just say, "We don't know."

"Just look at the chart and you will know she needs care immediately to save her life," Joyce pleaded. "You can't leave her to die. Her infection will spread and cause sepsis. Sepsis is deadly. You know it better than I do."

"Her vitals look fine," said the nurse who was checking patients. It was clear the nurse thought the mother's condition was not that urgent and had therefore had put her far down on the priority list. But how could she tell Joyce and her mother about that openly?

100

"Please come and see my mother," Joyce said upon returning to the nurses' station. "She is groaning in pain. I think she is dying! She needs to see a doctor!"

"Her vitals are fine," the nurse who came to check on her repeated, meaning she was still breathing, her eyes were still wide open and her heart was still beating.

Joyce found the nurse indifferent and uncompassionate. In a case like her mother's, a stubborn nurse could sound cruel, but nurses here had to deal with so many patients, and doctors could not see all of them at once. Some ER patients, desperate to jump the queue, might even lie about the severity of their case. The nurses had learned not to trust the patients' words but rather to stick to the rules about which patients were prioritized.

Finally, after a torturous hours-long wait, Joyce's mother was examined by a doctor. It wasn't clear whether it was under mounting pressure from her daughter, but there were some who had to wait even longer. The ER doctor was a young man who seemed to have never seen a case like hers. Joyce thought of repeating to him the same information she had told the nurse, but she refrained, unsure if that would be mistaken as a challenge to his authority. He looked like a new medical school graduate.

During the many hours of waiting, she did not bleed, did not pass out, and showed no actual sign of dying, but the patient's life was being eroded by an insidious kidney infection that spread and became a deadly case of sepsis. Two days after she was finally seen by a doctor, at the age of fifty-five, she died in the hospital of multiple organ failure.

Steels took her body to the morgue, locked the door, and worked on it. "Still warm and soft. Now, let me see if I can bring you back to life," he said to the corpse. "Let's begin. Ah, that's good. Now, the left one first. Nice and soft and still springy. Feels good. Now the right one. Get closer to me. And now, the bottom. You don't cooperate. My dear lady, no chance for you." When he had finished his task inside the morgue three hours later, he opened the door and went out with his gurney again. "Too bad. No chance. No hope," he mumbled, shaking his head.

There were no more bodies to pick up that day, so he went home at the regular hour.

Monday saw Steels working hard again. He appeared at the emergency area with his morgue gurney and sat on a stool seven or eight feet away from the patients, helplessly watching them suffering.

Riana, a 39-year-old patient, was an easily satisfied person. She felt lucky to have seen a doctor briefly and been told to wait. She knew she had a chronic heart condition, and despite her excruciating pain, she waited patiently—until she died, still waiting to be seen properly.

When a doctor finally came, it was to sign a death certificate.

With the death certificate in hand, Steels carefully placed her body onto his gurney and pushed it to the morgue. As usual, he closed the door, locked it, and began to work on it.

"Still warm and soft," Steels said inside the morgue. "What a shame! Such a pretty young woman! If you were my wife, I would have taken better care of you than this. Come on, open your eyes and look at me. Now here. That's good. Now, the left one. Great. Now, the right one. Ah, beautiful! Now the bottom here." Steels ran his hands over all her sensitive places. When he touched her privates, her heart started beating, and her eyes suddenly opened. "Oh," she moaned, wrapping her hands around his bare back.

Steels had the habit of working naked when he washed a female body. He thought of this as not just a moment of joy for him, but also for the deceased, who would soon leave the hospital. Some had died because they had not received timely treatment, and he thought he should treat them differently before their departure.

"Oh, I am so glad you are still alive!" he exclaimed. "Oh, wonderful! Enough? Now let me get up and get you dressed. Then I will take you back to the doctor. I hope we can be friends." He put on his scrubs quickly. After that, he aimed the shower head at her privates for a quick wash and then dried her with a towel. "There you go," he said, dressing her up neatly.

Five minutes later, the living, breathing patient was back in the emergency room. The doctor was shocked and puzzled at the reappearance of a woman he had pronounced dead a few hours before, but he treated her without delay this time. Then, he grew scared and thought, *Oh, my! If this incident becomes known to the public, my career will be in jeopardy!* He sent her to ICU immediately.

The patient came back to life all right, but she lived only for another month before she died again, this time in her own bed at home, cherishing the brief dalliance with Steels in the morgue. She had been a virgin, but now she felt she was a real woman who had lived a full life.

Though it was another miracle, this patient was not headline news. . Few knew about it. It was not until after the patient's death that rumors started to spread in the hospital. "Is Steels some kind of angel? He has brought two dead patients back to life. For that alone, he's outdone the best doctors in the hospital."

Steels had become a star that shone everywhere he went in the hospital. Patients who'd heard the rumors looked at him with admiration, thinking if they had to die in the hospital, they wanted to die in his hands. Steels continued to enjoy his work in the morgue. He thought he might be the happiest man in the world. The job was easy; his pay was good; every patient he dealt with, young or old, was a beautiful woman. His colleagues were all great, charming women. Seeing any woman, old or young, alive or dead, always made him happy.

On Labor Day, he came to work at 8:00 a.m. as usual. Again, he went to the emergency waiting area and took up his spot, watching the patients complaining and moaning until they were finally seen by a doctor. The most serious cases, strokes and heart attacks, were the first to be treated.

At 10 a.m., a healthy-looking woman in her thirties screamed, "I'm in pain. It's attacking my shoulders and shooting right through my arms and legs. I need relief!" But the waiting room was filled with people. The polite nurse checked on her and respectfully asked her to wait until the doctor was able to see her.

The patient knew waiting in the ER was a matter of course. She tried to make herself comfortable in her chair, but after seven or eight hours of this, she felt sweat wetting her blouse, then a sudden weakness. Another attack of excruciating pain was coming on. She gritted her teeth and said to herself: *Be tough, you'll see a doctor soon.*

She was a conscientious person who disliked causing inconvenience to others. She swept her eyes across the numerous patients in the emergency room and said to herself: *I wouldn't want to be an ER doctor myself. The sight of this crowd would make me faint.* Suddenly, she felt an acute pain in her chest, and she blanked out. She never woke up and did not need the doctor anymore.

Again, a doctor came to record the death.

Steels took her to the morgue, locked the door, and worked on her body as he did with the others. As soon as he entered her body, she seemed to shiver. Miraculously, her body was becoming warmer and warmer, until she opened her eyes and was able to move her limbs and speak.

"What are you doing to me?" she scolded him.

"You died before I brought you to the morgue. I have given you treatment and brought you back to life," Steels said, waiting for a thank-you.

"No. Leave me alone. Get off me at once," she demanded. "I am getting married tonight. My fiancé doesn't even know I'm here."

"Oh, congratulations!" said Steels, shamefaced. He put his scrubs back on, and when the patient was dressed properly in a hospital gown, he pushed her back to the doctor who had signed her death certificate and told him she had come back to life.

The emergency doctor was more dumbfounded than last time. *How is it possible so many patients have come back to life in Steels' hands?*

"What did you do to that woman to bring her back to life?" the doctor demanded.

"I didn't do anything. When I was washing her body, it just became warm and her eyes opened and she started to speak. I don't know how it happened."

"What a mystery!" the doctor said, frowning at Steels.

The patient's symptoms had been alleviated, but the hospital kept her there for three more hours, just in case. She was discharged at 5:00 p.m., thankful her wedding would go ahead as planned but upset she had lost her virginity in the morgue.

A proud Steels came to work at the same hour the next day. He was working hard on another female corpse when he heard banging on the door. Frightened, he leapt off the body on the gurney. The door burst open and four police officers appeared. Surprised but not shocked, he got up from the floor and quickly put on his scrubs. Then he covered the naked corpse with a sheet.

"What were you doing with the body?" asked the police.

"I was trying to bring her back to life."

"You are under arrest for indecent assault on a human body," one of the officers announced as he was handcuffed.

It was a peaceful arrest, but it shocked the hospital that had been proud of him for playing a mysterious role in bringing in a $100 million donation.

Steels appeared at the Old City Hall Court in Toronto the following morning. The Crown attorney laid out a long list of charges against him, of which he would later remember only sexual assault and breach of trust, but Steels would not admit to any wrongdoing. He claimed repeatedly that he was giving the deceased women "resurrection therapy" and his success rate was high.

"Come clean. Did you sexually assault a corpse?" asked the prosecutor.

"No. I did not," Steels said.

"Why did you climb onto the body of that woman and behave like a rapist, then?"

"I admit I entered the deceased's body, but it was not rape," said Steels. "It was part of my resurrection therapy."

"What is that? I have never heard of any kind of therapy by that name."

"It's like sex therapy. It is effective for some depressed women, especially ill patients who have been deserted by their families and doctors. It may work only within five minutes after the patient's death and only when their body is still warm and soft. I follow a self-created standard procedure in stimulating deceased women to bring them back to life. I don't charge a fee. I do it as a volunteer. I never had a chance to ask for their consent, or consent from their relatives."

"You think this is quite the joke, don't you?" said the prosecutor.

"No," said Steels. "Everyone knows that somewhere between eight thousand and fifteen thousand patients die in Canada every year because crowding in the emergency department delays them getting treatment," he continued. "My patients are among these pitiful people. Their conditions were such that they couldn't wait so long. I think some of them may be declared dead before they really are. I've seen it with my own eyes. These are beautiful, lovely people. I have a simple therapy that works for some of them. I love them. I try my therapy on all of them. I enjoy doing it."

The judge seemed bemused.

"Why did you steal their jewelry, then?" The prosecutor started a new line of attack.

"I didn't steal anything or keep anything for myself," Steels said.

"What did you do with all the jewelry you removed from the bodies?" the prosecutor asked.

"I gave it all to the Salvation Army. I worry that it's not clean, that there's bacteria on it. I remove all jewelry from every corpse and give everything to the Salvation Army. You can ask them if it's true."

The judge called a brief recess while the prosecutor instructed a clerk to call the charity, which soon confirmed that he was a repeat donor of valuable items.

Meanwhile, a brief note was passed to the prosecutor. The victim who had reported Steels to the police had abruptly requested that they drop the charges against him. She said she would not testify against him in court.

The newlywed couple, who had been sitting in the back of the courtroom, had been discussing the revelations. The groom was consoling his bride after hearing the details of what had happened to her before and after her apparently fatal heart attack. She held that Steels had taken advantage of her and that she'd caught him in the act of rape. But she could not deny the fact that he had also brought her back to life. "What if his sex therapy really works?" he said to her. "I suppose that donating everything he took off the bodies shows he's not a thief."

"I'm not so sure about that," she said.

"I can't try to send someone who saved my wife to prison. I just can't," he said, grateful tears spilling from his eyes. He didn't want to think what his life would be like without her. He struggled with the idea of pressing charges against Steels, regardless of his methods.

His wife, on the other hand, was still outraged, not because she was ungrateful to Steels for saving her life, but that he had violated her body and stolen her virginity—something she cherished, believing that it belonged to her husband only.

"You are just as great as ever," her husband assured her. "And I love you just as much as before. I love you more than words can express. You must believe me and just turn the page. What has happened has happened," he said. "I'm just glad and grateful that you survived your heart attack. That's what really matters to me." Then she burst into tears again.

When the hearing resumed, the prosecutor asked the judge for additional time to investigate the case. "Your Honor, as court has heard, Ms. TS woke up in the morgue and found Steels on top of her with his penis inside her," he told the court. "It was an undeniable act of rape. She called the police after she returned home. Nonetheless, she and her husband have just informed us that they will not testify against the accused in court."

The judge cleared his throat and announced, "This hearing is adjourned. Given the complexity of the case, I order that a team comprised of three qualified medical scientists and five experienced doctors be created to conduct a study of the accused's claims about the effectiveness of sex therapy on newly deceased patients, including women and men. The team will submit a report to this court by February 28 next year. The report shall include recommendations regarding Steels' qualifications for practicing sex therapy on deceased women patients.

Until then, the charges against the accused are suspended and Mr. Steels, you are free to go."

Steels grinned with the air of a victor.

Heroic Mother and Daughter

Todd and Conna had no chance to call the police, but a passerby did it for them. Within five minutes three police cruisers arrived at the scene. Nonetheless, the officers were helpless—the $700,000 Rolls Royce was gone and the carjackers had escaped. As in other cases, the officers listened to the victims sympathetically and then wrote out a car theft report.

The couple had been returning home with a senior friend after seeing a musical production downtown. On their way, they dropped their friend at Spring Garden Avenue, just off Yonge Street in North York.

"Is it safe here?" Todd asked Conna as he parked in front of a fashion store. The city was not what it used to be, and their 2024 luxury car was a coveted target for carjackers, so he was cautious whenever he parked.

"It looks like a fairly busy place with so many people around," Conna said. "And look, there's another car parked in front of the antique shop next door. Seems safe enough."

Todd nodded and got out of the car to open the door for their friend at the back. He left the engine running, for he only intended to help his friend get out and would immediately return to his seat. Conna remained in the passenger's seat. The senior friend had just exited the car when five men wearing black face masks swarmed Todd, demanding, "Give us the key!"

"Are you kidding?" Todd said, thinking the slim figures might only be mischievous teenagers. "I have some cash here, take it."

"F--k you! Give me the key fob." One of the men, a taller one, struck him in the face, sending Todd several steps backward, but Todd refused to give up his fob.

At this moment, another of the men popped his head in the passenger's side and threatened Conna, "Give me your key, or I'll blow your head off!"

"I don't have a key," she said, shrugging her shoulders.

"Okay, bitch!" A third man, who was now brandishing a gun, threw open the driver's door and sat down behind the wheel, pointing his weapon at Conna's face.

"Give me your key fob, your watch, and your ring, you bitch! Now!" Conna and Todd were stupefied but resolved not to surrender.

"I'm not giving you my ring," Conna said calmly. "You don't scare me. Get out of my car with your phony, fake gun."

"Fake gun!" repeated the intruder angrily, hitting her in the head with its handle. "Feel it, damned bitch! Is this a fake gun?" Then he took out the bullets and showed them to her. At this point, Conna realized she and Todd were in real danger. She handed over her key ring.

Another carjacker jumped into the back seat behind her. The one behind the wheel put his foot on the gas pedal and accelerated rapidly. Inside the speeding car, the man behind Conna reached over the seat to unbuckle her safety belt, opened her door, and pushed her out. Her arm got caught in the seatbelt and she found herself being dragged along the street. She finally fell free after the driver hesitated briefly while running a red light.

She fell hard onto the pavement, but managed to crawl to the sidewalk as Todd, who had been running desperately after the car, finally caught up to her. Though trembling in fear and anger, she felt thankful there had been no oncoming car in the intersection. Otherwise, she could have been run over and killed.

Conna's beautiful creamy dress was torn, exposing her underwear and revealing bloody scrapes and rapidly rising bruises.

Todd was checking her over as she got to her feet, concerned that she had been seriously hurt. Dazed from the ordeal, she was regretting their choice to drive the Rolls Royce that night. "If we had driven the Lexus," she told him, "those guys might not have been interested in our car."

Todd shook his head and sighed.

After the police left the scene, the couple took a taxi home. On the way Conna cuddled in Todd's arms, rubbing her bruises on the right arm. "This is not the same city anymore!" she moaned.

"Oh, God," Todd shouted in disbelief as the taxi drove into their driveway. The fare was $11, but he thrust a $20 bill into the driver's hand and muttered, "Thank you" while staring at the garage.

After opening the taxi door for Conna, he ran toward the door, which had been hacked open. Before they had left for downtown, it was a secure, functioning door. Conna followed at his heels.

"The other car is gone too, Conna!" He stomped the concrete floor as if to break it. "It's gone! Oh, God!" Conna, a tough woman who seldom shed tears, burst out crying. She had thought driving the cheaper car, might have spared them from this ordeal, but now she realized both vehicles would have been stolen anyway. Her sobbing scared Todd.

"All right, Conna, all right." He comforted her in his arms. "Everything will be all right." He stroked her hair and kissed her.

"We need to call the police," he said after they cautiously checked inside the house and found it undisturbed.

When the 911 operator heard that everyone was safe and there were no intruders in the home, she advised them that it might be some time before police officers could be dispatched to their home. In the meantime, they could report the car theft on the police website.

The sudden, violent loss of two cars drained Todd's confidence in the public safety system he had trusted. He felt weak and hollow, knowing life could never be the same after this.

"How are we going to go to work tomorrow?" he said to Conna. But she knew he didn't need an answer. They called their insurance company to put in a claim and were told their coverage would pay for a rental until they could replace their vehicles. But it might take a couple of days to verify the claim and make those arrangements. So they considered finding another way to go to work the following day.

"Can you ask Vans if he could lend us the car you gave him last week?" Todd suggested

"That would be embarrassing, but I will try," she said.

By now it was 12:20 a.m. Conna felt bad about calling him at this hour, but Vans was her brother, and he usually went to bed late, so she called anyway.

"I'm awfully sorry, Conna," Vans said after hearing her horrible story. "The car you gave me last week was stolen three days ago. Apparently Toyota Highlanders are a popular vehicle for thieves these days."

"Oh, my God!" Conna could not believe her ears. "So between us, we've have lost three cars in three days! What is becoming of this city!" She burst into tears again.

"Conna, I actually know where my car is."

"Really?"

"It's somewhere at the harbor in Montreal," he said unenthusiastically.

"How is that possible?"

"On Thursday morning, I was about to go to work at 8:15, as usual, and my car had disappeared off the street. I have no clue how it was stolen," sighed Vans. "In the beginning I thought maybe I'd forgotten where I had parked it, so I searched all over the neighborhood—five blocks around my home. I walked up and down every street, hoping to find it somewhere, even if it had been stolen. After fifty minutes of anxious, fruitless searching, I was certain that I had parked it right in front of my house. Conna, they just stole it right from under my nose!"

"These goddamned thieves!" Conna said. "I just can't believe it."

"I was lucky because the police came over right away when I called. They told me that the thieves have been using sophisticated equipment to steal cars that function with keyless entry, like the Highlander. They probably just stood near the front door of my house and used a small device, a radio frequency amplifier, to capture the signal that was being emitted from the keyless fobs that I keep on a hook just inside the house. When it captured the signal from inside, it extended it to enable it to reach the car. The car door then opened and the engine started. Then they just drove it away! As easy as that."

"How terrible!" Conna sighed. "How is it possible to prevent it?"

"The officer told me some safety tips, such as keeping the keys in a Faraday bag as far away from the front door as possible, parking in a garage, if you can, and using a steering wheel club."

"What have the police done for you?" asked Conna.

"All they did was write a quick report and told me to submit my claim to the insurance company."

"Seriously?"

"Conna, the police are under tremendous pressure," said Todd. "You don't know how many car thefts they deal with every day. You don't know how dangerous it is for them to catch these armed criminals. And you don't know how quickly the court releases them. Police morale is low. The whole system just isn't working."

"But the police have guns," Conna said. "The carjackers had guns. They wanted to kill me. Why can't the police shoot and kill them?"

"Conna, it's not that easy. Let me just tell you my own story. I detected the exact location of my car on the same day it was stolen and reported it to the Toronto police, but they could not get it back for me."

"Why then? I don't understand," said Conna.

"They could not get it back for me because they could only deal with cases in Toronto."

"Vans, your car was stolen here in Toronto. Doesn't that make it a Toronto case?"

"Yes, but when it arrived in Quebec, it was outside the jurisdiction of Ontario police. The Montreal harbor is under RCMP jurisdiction. The city police and the provincial police have no authority at the harbor."

"Then, why didn't you call the RCMP?" said Conna.

"I did, but they said there were too many containers at the harbor. They couldn't easily single out the one that had my car. They would have to open every container of goods to search for it. Too much work for them. They just could not do it. They just told me I'll get my money back from the insurance." Vans sighed.

"This is the funniest thing I have ever heard of. Three levels of police know where a stolen vehicle is and none of them can get it back. What a slap in the face!"

"Conna," said Vans, "I know you're really shocked by this experience. But you are not alone. I've been reading about car thefts these past few days and I have learned a lot."

"What have you learned?"

"Too much to tell you, but they are mostly sad stories, quite different from our own. If you like, I can tell you a few."

"Yes, please. I'm all ears."

"The first thing I have learned about is our broken system," said Todd. "It does not really protect innocent citizens. It protects the thieves mostly. Frustration and resentment about this was mounting all over the country until the Prime Minister called a summit on February 8, 2024, with police and municipal leaders and other government officials. He acknowledged it was an unprecedented problem and hinted at stiffer punishment. Indeed, he quickly allocated more money to help police buy better equipment and called for better coordination and cooperation between the three levels of police, but he did not bother to toughen the law. Just look at what happened after the meeting.

"At dusk on February 24, 2024, Bro Young had just finished grocery shopping in a large supermarket at Markham Town Square when a black Honda Civic pulled up next to his BMW. Young said three or four men got out of the black car and went up to him. One of them pulled out a gun and pointed it at his head, demanding his car key and cellphone. He gave them the key, but fought back when they insisted on his cellphone too. "I had no time to react. Just so sudden!" he said. In less than a minute, the car was stolen.

112

"That's just the way it happened to us," Conna said.

"A few weeks later, another BMW, an M4, was robbed at Midland and McNicoll. A young couple was sitting inside the car, but two violent carjackers brandishing handguns charged at their car. One got into the driver's seat and they just drove away with it. Again, it took less than a minute.

"The following week, the drivers of two luxury vehicles, a Lamborghini SUV and a BMW M4, were dragged out of their seats with guns pointed at their heads while they were parked at a Shell gas station in the Sheppard and Yonge area. All of this took place in broad daylight with at least fifteen other drivers around.

"Here's one that's a bit different. Last Thursday, a brave young mother who was with her 3-year-old daughter fought off two armed carjackers outside their home."

"Well, that was brave! What happened?"

"Give me a second, I'll read you the story from a news website. Here it is.

"'My husband and I drove over to my mother's home to pick up our child after work last Thursday evening. As usual, we would return home at about 11:00 p.m. Nothing seemed out of the ordinary in the neighborhood. Like before, it was peaceful and quiet, but when we drove into our street, we saw a car facing us, parked on the other side of the street. Seeing us entering the street, its driver followed up and parked on my next-door neighbor's driveway.

'I thought it was our neighbor's car and didn't think much of it. Out of habit, I opened the back door on the right and got out of the car, but then, as I was taking out my child, I heard sudden, rapid footsteps from behind. Instinct told me they were rushing toward me. I sensed something wrong and instantly decided to get back into the car, but it was too late.

'Our child's legs were halfway out but were stuck in the door, so I could not slam the door shut. I started screaming, "Baby, quick! Get back in." I tried to free her from the door and drop her down, while blocking the right rear door with my body as tightly as I could. I held the door handle with all my might. Meanwhile one of the carjackers was trying to force me away from the door. A second man was heading around the car toward the driver's door when our child finally got back into the seat. I don't know where I got the strength, but I finally shut the door, shouting to my child from outside, "Carjacking! Quick! Lock the doors!"And she did!

'My husband, who had been sitting in the front seat unaware of what was happening, was stupefied when he heard me screaming at the carjacker, "What are you doing here?" The guy was still trying to force me away from the car, but I protected the door with my body. At this moment, I forgot about my own safety altogether. I just needed to protect my child from these dangerous criminals! I had to keep the door shut to keep them away from my child!

'By now my husband realized what was happening, locked the driver's side door and started honking the horn. I'm sure the whole neighborhood heard him honking and me screaming for help!

'About eighty percent of our community is of my Asian ethnicity, and we are close-knit. In my desperation it was all I could think to do—attract enough attention to scare away the carjackers before they could seize our car. "Help! Help! Help!" I kept crying.

'My neighbors were coming to their windows, looking toward our direction. The two masked men panicked as they swept their eyes across our neighbors' houses, realizing that our car doors were all securely locked and there was no way they could open any of them! Sensing imminent danger, they gave up, ran to their car, jumped in, and sped off in panic.

'I stood there stupefied, trembling! To be honest, I wasn't consciously feeling fear when I was fighting them off, and my hands weren't even shaking when I was crying for help. But I just could not help it after they left!

'I glanced down at myself in embarrassment. During the whole ordeal, my bag was hanging on my right shoulder, right next to the carjacker, but he didn't try to grab it! If he did before he fled, he could have taken it effortlessly.

'I opened the car door, trembling, and hugged my child tightly. Fortunately, she wasn't harmed and didn't seem distressed. Helpful neighbors all came out to console us and offer us assistance. The kind couple living opposite our house called the police for us.

'The police came in three minutes. Five or six police cars arrived one after another.

'The police took our IDs, asked us what had happened, and started collecting fingerprints on the car. They didn't stop working until after midnight.

'We were the lucky ones, and also the unlucky ones. We were lucky, because none of us was hurt and our car was not stolen, but we were also unlucky, because my car was targeted amongst the ocean of vehicles and because the ordeal has left a shadow on me. I dare not drive out alone anymore. I have become very alert to danger. I feel insecure and always want to get back home before dark.

'This is my eighth year living in Toronto. When I first came, I found everything was great: prices were low, wages were decent, people were friendly and helpful, and overall life was comfortable.

'But what has happened to you, Toronto? Just mentioning the issue of law and order scares the wits out of everyone!

'It is my friends who say that we are the lucky ones among the unlucky ones. One of my friends was confronted and attacked outside his car. They struck him in the head with a club. He lost consciousness instantly, and they drove off with his car. Another friend who was sitting behind the wheel was surrounded by four men who were standing all around the car, one pointing a gun at his head. They simply dragged him out of the driver's seat and sped off in his car.'

"An unbelievable story, isn't it?" Vans said to Conna.

Conna was silent for a moment. Then she said, "The mother is not only a hero, but also such a great story teller. This city, this province, this country, the entire system, has let down everybody—men, women, children, everyone! But who is responsible for all these violent crimes?"

"Perhaps our lawmakers know the answer," Todd concluded.

Surprise Arrests

The street was deathly quiet at 1:30 a.m. Mr. Torunto, the busiest person in his family, had just finished his day's work and household chores on the main floor. He was tiptoeing upstairs, where his wife and children were sleeping, when he heard three deafening knocks on the front door. *How annoying*, he thought. *Who can it be at this hour?* He rushed to the front door as a second round of loud knocks came. He lifted the curtain on the door window and was taken aback.

A large group of police officers was swarming his front door. In front were two officers holding automatic rifles pointing downward with their fingers on the trigger. Uneasily, he opened the door a crack, keeping it chained from behind.

"Hi?" Mr. Torunto greeted them, hoping this was a simple mistake and that they had come to the wrong house. The police slogan was "To serve and protect." He was sure they would not harm anyone in his family, for he and his family members were all lawful citizens who had not broken any law.

"Police. Open the door!" one officer ordered.

He wondered if they could be robbers pretending to the police to gain access to his home. "Do you have any ID?" he asked, knowing it was his right to ask for identification. An officer next to the two rifle-carrying officers presented his ID card. Mr. Torunto looked at it, but could see nothing because it was dark. He grew anxious and agitated. Why were they here?

He thought back to his mistakes in life, but could not think of anything that could justify his arrest. He had paid his taxes every year. He had not engaged in any illegal activities anywhere, anytime. His wife was an honest homemaker and did not work, so she had no trouble with anyone at all. His daughter was a model student at school, and so was his son, who went to bed on time and got up without being prodded. The children's grades were always good and their teachers all spoke highly of them. So why would the police come to his door like this, at this hour of the night? The only logical reason, he thought was to arrest him, for he had published essays and books that might have offended some readers who might have complained. *But isn't freedom of speech guaranteed by the Charter of Rights and Freedoms?* he said to himself.

"Open the door, sir," they ordered again. He could see they were losing patience.

"Could you give me a few minutes and let me call my lawyer?" Mr. Torunto pleaded.

"Open the door now!" It was their third and, most likely, last order. If he did not obey, he could be in more trouble. They were carrying powerful rifles that could easily shoot and break his chain, or even kill him.

Mr. Torunto removed the chain from behind, opened the door, and raised his hands.

"Is Ted Torunto here?" the officer who had shown him his ID card asked as soon as they entered his house.

"Yes, he is my son," he said.

"Which room is he in?"

"He is sleeping in the room right above, upstairs," said Mr. Torunto, pointing to the ceiling. "I will show you the room." Suddenly he worried why his son was being targeted. He would die for his family if he had to, but why were they asking about his son instead of arresting himself?

"No. You can stay here. We will go up," the officer said, showing him a printout with the words "some people do not deserve to live" highlighted in light purple. "Your son posted this on the internet. We have reason to believe he's a danger to the community." Several officers marched upstairs. Mr. Torunto's heart throbbed with fear. He hoped they would just ask Ted some questions and leave.

Moments later, the two officers armed with the giant rifles came back downstairs with his son, his hands cuffed behind his back. Mr. Torunto was dumbfounded. He felt dizzy, trembling. What was happening? His son was only fourteen.

All he could do was hug him and say, "Be tough. I'm going to get you out of this as soon as I can." To his surprise, his son didn't look terrified. Not happy, but brave enough to give his father some confidence that he would survive whatever ordeal awaited him.

It was wintertime and Ted was wearing his pajamas only. Mr. Torunto got his winter jacket from the closet and put it around his shoulders, because his son could not do it himself. The senior officer searched the pockets and found a heavy cylinder three inches long and an inch in diameter wrapped in white paper, with a sharp nail sticking out of each end. Looking satisfied with the discovery, he instructed another officer, "That's possession of a dangerous weapon right there." At this, Mr. Torunto regretted offering the jacket to his son, which might result in upgraded charges, still unknown to him. He stood by the door trembling, feeling the earth was spinning. A catastrophe had befallen his happy family!

117

"We've explained to your son why he's being arrested, on the basis that he uttered death threats, and that he has a right to remain silent and to have legal counsel," an officer told Mr. Torunto as they walked the boy out of the house. He handed him a card with the address. "He'll have a first appearance in court tomorrow morning. Unless you want the court to appoint a lawyer for him, you might want to call your own lawyer pronto."

It was about two a.m. The family had never had any trouble with the law and never needed a criminal lawyer. How would he find one now? In desperation, Mr. Torunto thought of his real estate lawyer. He hated to bother him at this hour, but without finding a good lawyer quickly, his son would be in more trouble.

Mr. Torunto struggled to find the lawyer's number, which he knew was recorded in one of those tiny address books. Trembling and panicked, he couldn't seem to find it until his wife, who had been hiding in their bedroom during the ruckus, managed to find it. To his relief, twenty minutes later he was connected with his lawyer, who sounded surprisingly calm.

"I'm sure your son will be fine," he said. "I am not a criminal lawyer, so I cannot help you." But he went on to recommend one, a Ms. Thompson. Though he hated to disturb her so late at night, Mr. Torunto felt he had no choice. Fortunately, she did not sound sleepy or annoyed at all. It seemed she was used to working around the clock on such cases.

After hearing the details, she accepted his son's case and said, "The initial fee is $4,000 plus taxes. You can give me a check when we meet tomorrow morning." The money would have to come out of his son's university fund, but the priority now was to bring him back home, hopefully without a criminal record.

At 10 a.m., Ted appeared in court before a female judge to be formally charged. The Crown prosecutor presented the case, repeating the same quoted words they had shown his father. Ted was charged with uttering death threats. Mr. Torunto was so agitated that he later could not remember much about the details of the charges.

"Did the accused target any specific person in his writing?" the judge asked the prosecutor.

"No," answered the prosecutor. He went on to explain that it was reported to police by someone who felt concerned that he meant to carry through on it.

That person was a boy in Ted's class who was a new immigrant. To earn social validation in Canada, he and four other friends had set up a website where classmates would post entertaining messages, the funnier the better. Every student tried to outdo the previous posts.

Ted was a very funny person, who had been the class joker since Grade 1. At home, his jokes often had his parents and sister roaring with laughter. He was also a polite, gentle boy who never uttered a rude word at home or to any teacher.

However, in the competitive post that had landed him in court he used nothing but coarse language, including the phrase "some people do not deserve to live," which was out of character.

"Why did you post that statement?" the judge asked him.

"It was just a joke," he said. The judge asked no more questions.

At hearing this, Mr. Torunto was relieved and disappointed at the same time. Relieved because his son was not involved in any illegal activities; disappointed because he'd shown poor judgment and made jokes that were easily misunderstood and misinterpreted. Humor is the highest form of intelligence, but it is appreciated only by those who understand it.

Whoever had reported his dark humor to the authorities did not understand it, let alone appreciate it.

During a break in the hearing, Mr. Torunto asked their lawyer if she could get the Crown prosecutor to drop the charge, since it was all a misunderstanding, no harm had been done and no law had been broken. "I talked with the principal of his school this morning and he was sad to hear about this. He assured me that Ted has always been a model student and he has no idea how this happened."

"They won't drop the case just like that," the lawyer said. "The process has started and it will have to take its course." How disappointed Mr. Torunto was. He knew that the authorities would want to find something wrong with his son to justify their arrest.

To bring the case to a quick close, though it violated his conscience, Mr. Torunto agreed that his son would have to show "remorse" and correct his "wrongdoing." Accordingly, with his lawyer's urging, Ted accepted all conditions imposed by the judge. Among them, he accepted his father as his supervisor and had to obey any instructions he gave; agreed that he would never contact the person who had reported him, and would see a social worker several times to assess his mental state. Mr. Torunto remembered the torturous six-year court journey of a

119

homeowner who had been prosecuted for injuring a raccoon that had been destroying his garden and refused to acknowledge he was wrong. Early "surrender" might be better, he thought.

Upon returning home with his dearly-missed son, Mr. Torunto called a good friend in Alberta for a second opinion about his intention to give in instead of fighting to hold them accountable for his son's unreasonable arrest, but he only heard a voice message: "Sorry. I can't talk now. I will call you later." As soon as he hung up, his phone rang with a call from the school principal, who informed him that according to school policy, his son would be suspended from school for a week, simply because he had been arrested. He had no objection, for his son had endured too much emotional turbulence and it was good to let him rest for some time at home.

The next day, the principal called again to say the suspension was reduced to three days. During his absence from school, he would receive his assignments, which he would do at home. Ted saw the social worker, who found him to be perfectly normal and decided he did not need assistance from any other professional. She issued a letter that could be presented to the judge. Ted also volunteered to fundraise for charities. He sold used books and other stuff given to him by his parents and made $200. With the money he bought 250 pounds of spaghetti and donated it to the Salvation Army. He also wrote an essay reflecting on the nature of humor and what he had learned from his black humor, or rather his realization that such humor was not for everyone. At his second court appearance, two months later, the judge accepted the deal struck by the prosecutor and Ted's lawyer and dropped all charges. No criminal record was registered. The school also decided to cancel his suspension, erasing it from his files.

Two weeks before the case was closed, a police officer had come back to Mr. Torunto's house and given him a handful of coins with two nails, placed in a sandwich bag. The baffled father did not understand what they were for, but suddenly started laughing bitterly.

"So, these are the parts of the 'weapon' they found in Ted's pocket that night—a weapon made of coins with two nails wrapped in paper!"

In summer, the Toronto Police Association, which was raising funds for police widows and orphans, sent Mr. Torunto an ad for a summer sports ticket. As he had done in the past, he donated $10 to them instead of buying the ticket. It was his way of showing support for the police, and he had always done it happily. This year, he felt differently. He felt bitterly wronged by the overreaction of the police toward his son's childish internet post, but he sent the same donation to the police anyway. After all, arresting people was their job. Finding the accused guilty or not guilty was the court's job. At the end of the day, Mr. Torunto forgave them for what had happened. His son continued to grow and improve and eventually went to a top school that made him an excellent Canadian professional, of whom the judge, the prosecutor, the police and his high school teachers would be proud.

After the unfortunate incident, Mr. Torunto would tell his son from time to time, "Ted, be careful with who you are joking with. In university or at work, now or in the future. Joke only with those who understand jokes." Ted understood why his father kept repeating the advice and never complained. He would say "okay" as if it was the first time he had heard it.

On the Labor Day after the incident, Mr. Torunto was in a cheerful mood after dinner. He thought of his good friend in Alberta when he heard his phone ring. "Oh, it's you Edmon!" he exclaimed, glad to hear from him.

As it turned out, Mr. Edmon and his family had also encountered rough treatment by police, but in a far more horrific manner. At the time Mr. Torunto called him for advice, Mr. Edmon had lost his freedom and was unable to answer his phone. He apologized repeatedly and explained.

At 5:00 p.m. that day, he had been heading out and was about twenty feet from his home when he saw a police vehicle-mounted battering ram appear at the corner of the street. From a distance it looked a bit like a tank on the battlefield. It was driving at full speed toward him. Suddenly, it stopped in front of his house, adjusted position, and aimed the ram at his own door.

"Why did it stop in front of my house? I had no idea." He quickly ran closer to the vehicle, intending to find out why it was there, but before he could speak to anyone, its long metal arm had reached his front door. At this moment, a 15-member tactical team descended on the house. Ten officers swarmed into the backyard. Another five or so jumped up to the front porch as the ram cracked open the front door. It was a powerful ram that could easily push open the best security door sold at Home Depot.

Spotting Mr. Edmon close to the vehicle, two officers turned toward him and pointed their assault rifles at him. "Freeze!" they ordered. "Hands up!"

121

Terrified, Mr. Edmon tried to tell them that there must be some misunderstanding, but they would not listen. The black barrels of their huge rifles looked threatening. If their fingers pressed the trigger, he thought, his life would end. He trembled and, without thinking, dropped to his knees and raised his hands. They handcuffed him without mishap.

In the backyard, the officers were dealing with his children and their grandmother, who had been sitting there, enjoying a snack. One officer dragged his teenage son from the wooden deck and dumped him facedown on a paved area, tearing his shirt in the process. They zip-tied his hands at the back. They ordered the younger sister to lie flat facedown with her arms to the sides. "You won't kill me, right?" the terrified girl asked.

"No," the arresting officer said. What a relief the trembling girl felt!

Their 90-year-old grandmother was also ordered to lie on the pavement. She was thankful not to have suffered a heart attack, but she was shaken, never having imagined being subjected to such humiliation and abuse.

"What the hell are you doing here?" she cursed them. "What kind of soldiers are you, bullying an old woman and children like this? If you're so tough, go catch the rapists, carjackers, murderers, and home invaders! Go fight on the battlefield!" She despised them; she hated them. "Treating my innocent grandchildren like terrorists! Aren't you ashamed of yourselves?"

In the end, the police explained that the surprise raid was launched after they received a report that someone in the house was being kidnapped and needed to be rescued. The police chief said they did not have the luxury of time to investigate the incident and that their priority was to save a life before it was too late. They were racing against time to ensure everyone in the house would be safe, and that was why and how it all happened. Police, he said, had done nothing wrong.

The hell indeed!

"Should we sue them?" Mr. Edmon asked a stupefied Mr. Torunto, who instead answered with his own question. He told his friend his son's story and then asked, "Should we sue my son's classmate who caused his wrongful arrest?" Mr. Edmon gave no advice. He just cleared his throat on the phone to let Mr. Torunto know that he had heard everything. Both wondered in disbelief: Is the country ruled by law? What law is it then?"

They felt violated. They felt victimized. They remained silent.

Brutal Animal Cruelty

An infuriated Don Tran swung his shovel at a family of raccoons that had destroyed the vegetables and flowers in his garden. He missed the raccoon mother but hit one of the kits. Terrifying animal shrieking was heard in the chilly dawn air in the Lansdowne neighborhood in Toronto.

"Hey, what are you doing?" Tran heard someone shouting at him. He followed the direction of the voice but saw no one.

"The raccoons have destroyed all my plants again," grumbled Tran.

"You can't do that. That's animal cruelty," said the hostile voice.

"Humph!" Tran snorted, surprised at the unknown person's reaction. "Animal cruelty indeed!" Amid his displeasure and frustration, he found that he had wounded one of them. It lay in pain on the lawn next to the ruined vegetable bed.

Tran's wife heard the commotion in the backyard and the dialogue between him and the stranger. She ran out to see what was happening. "Oh, Don," she said, "I hear Canadian neighbors can be very sensitive. Some can even be mean. Don't hurt the animals. Or they may call the police and cause you trouble."

"This is Canada," he said proudly. "Canadians have human rights. I am protected by the law and by the Charter of Rights and Freedoms." He threw a contemptuous glance at the wounded animal. "I have confidence in the Toronto police. I have confidence in the justice system. The innocent will be protected. You know I love animals, but they don't love me. Just look at what they have done to my plants."

"Oh dear!" she sighed.

Tran raised his shovel to scare the last kit away, but it started screaming again and did not move. "God damn you all!" he cursed it. "Get lost." But it seemed unable to move. If he could do it without getting into trouble, he would have killed it. "Everything's ruined. All ruined!" He had spent more than $300 on the roses, pepper and cucumber seedlings, among other plants, not to mention the time he'd invested and the expensive gardening tools, fertilizer, and pesticides.

The raccoon mother had run away with her three unhurt kits when a police cruiser arrived in front of Tran's neighbor's home. Constable Vito King knocked on the neighbor's front door and talked with the neighbor. Three minutes later, Tran heard loud knocks on his own front door—the kind you hear when the police come to arrest you.

Shovel in hand, Tran dashed to his front yard via the north lane, surprised to see the police officer. "Good morning, sir," Tran greeted him humbly, hoping the officer would be kind.

"What's your name, sir?" asked the officer. Tran answered him.

After checking Tran's personal identification, King said, "Your neighbor called to report that you were assaulting raccoons."

Tran was frightened by the sight of the officer's handgun, taser baton, and handcuffs hanging on his belt, instruments that could take a life, paralyze him, or end a person's freedom. Tran did not like the word "assaulting" but dared not talk back.

"The raccoons were destroying my vegetables, flowers, and all the other plants," said Tran.

"Where are your plants?" asked the officer. Tran took him to his backyard, where all the plants had been rooted out, eaten, or destroyed in one way or another. Next to the ruined plant beds lay a small raccoon that started screaming again as they approached, startling the officer.

"Did you hit it?" the officer asked, pointing at the kit. "It looks injured."

"Yes," Tran answered, now as scared as the kit. "The raccoons were ruining my garden. They destroyed all my vegetables and flowers." He thought that would justify what he had done.

"What weapon did you use?" asked the officer.

"The shovel," said Tran, wondering why he used the word "weapon."

"Drop your weapon, Mr. Tran," the stern officer ordered. Anxious and confused, Tran obeyed, dropping it at once. He fixed his eyes on the officer, wondering what he would do next.

"Mr. Tran, you are under arrest," announced the officer, handcuffing him at the same time. It was a peaceful arrest,

Panic-stricken, Tran was confused. "Why?" he said, "I haven't done anything wrong."

"You will be charged with animal cruelty and possessing a dangerous weapon," the officer announced. "Let's go."

Tran could not believe his ears. His head started spinning, but soon he regained his calm. "Damn it!" he cursed under his breath. "Can I go to work today? Can I even eat my breakfast?" His fear of losing his freedom had come true with the cold, hard metal locked around his wrists. Ironically, Tran had immigrated to Canada for freedom and democracy. "The raccoons have ruined my garden," he muttered to himself. "And are you going to ruin my life? You cuffed me like a criminal. You took away my freedom for no reason, as if you had the goddamn right. What do you think

124

you are doing? Are you working for the animals or the people? Are you a man or an animal?" His helplessness turned to anger, hatred, and then contempt toward the officer.

"Let's go," the officer repeated.

Tran started to move, but his mind was blank. He had no clue what he had done wrong. The raccoons had invaded his yard and destroyed all his plants. He was just trying to drive them away. Accidentally his shovel touched one of them. That was it, and he was now charged with animal cruelty.

Animal cruelty, indeed! He wished he could protest, but he was afraid that would only make matters worse. He hung his head and dragged heavy feet toward the police car, with the officer following at his heels.

Near the lane entrance, Tran heard noise from his driveway. When he raised his head, he saw a large crowd in front of his garage. The neighbors had come to support him.

"Be tough, Don!" someone shouted to him. "We are with you." Tran was moved to tears as a warm current ran through his spine.

The next day, Tran's arrest made headlines throughout Canada. When asked about his arrest, the police announced, "Mr. Don Tran has been charged with animal cruelty and using a dangerous weapon. While the mother raccoon was taking away the injured kits, he kept attacking them with a shovel."

"How many raccoons did he kill or injure?" asked a news reporter.

"At least one injured kit was taken from his yard for emergency treatment," said the police spokesperson. "We don't know much about the rest because the mother had taken her other kits away. All we know is we rescued the injured kit with a broken leg and it could have died. [The fact: Tran had only injured one kit and it did not have a broken leg.] A neighbor called 911 reporting that Tran was assaulting a family of raccoons repeatedly." Color photos of the wounded kit taken from Tran's backyard were then presented to the media, cementing the impression of animal cruelty.

Tran had been thrown into a cell furnished with just a bare metal bed, waiting for his first appearance in court the next day. Shivering in the dim, cold room, he heard his stomach growling. During the same period, the baby raccoon had been fed three times. Members of the wildlife rescue team had carefully placed it in a cozy cage before taking it straight to Procyon Wildlife Veterinary and Rehabilitation Services in Beeton, Ontario, seventy kilometers from Toronto. There it underwent a thorough examination followed by immediate treatment.

Tran appeared in Toronto Old City Hall Court the following morning to hear his charges.

"The accused, Mr. Don Tran, continued to attack the raccoons with a dangerous weapon with the sole purpose of causing pain and suffering," Crown attorney R. RacLover told the judge. "The mother raccoon was seen carrying two motionless three-month-old babies afterwards, one likely dead. Animal Services rescued the third kit after a neighbor phoned police." Tran was described as an undeniable animal hater who enjoyed torturing and killing raccoons for pure pleasure in the cruelest manner one could imagine. The charge he was facing came with a penalty of up to ten years' imprisonment if he was found guilty.

When the judge asked for his plea, Tran refused to admit guilt.

"Your Honor," he said, "the prosecutor is lying. I did not kill any raccoon and I did not intentionally try to hurt any of them." Everyone present was shocked at hearing him accuse the Crown attorney of lying. Tran was defiant, confident the judge would side with him. At the hearing, he was released on bail.

Tran was upset that his charges were not dropped. "Bold-faced liar," Tran continued cursing under his breath, as he walked out of the court house. "And he represents criminal justice and fairness on behalf of the Queen! I will expose your shameless lies to the whole world. Yes, you can continue to lie in court, but if you think the court can be fooled, you would be the most stupid fool yourself."

An official forensic report was made public the following week, stating that the wounded kit was two months old, not three months old, as stated by the Crown in court. Three toes of its left leg were broken, but contrary to the prosecutor's presentation, it did not have a broken leg. No other wounds were found.

The veterinarian, one of the best in Canada, had already worked out a treatment program for the kit, putting a cast on its wounded toes immediately. The raccoon was kept in the center for complete rest and well fed. In three weeks, thanks to the staff's meticulous care, it had recovered, news cheered by animal rights activists all over Toronto and throughout Canada.

Unsurprisingly, the cruel animal assaulter was not as lucky as the baby raccoon. Though by law Tran was innocent until proven guilty in court, he was treated like a murderer during his trial. Yet, he never lost confidence in the Canadian court. "Canada is ruled by law. I am innocent," he would say. "I will prove my innocence in court."

After the first court hearing, the prosecutor realized the charges against Tran were not well founded. Calling his shovel a dangerous weapon had backfired, and asking for ten years' imprisonment for wounding three of the kit's toes would offend many Canadians. The strategy now was to pressure Tran into pleading guilty to his charges, thus justifying his arrest and trial.

Tran had to wait months for each new court hearing. As the case dragged on, he grew worried and began to lose confidence in the criminal justice system. A list of other odd twists in the justice system often flashed across his mind: the bicyclist in Markham, Ontario, who hit a pedestrian on the sidewalk—who died afterward—and was merely fined $10. A mentally ill person could kill someone without being found criminally responsible for his killing and would not end up in prison. One such mentally ill killer dug out a victim's heart and ate it on a Greyhound bus, and he was found guilty but not criminally responsible. Instead of going to jail, he went to a psychiatric facility for treatment, where he enjoyed seven years of free food and care. After that, when he was deemed safe to the public, he was released into the community. If he were to kill another innocent person, he could well just go back to the psychiatric hospital again. On the other hand, Tran had heard about an innocent young man who was thrown into jail for life for a sexual assault and murder that, as it turned out, he had not committed. Tran dared not think anymore.

"Ten years isn't impossible," he thought, shivering. "Criminal justice in Canada!" He sighed, shaking his head.

Despite his frustration, Tran refused to be intimidated. "I haven't killed anyone. I haven't hurt anybody. I have not broken the law. I have not killed an animal. I have only wounded a raccoon that was destroying my garden. I have the right to drive away a home invader or a trespasser from my property, but why not a raccoon? Doesn't the law protect personal property and wealth? Doesn't a Canadian citizen have more rights than a raccoon! I will stand up for my rights!"

The average Canadian would appreciate Tran's confidence in the criminal justice system, but Tran did not know that justice sometimes depends on having a good lawyer and that the better your lawyer is, the more expensive they are. In any case, it's generally those who win who feel there is justice in the system.

Nonetheless, Tran did not have the money for a good lawyer. He was middle class and owned a home; therefore he didn't qualify for legal aid. Carrying a $500,000 mortgage, he had little cash. In fact, he had to borrow the initial $5,000 to hire a lawyer, and that only paid for the first two hearings. After spending $20,000, he fired his lawyer and represented himself in court instead.

At the following hearings, Tran was confronted by a prosecutor who used legal jargon he did not fully understand. The judge also used unfamiliar jargon. Tran would visibly sweat in court, sometimes to the point of soaking his shirt, but he always survived.

As a father to two children, Tran had to put food on the table for his family and pay the mortgage, no matter what happened. The first time he represented himself in court, he learned a trick. Whenever he did not understand the prosecutor or the judge, he would just say, "I did nothing wrong. The raccoons were destroying my garden. I just tried to drive them away." Though these statements might not answer their questions, his repetitive and often irrelevant defense was a forceful denial of the accusations against him, making it difficult for the judge to deliver a conviction. Thus, the trial went on and on.

Every court hearing was boring. The prosecutor would repeat the same charges and accusations while Tran would just deny everything by repeating the same words.

Tran had aged almost six years since his first court appearance. Still, neither side was prepared to give in. On April 1, when he looked in the mirror in the court's washroom after his 18th court appearance, Tran could hardly believe his eyes. He had changed: the shine in his eyes was gone; the confidence on his face had disappeared; he looked pale and fragile, and his hair had turned gray.

Where is my former self? he wondered, rubbing his wrinkly face and brushing his gray hair with his fingers. If he were a woman he would cry, he thought. *Because of that useless baby raccoon, they have ruined my life—six years of my prime! They all want to make me into a criminal; they have presented me as a criminal; and they have been treating me like a criminal!* This strong man, who had never cried, suddenly found tears welling up in his eyes. *The Crown is bent on proving me guilty. He will never give up until I am found guilty or admit guilt. The judge does not care about me. They work together against me.*

Tran was looking feeble and moved slowly. Wearing a long face, he gritted his teeth or bit his lips all day long.

Oh God, I may as well admit guilt to end this damn case, he suddenly said to himself when he got up on Canada Day. *What difference does it make if I have a criminal record anyway?*

He just did not understand how this endless trial benefited those who were bent on proving him guilty of wounding a kit, a case that had already lasted almost six years. "The kit intruded into my property and damaged my plants. Didn't I even have the right to defend myself and my property? What kind of law is this?" Tran murmured for the thousandth time, feeling his tears streaming inward. The more he questioned the case, the more listless he became.

His heart sinking, he realized that he had been battling an army of well-paid, well-fed, well-clad officials that he could never defeat. He had fought them eighteen times in court. He raised his head and saw a thick dark sky before him. He felt like he was about to faint and quickly put his hands on the brick wall beside him to keep from falling. He made two tight fists to consciously improve his blood circulation. Then he took several deep breaths, straightened his shoulders, and felt a warm current all over his body.

Thank God, he said to himself, grateful not to have fainted. *No. My children need me. They are still in school.*

On September 15, as before, as soon as he left the court house, news reporters asked him the same questions: "Has the court ruled on your case? Do you think you are guilty as charged?"

"I can't stand it anymore," he told them, breaking down. "My heart is bleeding. This system has broken my heart, torn my liver, and ruined my life. They want to torture me to death." He lowered his head, tears streaming down his cheeks. The reporters grew worried about his mental health; he used to be gentle, polite, and confident after each hearing.

Then came his 19th court appearance. The now fifty-five-year-old Tran finally admitted to beating three (in fact there were four) raccoons with a shovel, as charged. As the story goes, he had struck a deal with the prosecutor. He would admit guilt in exchange for them dropping the charge of possessing a dangerous weapon, and he would then receive a conditional discharge on the charge of animal cruelty.

Then came his judgment day in court. He was ordered to pay $1,365 in restitution to Procyon Wildlife, where the wounded raccoon was treated. He was also ordered to complete a hundred hours of community service at a humane society shelter. The prosecution had originally recommended

129

forty hours, but the judge thought that wasn't enough. Was it a good deal for him, given the severity of the crime he was originally charged with?

News reporters waited outside the courthouse to ask the court audience, lawyers, and Tran to comment on his ruling. Tran made no comments.

"Mr. Tran," asked a reporter from The Canadian Press, "can you comment on the statements made by the spokeswoman with Lawyers for Animal Welfare? She said that 'the Crown should have stuck with indictable charges' and that 'the accused should be punished to the full extent.'"

Tran had an answer in his head, but he did not say it out loud: *These people made the most of a totally broken system. Under the pretext of protecting the animals, they live off them. You know animals do not hire lawyers. It is animal owners or those that get into trouble with animals who hire lawyers. The longer a case lasts, the more they can blackmail you. They only care about money. They never cared a damn about raccoon rights or human rights. It's all greed. There is no criminal justice.*

"Do you hate your neighbor who called the police?" another reporter asked him.

Again, he remained silent. *What good would it do if I said he is the cause of all my injustice? He deserves punishment, not me. He lied to the police. I did not hurt all the 'four' raccoons. I only wounded one of them, all by mistake. I did not wound the second one. None died. Saying one was probably killed was a shameless lie. Saying that I kept attacking them while the mother took the kits to a safe place was just another bold-faced lie. He deserves to rot in hell!*

"Mr. Tran, were the details in the charge against you accurate?" came another question.

Once more, he said nothing. *Accurate? Does it matter to them? They are above the law. They are above the prime minister, next to God. The police report was based on lies and the prosecution drew details from that report, and you somehow expect their details to be accurate and the charges to be fair! Are you an idiot?!*

"Was it a surprise to you when your community service was raised from the forty hours originally recommended by the Crown to one hundred hours by the judge?"

Silence again. *I used to think Canadian judges were fair and would protect the innocent. I have tasted the real fairness of real Canadian criminal justice firsthand. I had this judge who was no smarter than any one of those who were bent on ruining my life, who would rather lie and cover up and protect each other's negligence and other wrongdoing instead of being honest and admitting mistakes and correcting them. They would not let me go, not because I had done anything wrong, but they had wrongfully arrested me and laid fake charges against me. For that they had to force me to plead guilty just to justify their wrongdoing. You wonder why I admitted to all the wrongdoing they had fabricated. If I did not, the judge would eventually impose a much worse sentence. She didn't need to explain anything. She could do anything, right or wrong, because she is a judge. Theoretically, I can appeal, but do I have the money and time to appeal? And if this court cannot be trusted, why would I trust the appeal court? The ruling finally proved they were right in arresting me and charging me. Stay clear of all of them, my friends.*

Tran was about to wave goodbye to the reporters, friends, and neighbors who had come to receive him when another question came.

"Overall, do you think the ruling was fair for you?"

He looked back again, sniffing in silence. *Isn't it annoying? Haven't we had enough? Overall fairness? I have seen nothing but the dark side of human nature! It's all about human greed and cruelty, not animal cruelty. Nothing was related to raccoon protection or rescue. It's all about filthy money. Treating the raccoon's wounded toes for $1,300. There's a raccoon removal service where removing a raccoon from your attic costs $1,000, and a raccoon mother with kits, $2,000 or more, and all they do is leave them in front of your house so that they can dig into another neighbor's attic and create more business. If you trap them in the wrong way, as they claim, and if you attack them when you are attacked, they arrest you. This way, they keep themselves busy. That would justify their six-figure salaries. The animal lawyers then come to help you if you can afford the legal fees that easily amount to tens of thousands of dollars. An animal forensic report could cost thousands of dollars or even more. Who among these people really cares about the wounded kit and other wild animals, except for their wallets and ways of securing payments? Tell me, did I commit animal cruelty or did they commit human cruelty?*

Animal rights? Human rights? Bullshit rights!

Telling the Truth in the Dark Room

It was 9:00 in the evening at airport customs in Boston. Young, who had been doing post-doctoral research in Zurich, Switzerland, was nervously excited as he filled out the declaration form. It was not the best atmosphere for foreigners, for there were fewer passengers than customs officers. Typically when the officers are overwhelmed by the number of passengers, they ask fewer questions and let them pass more easily.

He followed a Swiss woman into the short queue, and they were soon at the booths. The American officer glanced at the Swiss woman carelessly, checked her passport, and let her pass. Then came Young's turn. The officer swiped his passport, looked at his photo, turned over to his visa, and then paused. He pushed a button, and soon two tall, strong officers appeared. *This does not bode well*, Young thought.

"Can you come with us?" they ordered.

Young followed at their heels. Soon he was sitting in a dark room, where the interrogation started. They asked which university he had attended, where he had completed his master's degree, and then his PhD. They asked him what journal essays he had published, starting from his first year of graduate studies. Knowing his future career was in the hands of these two strangers, he thought he might have a better chance if he answered truthfully, and so he did.

They asked if he could give them his password for his smartphone. You can easily guess what his answer could be. Then, they took his cellphone, along with its password, to the IT experts working on the other side of the corridor. When the two officers came back, they asked Young, "Did you watch the launch of a satellite?"

"No," he said.

"Why did we see a photo of a satellite being launched on your phone then?" They looked straight into his eyes.

"Oh," he said, surprised. He had previously deleted any unnecessary information, including contacts and browsers, that might arouse suspicion from the American customs officers. To his surprise, they had found this photo. "It was a photo I copied from an internet news article, which I then shared with a group of WeChat friends."

They said no more about the issue. They went back to their IT colleagues and then returned again. This time, they focused on the journal essays he had written and published, including unpublished ones and research that he had done and had been doing and what he intended to do at Harvard University. So far, he seemed to have held himself together, though each of their questions felt like a thunderbolt that might strike him down. His heart was throbbing rapidly, and sometimes his mind would go blank, though he always recovered quickly thanks to his young age and shrewdness.

Now he felt like a deflated balloon. He had been a top student in nearly every school he had attended, and he had led most research projects he had been doing and thus gained due recognition and respect from colleagues and supervisors. But now, any answer that failed to please these two men would ruin his entire trip and negatively impact his career instead of improving it. *This is such a humiliating experience, something neither I nor my relatives and friends would be proud of,* he told himself. *But telling the truth is still the only option.*

"Well, my research is in AI," he told them.

"What applications is that intended for?" they pressed for details.

"I started my project during the Covid-19 years. It was used to monitor the behavior of people during this period. It would identify individuals in one place and match them elsewhere amongst a crowd, for example."

They looked stone cold but asked no more about his research. Their facial expressions convinced him that they seemed to understand the nature of his research. He felt relieved that he had told the truth, and perhaps they appreciated it. Again, they went back to their backroom and instantly returned with another folder containing various printouts.

"Most post-doctorates apply for a J-1 visa. Why did you apply for an H-1 visa?" they asked.

That was the most difficult question, one he had hoped to avoid, but now he had to answer it. Up till this moment, he had defended himself quite well, probably because he had been telling the truth, which was the easiest to do. Perhaps, as long as they could not find anything illegal in what he had done, they would have to let him pass, he thought.

"Honestly, I preferred an H-1 visa, because if I had applied for a J-1 visa, my application might have been rejected due to Proclamation 10043." He was kind of relieved that he had managed to answer the most fearful question, but he was unsure whether they liked it or not.

Then, their eyes brightened a little and the muscles on their faces loosened. Perhaps they liked it, he thought. They went back to the backroom once more and came back with another colleague in civilian clothes. *He must be their supervisor*, Young thought. He felt his heart was jumping up to his throat, his face burning.

"Do you fear being prosecuted and tortured if we send you back to where you came from?" the man asked him.

"No," Young answered.

"Do you want to seek political asylum?" he then asked seriously, staring at him.

"No. I don't," he answered confidently, apparently taking the official by surprise, who then said, "Thank you." The official turned to the two officers, whispered something, and left.

"Sir, do you mind standing up against the wall here?" They beckoned him to come over and stand against the wall, which had measuring marks on it.

He did not know what they were up to, but he had to cooperate with them anyway. One of the officers clicked the camera. Within a few seconds a photo of Young was stapled onto a form.

"Please sign here." The active officer pointed at an X indicating where his signature was required, while the other stood next to him watching him with fixed eyes.

Young signed as he was instructed. "And also, your fingerprint next to your signature, please," he said, producing an ink pad on which he rolled Young's index finger.

Young did what he was told, hoping he was finally at the end of the interrogation, which had gone on for hours. He was relieved in a way. Probably they had run out of questions. If they could not find anything wrong with him, they would have to let him pass. One way or another, Young felt relieved and even a little relaxed. *Do whatever you want with me.*

"Mr. Young?" they started again.

"Yes, sir," he responded.

"As you have admitted," one of the officers said firmly and loudly, "you have committed a crime of visa fraud. You have illegally obtained an H-1 visa instead of applying for a J-1 visa." He glanced at Young to see how he reacted. Young felt like a hollow man. He had endured so much for so long, and he was tired, hungry, and helpless. He was like a bird locked in a cage, and they could do anything they wanted with him.

"In accordance with the law, you will be deported to where you have come from. Your entry into America is prohibited within the next five years. Do you have money to buy your return ticket?" The officer suddenly softened his voice.

"I have a return ticket," said Young.

"When is your return date?" the officer asked.

"Three months from now," Young answered.

"I will move the date to 2:00 p.m. today for you," the officer said confidently.

Young was surprised how much power he had. Getting a ticket for the same day was never easy for any passenger, but this officer sounded as if he were the boss of all the airlines. With this, they handcuffed him and escorted him out of the dark room, straight to an airplane flying to Germany, not to Switzerland. They said something to the captain, asking her not to return the passport to him until he was on a Swiss plane back to Zurich. "We'll go skiing with you in Switzerland," they said before they left him.

Young's suffering on his deportation trip was dwarfed by what he had just endured mentally in the dark room. Two days later, with assistance and support from friends and strangers, he finally got back to Zurich, where his previous doctoral supervisor happily renewed his contract, allowing him to continue doing his research project with him.

At least Young did not have to live on the street. He was moved to tears by the kindness of his Swiss supervisor, who then told him about how his colleague's son had been treated while similarly trying to enter the United States. "This middle-aged man was born in America, but never grew up or lived in America. Two years ago, he went to visit America, but when the American immigration officials noted his birthplace, they took him to a dark room where he was questioned like a criminal. They did some calculations and finally told him that he owed America $460,000 income tax and must pay immediately. Of course, he would not pay it; or rather, he could not pay it. He just did not have that kind of money to pay them. He hadn't lived in America since his early childhood, but as a citizen, officially he was supposed to have been paying taxes all those years. In the end, he hired a lawyer to fight them. It took him more than a year, and the American court finally ruled that he did not have to pay the money he owed. But he was prohibited from entering America again."

Strangely, Young felt a little better that a U.S.-born American had been treated the same way as he was. He decided to share his experience with his WeChat friends, one currently in the United States doing post-doctoral research and two others, who would follow suit soon, hoping that they would delete all irrelevant browsing history and contents from their phones, so as to avoid trouble at U.S. entry points.

Soon after he sent out the message, his scholar friend in the United States replied: "I was deported by the American government two months ago."

Screaming Woman in the Clinic

A police cruiser arrived outside the Century Square Mall. Two police officers got out and hastily entered the mall through the eastern entrance. Then, they quickened their pace toward the basement department store, where a shoplifter had been apprehended by the mall's security guard. They were turning left when they heard panicked screaming from behind them. They turned about, followed the direction of the voice, and were immediately led by the sound into the CS Acupuncture Clinic.

Seeing no receptionist there, the older officer knocked on the front desk, hard. Out came a man in his late sixties, dressed in a doctor's coat. "Yes, sir?" he greeted the officer. "What can I do for you?"

"We are police," said the officer, showing him his ID. "We heard a woman screaming just now. Is she in your clinic?"

"Yes, sir," he said, "she's my patient. I am the acupuncturist."

The officers asked for his name, address, and his driver's license. Then they asked, "What was going on?"

"What do you mean?" The acupuncturist did not understand.

"The woman's screaming! We heard her screaming just now. Why did she scream?" The suspicious officers looked him up and down. "She sounded like she was being assaulted."

"No one assaulted her. I was with her all the time. You probably heard her reaction to my needles. Some patients may give out a cry when the needles touch them," he explained.

The officers were not convinced. They wanted to make sure the acupuncturist was not covering up anything. They whispered to each other, wondering if they should handcuff him, but they did not.

"Can we talk to your patient," they asked the acupuncturist, "the lady who was screaming just now?"

The acupuncturist led them to the treatment room, where she was lying on a black leather treatment bed with two small blankets over her body, one covering her upper half and the other her lower half.

"My God, what are you doing here?" cried the lady when she saw the officers.

"We want to talk to you," they said.

"About what?" she said.

"You screamed just now, didn't you?" they asked.

"Yes, I did," she said. "I always scream when I receive acupuncture treatment, but why?"

"Did the acupuncturist harass you in any way?" they asked.

"For God's sake, what are you talking about!" she protested.

"Don't misunderstand us. We are trying to protect you. Just tell us the truth. Don't be afraid," they assured her.

"I'm not afraid of anything. I'm just afraid of the needles," she said.

"In which part of your body did he put the needles?"

"On my belly, around the hips, anywhere he wants to. But why?"

"Anywhere he wants to?" The officers became alert now. Something smelled fishy. "Did he ever touch your privates?"

"Oh, my God, the last person you should suspect is Dr. Kao. He is the most professional and the best acupuncturist in the world!" She became really annoyed, not knowing how to get them to leave. They had spoiled her treatment session. "Okay, gentlemen, you want to know if he had touched my privates. Now see for yourself. Here are my privates." With this, she pulled away the blankets and exposed her bra and underpants before she tore both away to expose her privates to them.

The officers, taken aback, quickly looked away. "We're sorry," one of them said. "We didn't mean to disturb you. We just wanted to make sure everything is okay with you."

"Thank you!" she shouted angrily.

The two officers still wondered why she had screamed so loudly just now. "There has got to be a reason," one whispered to the other. In the waiting area, they told Dr. Kao, "Everything is fine. Sorry for the inconvenience."

Knowing the police officers were still puzzled, Dr Kao said, "The reason some patients cry out has something to do with blockage in the meridians. In acupuncture, we say blockage means pain. No blockage, no pain. If there is blockage in the meridians, the pain is more acute. Some patients are very sensitive to this, and when it is combined with a degree of fear of the needle, they scream. Once the blockage is cleared and the pain is gone, their ailment is cured."

"Thank you so much for educating us on acupuncture." Both officers smiled in embarrassment, quickly heading back to the department store to investigate the shoplifting case.

Landlords and Tenants

May and Her Tenants

To rent, or not to rent? That was the question.

May Dunn of Queens, New York City, bought a three-storey investment house in the Bronx in 2019. Soon she rented it to three individuals, one on each floor. Each tenant signed a standard lease prepared by her lawyer, which she figured should suffice to protect her if she had to take them to court, should they fail to pay rent or cause unexpected trouble.

The man living on the third floor was a professional who had a permanent job with a decent income. He paid rent on time every month until the third year, when he surprisingly told her that he wanted to move out.

"All right," said May. She had no hard feelings, for he was a good tenant who was always polite and respectful. Both parties signed a Surrender Agreement as required by the rental act.

Nothing was out of the ordinary on his day of moving. He moved out his belongings and then returned his keys to May. Before he left her house, she went into his room for a routine inspection. To her surprise, she found he had left many women's items there. Only when she insisted did he tell her the truth: they belonged to his girlfriend. They had broken up, but he could not kick her out. That was the reason he had decided to terminate the lease and move out.

"But the lease clearly says the room was only rented to one person—yourself!" May was shocked. "How could you have brought her in without my permission?"

He left anyway, but his girlfriend's belongings were still in the room. To avoid trouble, May consulted a lawyer who specialized in landlord-tenant disputes. The lawyer told her that as long as the tenant had signed the Surrender Agreement and returned the keys to her, she had the right to change the lock and throw out anything he had left in the room. The consultation cost her $500. It was just for peace of mind.

Immediately, May had the locks changed. Then she went back to her Queens home. At 6:00 p.m., she got another surprise, this time a visit

139

from the police. The officer told her to immediately open the door for her tenant, or he would call a locksmith to open it for her.

May was panic-stricken. What she feared most had happened. She immediately went back to her rental home.

"She is not my tenant," she told the police officer. She showed him the Surrender Agreement the ex-tenant had signed. "I don't know her. She has never paid any rent. I have nothing to do with her."

The officer asked the woman for proof of residence in the house. She showed him a bank statement that had been sent to that address more than a month ago. That was enough!

"Open the door for her immediately," the police officer ordered May. "According to the law, anyone who has lived in a rental place is a tenant, whether they have paid rent or not. You have illegally locked her out," he explained. "If she was present when you locked her door, it would be an illegal eviction, which is a criminal offense, and you would have been arrested."

A stupefied May obeyed his order at once. She could not believe that a lawful landlord had become a lawbreaker, while an intruder who had been living in her house without her permission and without paying rent had become a legal tenant. She did not know whether she should hate this intruder, or the law, or the lawyer she had paid $500 for his advice to change the locks. She broke down but managed to hold back her tears.

Her battle to evict the intruder had only begun. She dared not go back to the same lawyer. Instead, she consulted a more reputable one with more success stories in dealing with evictions. He told her that during the Covid-19 epidemic the court was not open, and that, even if it were, it would take at least one to two years to evict her tenant. Then there were the issues of property damage, legal fees, and stress. The process would be long and frustrating, so a better option was to pay her a lump sum to get rid of her.

May hated the idea, but reluctantly accepted his advice in the end. She called the tenant repeatedly, but she would just scold her or hang up on her. The helpless landlady finally asked the lawyer to negotiate with the tenant on her behalf, promising to pay her $500 upfront and another $500 when a deal was signed.

The next week, her lawyer told her that after three long, difficult talks with her tenant, she had agreed to accept $5000, but wanted to stay for another three months. May was willing to pay her $5000, but wanted her to leave immediately. He lost his patience when he heard her response,

"It was not easy for me to negotiate this deal with her. Why would you mind her staying three more months?" Having no other option, the desperate landlady accepted the deal. Then she paid the lawyer the balance of her legal fees.

The day May had anxiously awaited finally came. Her lawyer had prepared the agreement for the tenant to sign. May had obtained a bank draft in the amount of $5000 for her. After contacting the tenant, the dejected lawyer told May that the tenant had told him that her grandmother was ill and hospitalized and that she had injured her back and could not walk. She had promised only verbally that she would leave in three months.

Another three months had finally passed. What May had feared happened again. The tenant said she could not find a new place and needed to stay for another month. Meanwhile, her lawyer told May that the tenant was too difficult to deal with and therefore he would not represent her anymore. May begged him to file an eviction application in court for her, but he said it was too much trouble and he would rather not take her case.

Only then did May realize why it would take one or two years to evict a tenant. *Attending so many court hearings for such a long time for just $3000! No wonder lawyers would prefer making easier money elsewhere,* May said to herself. *It's sad—small landlords are not only bullied by tenants, but also by lawyers!*

In March 2022, May learned from a friend that the Housing Court for Tenants and Landlords had reopened. She lost no time in hiring a third lawyer to deal with her tenant. The previous unsatisfactory experiences convinced her that a more expensive, good lawyer who could kick out this tenant would be worth it. He was one of the top three who had evicted numerous unlawful tenants. *Why would I mind paying a few hundred dollars more if he gets her out?*

May's new lawyer started the procedure by sending the tenant a letter asking her to leave, and filed the case with the Housing Court. Their first hearing was scheduled in July, but the tenant did not show up. Therefore, a second hearing was scheduled in September. Neither did she come to the second hearing. In October, the judge ruled in favor of May Dunn, who thought her nightmare would be over soon, but the lawyer reminded her that the process was not over yet. The judge's ruling allowed the homeowner to regain possession of her property, but it would take five months to apply for a Warrant of Eviction, and then another month to request a marshal to force the tenant out. But at least it was a step in the right direction.

May submitted her application for a Warrant of Eviction without delay, but the warrant just did not come. It turned out that the judge's clerk had made a mistake in her files. It finally resulted in the rejection of her application.

"When I received the court's rejection, I really wanted to commit suicide," she said to a *World Journal* news reporter in a later interview. "Two years of miserable suffering caused by this cruel tenant who had inflicted horrendous pain in my life, unbearable pressure on the mortgage payments, skyrocketing utilities fees, property taxes, and insurance premiums, and the repeatedly disappointing results of the service delivered by my lawyers overwhelmed me all at the same time. I burst out howling uncontrollably in my office."

When May regained her calm, she contacted her lawyer, and the mistake was corrected. A Warrant of Eviction was issued to her in July 2023, and she applied for execution of the eviction order on August 15. However, according to the regulations, the marshal had to post an eviction notice fourteen days in advance. The notice stated that if the tenant disagreed with the judgment, they could apply to the court to reopen the case prior to the eviction. Her lawyer reminded her that her tenant's chance of reopening the case was basically guaranteed, because she had been absent from all the hearings.

Unsurprisingly, the lawyer received notice from the court that the case would be reopened and therefore the eviction had been delayed. The next hearing was scheduled in late August.

As expected, the tenant's reason for absence was "never having received a court notice." May presented her proof of delivering the notice by courier, the cost of which was $200, but the tenant requested another hearing anyway. The judge showed little interest in May's proof but just reopened the case. A new hearing was scheduled in early September.

However, the tenant played the same old trick again. She did not appear. The judge ruled in favor of May Dunn again, and again an eviction notice was issued fourteen days in advance. A week after the notice was posted on her door, again the tenant appealed to the court that because her grandmother was ill she could not attend the court hearing, and therefore she requested another hearing. Again, her request was approved, but again, she did not come to the last hearing.

142

Oh, God, May moaned helplessly, *how many rounds of this game can she play: absence—default judgment—appealing for reopening—reopening—back to absence ... I am just numb now.*

May's tenant finally showed up at the September hearing. When the judge asked her if she wanted to appeal the judgment, she repeated May Dunn's "history of illegal eviction." May countered her with the ex-tenant's signature on the Surrender Agreement and his letter authorizing her to throw out anything left in his room. "At this moment," May told the news reporter, "a miracle happened!"

The judge turned to the woman and said, "I don't need your evidence to prove her illegal eviction. Whether the landlord legally or illegally evicted her tenants has nothing to do with you being a tyrant tenant. You are not her TENANT! You have not paid a cent of rent for two years and a half, ever since you moved into her house. You should be evicted!" May nearly cried.

The tyrant tenant continued to plead to the judge, "I have no job, no income, no other place to move to. I beg you, please, allow me to stay for another three months. Just three more months, please."

The judge looked at his computer and said, "This case was filed in April last year, and it has not closed yet. I must close it today. I rule that you must leave May Dunn's house. You have fourteen days to move out. Fourteen days later, the marshal will come to the house to evict you."

On eviction day, the marshal came to May's house but did not find the tyrant tenant. Her blanket, however, was still warm. They changed the locks for May and said, "If she tries to break into your house or into this room, she will be arrested."

Five minutes after the marshal left, the now homeless tyrant tenant called May Dunn to scold her for forcing her to sleep on the street. May hung up on her, at long last ending her 26-month ordeal.

May wasn't sure whether to be happy or sad. She didn't cry or smile. She just felt she had been violated. She swore she would never be a landlord again.

The next week May Dunn hired a contractor to repair the damage in the house, which cost $30,000. Finally, it became a lovely house again when it was repainted. In early January 2024, she listed her $1 million home for sale. Due to high interest rates, the housing market was slow. Her real estate agent said that she would most likely sell it in early spring. Anyway, the house was hers again, and she was not worried at all.

Believe it or not, in the same week her house was listed for sale, a squatter, or unlawful occupant, took possession of her vacant house. Claiming to be her tenant, he changed the name on the utility bill, water bill, and other bills to his. The day he moved into her property, he even replaced her entire front door, including the locks. Then, he sublet several rooms to other homeless people.

May nearly fainted when she came to see her house with her daughter on February 29 and realized squatters had moved in. The front door was open and no one was at home when she arrived. She tried her keys, and as she had feared, they did not work. She felt a chill and shivered, but then, mysteriously felt a warm current surging all over her body. Though still terrified, she decided to defend her rights this time. She quickly called two TV reporters, three news journalists, and then a locksmith, who all arrived at about the same time. In ten minutes, May had the locks on the front door replaced. Then she locked it.

Hardly had the locksmith left when three squatters came. They kicked the front door open and smashed their way in past May and her daughter in the hallway. Once inside the house, the squatters called the police, telling them they had been illegally locked out.

The police arrived immediately, talked with the squatters and then May Dunn. They asked the men to show proof of tenancy, but they could not. The officers arrested one of them and escorted two away.

The police warned May that she could be arrested and charged with illegal eviction if one of the occupants could prove they were tenants of her house. She had not forgotten the definition of *tenant* in New York City. She was just waiting for them to prove their status.

To her disbelief, a fourth squatter rushed into the house out of breath, accompanied by the police who had just left a moment ago. This squatter claimed he had a lease, which he showed to the police.

"That's impossible. I had never rented my house," said May. The police looked at his messy, stained two-page lease and arrested May Dunn immediately—right in her own house, in front of her daughter, the journalists, and TV reporters.

The smiling self-proclaimed tenant told the journalists and TV reporters that he would leave May's house at once without causing trouble, if she paid him $16,000. He said he had changed the front door, fixed plumbing, and done painting, so at least he should be paid for the labor and material.

May's nightmare, which she thought had finally ended, just continued. She was conditionally released and would have to appear in court, where the judge would decide her fate. Even if she was found not guilty, the police warned that she would have to seek a court order to evict the squatters. May feared the squatters were plotting to steal her whole house, and they really could if they stayed longer than nine years. But now she had become a brave woman who feared neither the police nor the squatters. She would fight until she won. "When I get back my house I will pack and go—go north [to Canada]!"

May returned to her home in Queens, collapsing into the sofa. Then she got up and turned on the computer on the desk. The following caught her eyes on the news website.

Young Landlord Committed Suicide: *It is with sadness that SOLO (Small Ownership Landlords of Ontario) announces the suicide death of a young landlord, member of SOLO in the Hamilton area.*

Yesterday a young landlord, member of SOLO in the Hamilton area, committed suicide due to unbearable financial pressure. His death was a direct result of his tenant's non-payment of rent that led to the foreclosure of his home, which he had inherited from his father. This home was his shelter and it had a special value to him. Losing it meant losing everything in his life, emotionally and financially.

At the court hearing this week, in the absence of the tenant, he was granted a non-payment eviction order, but later in the day when the tenant appeared, the court squashed the order and allowed a stay. His hope to evict the nonpaying tenant was smashed. He fell into desperation, as he could not find the money to pay his mortgage. His life was stretched until it snapped in this justice system that appears only to protect tyrant rent gamers, not hardworking small landlords.

Many of our members have faced similar pain and suffering, and any of us could have ended our life in the same tragic manner. We demand fair treatment for small landlords, and we want the Ontario government held accountable for our member's avoidable tragic death.

May sobbed. Chokingly.

American Dream in the Making

The court case was labeled "Parto Vs. North Yorker Hotel." Mr. Parto was suing the North Yorker Hotel for rejecting his request to rent a room in the hotel as a resident with a six-month lease at a discounted rate. Whether out of arrogance, ignorance, or other reasons, the hotel did not send a representative to counter Mr. Parto at the hearing. The court is seldom amused if the accused who wants to win the case does not even send a representative on the judgment day. If a ruling is made against the absentee, they deserve it.

Parto stated that he had paid $300 for his room, No. 2222, for a night, and that the following day, he had requested a six-month lease after his one-day stay. The hotel manager told him that they would not lease him a room, for they had never done that kind of lease, nor did they have a policy to do so. They had asked him to move out his belongings; otherwise, they would do it for him, which was exactly what they did. Parto argued that the moment he submitted his written request for a lease, he became a resident there. He cited a 1968 state law and similar rulings.

The rules and regulations he cited were accurate. His support documents were sufficient and acceptable. His overall argument was forceful and convincing. Even if North Yorker Hotel had challenged him, it might not have won the case, let alone when absent from the proceedings. On June 22 that year, the judge sided with Parto, ruling that the hotel's removal of his belongings from his room constituted an illegal eviction. He granted Parto possession of his hotel room and ordered the hotel to give him a key and that he be provided with routine daily service such as nightly bedding change, daily cleaning, and free access to the swimming pools and fitness centers.

Realizing how serious the issue was, North Yorker Hotel scrambled to find ways to evict this unexpected guest, who had now become a permanent resident living there without paying another cent. Five days later, when Parto read the court ruling again, he got another surprise: the ruling did not even mention such words as "tenancy," "lease," and "termination date." It said that he had "possession" of the room, which confused him. Then, he called the court for clarification.

The court's representative told him he had **possession**, uttering the three syllables slowly but sharply. "You are not a renter," he was further assured. "You have **possession** of a building." Parto could not believe his ears. He was trembling in shock.

"So, I own it!" he murmured.

With the judge's order, Parto went to the government department where real estate titles are registered. He asked the officials to register the title of Room 2222 in his name but was told that, unlike apartments, hotel rooms could not be split, and therefore he could not register title to a single room. Then he reviewed the original registration on file and discovered that the hotel had no individual owner listed: the owner was Block 500, Lot 70.

What do I have to lose anyway? he said to himself. *If I have the right to register it all, then I will register it all.* That was what he did—through the Automatic City Register Information System. But he was rejected six times, until a city official told him to contact the sheriff's office. He told the sheriff's office he had been given a court order to register the title to the hotel. Obviously, someone did something for him, for his registration was successful after his seventh attempt.

Meanwhile, the hotel's legal team had been trying to evict him, arguing that the hotel was exempt from the housing law, but they failed to provide evidence from their May 1966 documentation that the room was rented for more than $88 per week at that time. Accordingly, the court dismissed the suit, handing Parto another legal victory.

In May 2019, having lived in the hotel room for free for nearly a year, Parto was identified as the official owner of the million-square-foot property in the Automatic City Register Information System.

What a nice bite of the Big Apple he had taken in this Land of Opportunity! Parto was not satisfied with possessing ownership of the 41-storey hotel. He could not wait until the next day to take possession of its profits. He managed to gain access to any information he wanted from the hotel's accounting department, where no one challenged his authority. He was informed that the hotel had earned $20 million in the past fiscal year.

"That payment is past due, and is due immediately," he wrote to the hotel lawyer, demanding the money without further delay. This was the first tangible benefit he was thirsting for. It would open numerous channels in his life. He explained to the lawyer that he needed the money to do urgent repairs and renovations the next day. He also emailed M&T Bank to name him as the owner of all the hotel accounts. He did everything he could to seize the hotel's money, including rent from its renters. In shock, the lawyer immediately contacted the true owner, Unifi Church, instead.

Two days later, the hotel's legal team was fighting Parto in court again. "I have done nothing wrong. The judge granted me the rights to the property, and I just registered its title in my name in accordance with the law, rules, and regulations. I did everything openly and legally." Meanwhile, he claimed that he was a descendant of Christopher Columbus, trying to take political advantage of the case in court. He exerted pressure on the judge and the lawyers as well. "In the final analysis, this is a case between Mickey Columbus and the Communist North Korean dictator," he declaimed confidently. If he succeeded for the third time in court, his American dream would indeed come true. "You are gently reminded that the original owner of the hotel was from North Korea, a communist state. I can never know the complex relationships he had with the dictators there. This Unifi Church was also involved in the assassination of the former Japanese Prime Minister. Tolerating the same regime that has been running the North Yorker Hotel is like ignoring another deadly time bomb that will sooner or later destroy another World Trade Center tower in this great city of ours." He went on and on.

The judge adjourned the hearing to a later date. Parto felt he had neither won nor lost. Playing the patriotic card was always a safe bet. If you succeed in discrediting your opponents in court, or better still, demonizing them, it's a good way to win a lawsuit.

Parto returned to his hotel room and continued to dream of the riches he would possess. Even just $1 million could give him the option of early retirement. He had been in America for less than ten years. He had not found a permanent job, never owned a home, and had never been able to rent a decent apartment. He could have accepted a special discounted rate to live in this hotel forever, but he did not want to waste the rights the judge had awarded him and the opportunity the city had given him. He would rather fight to the end. In America, he thought, everything is possible.

A week later, he heard a knock on his door. He opened it, only to face two police officers, who handcuffed him and took him away immediately. He had been charged with a long list of illegal activities, which could send him to jail for twenty years.

"Are you kidding me?" Parto said fearlessly when the officers were handcuffing him. "What have I done wrong? The judge gave me the order to register title to the property. The city officials registered it for me. I became the legal owner of the property and accordingly I have my rights. Why don't you arrest the judge and the city officials instead?"

The officers were silent.

Cause of Eric's Tragedy

Eric smiled with relief after signing on the dotted lines of the numerous documents in his lawyer's office. Like most clients, he had not read the papers he signed. All he knew was that he had bought a bungalow for $1 million and had obtained a mortgage of $500,000 from the bank. He still felt bitter that he had lost half of his two-storey house to his ex-wife, who had also "stolen" his twin girls. He had fought hard for custody of his nine-year-old daughters in court, but the unwritten law which the Coalition of Victimized Divorced Fathers called unjust, brutal, and rotten let him down in every step of the divorce procedures.

He owned his house before the marriage and thought he would be able to keep it because it was his wife who had been unfaithful to him. However, the court awarded her not only half of the house but also custody of the two children he loved dearly. He was also slapped with a monthly payment of $2,000 to support them, which he felt would guarantee an easy life for his ex-wife.

His ex-wife was cruel; the judge was brutal; justice was nonexistent. In his mind, she lied, the judge lied, and the court lied. He was the only person who knew the truth, but the final judgment found that he was a violent man who had often assaulted his wife and beaten his children, unfit to be a husband and father. If he'd had a gun at the time of judgment, he would have killed his wife, her lawyer, and the judge, and then himself. It was his unwavering love for his children that restored his sanity and saved his life. After his three-year battle in court, he had learned not to trust anyone. He had to take care of himself.

His mind was blank when he left his lawyer. For the lawyer, the deal was closed, but for him it was just the beginning of a new life with numerous uncertainties and challenges. He felt like a broken man, robbed of wealth, health, and worst of all, the joy of living with his daughters. What hurt most was that he felt his manhood and fatherhood had been ruthlessly raped by his ex-wife and the judge. He just hoped his two daughters would understand that he was a great father who loved them more than himself and that he had been victimized by a cruel family court system.

Comparing himself with some divorced men who ended up in homeless shelters, Eric felt grateful that he had managed to buy a home, albeit a rental property that was still occupied by a couple. He had found the bargain property in the online listings himself. His real estate agent prepared the sale and purchase agreement for him and the vendor to sign, and his lawyer had helped him with the rest of the paperwork. Before submitting his purchase offer, the agent and lawyer warned him of the potential risk in buying a rental property that he had not even viewed, though it cost ten percent less than comparable properties in the same neighborhood. Eric agreed, but he had a very tight budget and he knew that it was the properties that were choosing him and not the other way around.

Regarding the couple living in the basement apartment, he thought it might be an additional source of income. The ex-owner had told him that they had been paying $1,500 per month. Eric planned to raise the rent to $2,000, if they wanted to stay. In the current rental market, it would still be a bargain. If they didn't want to pay more, he thought, they could move out. He was positive he could easily rent it for $2,500 to another tenant.

Eric had estimated that $2,000 would cover his monthly mortgage payment, or he could use the rent as support for his children, which would ease his financial pressure significantly. In the end he brushed aside all worries, and now he had the keys to a property that would mark the beginning of his new life. He headed straight for his new home at 1331 Helton Road, which was within walking distance.

"I hope the basement is in good condition," he prayed as he stepped onto the front porch. "Repairs are expensive these days."

Knocking, he called out "Anybody inside?" just to make sure no one was there.

Hearing no response, he inserted the key into the keyhole of the deadbolt and was happy it worked. "So, this key is worth $1 million!" he murmured.

He pushed the door open and was taken aback. "What's all this?" he shouted. "Oh, God!" The home had not been vacated!

A pungent odor struck his nostrils. Scattered all over the living room were smelly soiled socks, underwear, pants and shirts. Disgusting, moldy take-out food boxes, coffee cups, and soft-drink bottles spilled out of the kitchen sink, covering the countertop and floor below. A corner of one basement room was covered with thick black mold. He felt nauseous. "So, this is the bargain I got!" He was prepared for some problems, but not to this extent.

151

"Filthy! Just filthy! How could someone live and survive in such a filthy place!" Then he ventured into the bathroom, A wet bathtub was covered with thick yellow slime that stretched upward, disguising the original color and pretty design of the wall tiles. The faucet over the sink was dripping, which appeared to be the cause of the decay in the laminated countertop, walls, and drawers. Then came the most shocking: the toilet bowl was full of revolting feces. Eric choked at the repulsive odor and retched. Holding his breath, he quickly ran out of the bathroom. At that moment he wondered whether owning this home might shorten his life.

So, this is my home! He sighed. *Are there really still tenants living here?"* he wondered. He decided to get out as quickly as he could, just in case.

Hardly had he stepped out of the front door when two police officers confronted him.

"What are you doing here, sir?" the officer on the left asked. His question suggested that they were assuming Eric was in the wrong somehow.

"I am the new owner of this house," Eric said, regaining his calm while pulling out the documents his lawyer had given to him.

"Do you live here?" Both officers looked into his eyes.

"No," he said, sounding deflated.

"Who lives here, then?"

"The tenants," he said, realizing too late that this might sound like a confession of wrongdoing. Suddenly, he felt weak and trembly.

"Did the tenants give you permission to enter the house?" the police asked.

"I am the new owner of this house. I just got my keys today," he said.

"We are asking you, have the tenants given you permission to enter the house?" The officers sounded annoyed.

"No," he mumbled, knowing his life was at their mercy now.

"We're placing you under arrest for invading your tenants' home," they announced.

"I'm so sorry, but it's my house," he tried to explain. "The tenants are supposed to be in the basement apartment, not up here. I own this property. It's all in writing, according to the law. I have done nothing wrong."

"You can tell the judge whatever you want to say," they said after handcuffing him. "We received a report that you illegally entered the tenants' home."

"Thank you, officers!" said a strange man who emerged from the west lane. "Thank you for taking him away." He was evidently one of the tenants in the house and had been hiding in the backyard, waiting for him. The moment Eric entered the house, he called the police and told them that someone had broken in.

Eric was locked up in a cold cell for the day. He appeared in court the following day and, after hiring a criminal lawyer to defend him, was released on bail. Apparently, entering without permission was a small offense and he was awarded one hundred hours of community service instead of jail time. The procedures lasted nine months, costing him $16,000 in total.

As much as he loathed the idea, the nonpaying tenants of the previous owner had become Eric's. He filed an eviction order against them with the Landlord and Tenant Board, but such orders were never easy to obtain. The tenants countersued, accusing him of negligence and failing to maintain the property in a manner fit for enjoyment of life—an argument that would justify their nonpayment. They presented to LTB color photos of mold, filth, ants, cockroaches, huge spiders, and mice droppings, among others, which easily backed up their claim that Eric was a negligent landlord.

Now Eric not only had to pay his wife, the mortgage, and property taxes, but also the tenants' utility bills, etc. Even if he went without food, he would still need $5,000 to cover his monthly expenses. He found himself drowning in debt, and neither the LTB nor anyone else seemed to care a damn about him. Everyone seemed as cold and cruel as those he had come across during his divorce procedures.

Like many other landlords who file eviction orders, Eric had to wait eighteen months for his first court hearing. But that was just the beginning of his legal woes. The tenants had failed to pay rent for thirty months and already owed him $60,000, but they told the judge, "We have the money to pay him, but as the photos show, our landlord has not fulfilled his obligations. The property is in need of repair. It is not fit for living. It is dirty, smelly, moldy, and unhealthy. We feel sick living in the house every day. We are holding our rent payment until he has fixed the property."

The landlord denied this accusation, but the judge disagreed with him, stating that the place was indeed not fit for living and that Eric must ensure it provided the basic comforts.

"According to the law, we have the right to delay our payment until he has repaired the property," the male tenant furthered their argument. "In fact, we are feeling sick, due to the dangerous mold in the house." The tenant grasped his chest as he pretended to faint and dropped to the floor. "I can't breathe. My heart, my heart, my heart … I am dying." He said in a choking voice.

"Are you okay?" asked the judge. The tenant shook his head, closed his eyes, looking as if he had fainted. The judge adjourned the hearing and called for an ambulance for the tenant on the floor.

It arrived in fifteen minutes. The paramedics found his vital signs perfectly normal, but according to standard procedure, they needed to take him to hospital.

Minutes later, the ambulance entered Sheppard Road. "Just a minute!" the tenant shouted, "Where are we now?"

"Sheppard Road, five minutes away from Central Hospital," they said.

"Can I get off here?" he said. "I live near here."

"But you fainted; we need to get you checked out," the paramedics said in surprise.

"I'm fine now," he said. "Please let me off here. I live across the street here. If you take me to the hospital, I will have to ride a bus or take a taxi to get back. I'm broke. I don't even have money to buy food."

They released him from the stretcher and opened the door for him. Quickly he got off the ambulance, smiling. They knew he had no health problems, but like the judge, they were required to follow up on his complaint. Thus he succeeded in postponing the court hearing.

As the tenant wanted, the hearing did not resume for six months, and after that, there were three more hearings. Like other tyrant tenants, the renter did everything he could to delay his eviction. At one hearing he requested that it be conducted in French. For another, he could not attend due to a Covid-19 infection. In his pocket, he had a list of reasons that could delay the procedures for at least ten more years.

Finally, after abusing the legal system for three years, the tenants accepted an eviction order. Without paying their rent in arrears, they just left, free of punishment. Eric could do nothing about it. The only thing he felt good about was that he had finally gained possession of his property.

"Only when you have dealt with a tyrant tenant will you understand what pain and suffering the system can cause," Eric told his mother afterwards. "It was even worse than dealing with my ex-wife when she was trying to steal my house and children."

Eric's life took a turn after he gained legal access to his house in July 2023. He had no money for professional garbage removal and renovations, but he was a handyman. For an entire month he worked day and night, first removing three truckloads of foul garbage, then replacing the drywall in all the rooms, including the two kitchens and the two bathrooms. When he finished the last brush of paint in the basement, he was so happy and relieved that he finally owned the home. He needed money, for obvious reasons. Therefore, without delay he advertised the two-room basement apartment on the Kijiji website for $2,000 per month. He was looking for a good couple.

The rental market was good after the Covid-19 years, but Eric had yet to figure out how to avoid bad tenants. He had posted a long list of conditions that would be included in the lease. The most important one was that the tenants must pay rent on the first of every month, keep the place clean and tidy at all times, and be polite and respectful.

More than a hundred people had expressed interest in his basement apartment. One tenant from overseas who needed the place three months later even offered to pay $100 more and one year's rent upfront, but Eric was worried that it could be a scam. Besides, a three-month wait was too long. A local man called at midnight, wanting to rent the place that same night, but Eric was scared off by his eagerness. A third applicant was a man who had a girlfriend open to sex with others and offered that Eric could join them. Eric felt offended and insulted; he blocked the phone number. The large number of phone calls was disturbing, and he felt rather exhausted at the end of the month.

Finally, a working professional couple came into his life. They were ready to pay first and last months' rent in cash and would accept all conditions without causing any inconvenience. They arrived dressed in suits and wore polished leather shoes. Eric grinned the whole time while they were viewing the place. They happily signed a lease for twelve months.

What followed was their honeymoon: Eric received the first and last months' rent in cash, and the tenant moved into the newly renovated basement apartment. The next month, however, the man said he had lost his job, so they could only pay half of the rent.

"How unfortunate!" Eric thought. It became a cause of concern for him.

The third month, the tenants said they couldn't pay even half of the rent, but they texted him a photo showing that their room temperature was below 20 degrees Celsius, which was against the law. They had a thermometer that monitored the temperature around the clock. Eric explained to them that the heating was controlled by the thermostat upstairs and the temperature could vary slightly from room to room, but the tenants insisted that they wanted no less than the lowest temperature required by law. Otherwise, they would withhold the rent. Eric realized he was in trouble again.

As good as their word, the tenants stopped paying rent, this time with a reason permitted by the law. Eric knew he was in a disadvantaged situation, so he offered to provide them with an additional heater. The extra cost was $100 in the coldest winter months. Eric offered to pay for it in exchange for prompt rent payment. The tenants took the electric heater but did not pay their rent as promised.

"There is mold in the basement," the male tenant told Eric three days later. "I hope you don't mind us withholding the rent until it is thoroughly removed. Mold is extremely unhealthy. It causes all kinds of sickness. It may even cause death."

"Mold?" How could there be?" Eric did not believe it. He had replaced the drywall of the entire house, including the moldy patches in the tenants' bedroom. It was all nice and clean on the day the tenants moved in. He had photos to prove it, but they sent him their own photos that showed a grey spot at the corner of their bedroom.

It was the same moldy spot he had fixed, next to the closet. It was far from the kitchen and bathroom, but how could there be mold within such a short time? But undeniably it was mold!

"What did you do to the wall?" Eric asked, sounding impatient and frustrated.

"We haven't done anything," the man said.

"You can pay your rent today, and I will get a mold contractor to look at it. If it is your responsibility, you should pay for the removal," Eric told him sternly.

The tenant said nothing, but neither did they pay the rent. They wanted to wait until the mold was removed.

Eric went online and soon became quite knowledgeable about mold issues in rental properties. He had read about more than ten ways mold could occur. He was most disturbed when he learned from a news report that there were tenants who deliberately and repeatedly wetted the walls or furniture to encourage mold so that they could refuse to pay rent. Nonetheless, by the look of it, he did not believe the tenants' mold was deliberately caused.

That same afternoon, Eric called a contractor for a quotation for removing the mold. He was shocked that fixing the spot would cost $9,000 plus taxes, totaling $10,000. Where could he find the money? But without its removal it would even be illegal to rent the place. The tenants could even sue him if they got sick in his moldy basement apartment. The more he thought about the problem, the more anxious he became. His head began spinning.

He was too impatient to wait until the next day, so he went downstairs to talk to the tenants again, hoping that they would withdraw their threat against him.

"I rented a perfect basement apartment to you, but it has become moldy now. I would appreciate it if you pay for the removal of the mold. If you don't want to pay but want to put up with it, that would be fine with me too," he said.

"But it's not our fault. Why do we have to pay for it?" they said.

Obviously, nobody wanted to pay for such an expensive job. The tenants insisted that they did not want to pay, and Eric repeated that he would not remove it. The mold continued to grow.

Then came the new month when rent was due again, and again the tenants refused to pay their rent. They even texted Eric that they felt nauseous when they smelled the mold.

Eric thought that they had escalated their accusation and he felt threatened now. No sooner had he finished reading the text than he dashed downstairs and banged on their door. The tenants were scared by the deafening banging but answered the door anyway.

"Do you want to pay for the removal of the mold or not?" Eric shouted. Horrific anger and hostility were spilling out of his wild eyes.

The tenants dared not look at him. They lowered their heads, repeating that it would be unfair for them to have to pay.

"Are you going to pay or not?" Eric shouted at the top of his voice. "You have one minute to answer me!"

They were silent. Eric left without saying another word. In a moment he was back with a short gun.

Seeing the black barrel of the gun, the female tenant begged, "Please don't. Please don't hurt us. I will pay. I will pay."

The panic-stricken young couple shot out of their apartment and ran as fast as their legs could carry them, but they were not fast enough.

Bang! Bang! Bang! Eric started firing.

The boyfriend fell; then the girlfriend dropped. They had planned to get married the next month, but that could never happen now.

Three neighbors called the police, who arrived in less than three minutes, followed by an ambulance. The young couple would eventually be pronounced dead on the spot.

Eric locked himself up in his house, refusing to surrender to the police who had surrounded his house. They tried to negotiate with him, but he was not interested in talking with them. Six hours later, he suddenly opened fire. The police returned fire. Then he rained more bullets on the police vehicles, and the police shot back too, until they heard no more shots from the house. Then, they broke open the front door and sent in a robot that found Eric lying motionless on the living room floor. He also was pronounced dead on the spot. The fierce battle ended with a third life lost.

At the news conference, the police said the tenants were innocent victims. As for the mold, though Eric did not know who had caused it or how it had occurred, an experienced mold contractor who had examined the foundation walls of his house thought it was probably caused by snow or rain water seeping in from outside, because that spot in the foundation had had visible cracks. Water gathered there could have got through and caused the mold inside.

With three people dead, the police had no interest in the cause of the mold. They just closed the case. Neither was the public interested in knowing the real cause of the tragedy.

The loss of the three lives was soon forgotten in the city.

A Landlord Speaks Out

In April 2020, Nawa Finn and her ex-husband sold their former marital home in Ottawa following their divorce. She decided to move into her investment property, which had been rented to a family for four years. She had never raised the rent and thought the tenant should be grateful to her for maintaining an exceptionally low rent of $1,500 per month. Nawa gave the family a seventy-five-day termination notice, telling them to move by August 31. She was positive that they would understand she had no other place to live and that they would move with gratitude for the past four years. She thought they might even remain friends.

On August 31, 2020, she arrived at her investment townhouse with a vague sense of anxiety. She put down her suitcase and inserted her key into the front door lock, but it did not work. She was taken by surprise and banged on the door impatiently.

"Who changed my lock?" she shouted.

"Hey, what do you want?" said a woman who answered the door.

"Well, I'm the owner of this house," Nawa introduced herself. "I gave you a termination notice seventy-five days ago. You should have moved out yesterday. I need to move into my house today."

"Oh," said the woman, surprised but not shocked. She shouted to her husband, who immediately appeared and apologized to Nawa.

"I am so sorry. We haven't found our new home yet. We just could not afford it," he said. "The current rent we are paying is barely enough for a small basement apartment, and we don't want to live in a basement apartment."

Shocked, Nawa suddenly realized she had done herself a disservice by charging too little rent. Apparently her tenant had got used to a budget with low rent. He either did not have the money or was unwilling to pay the fair market rate.

"What am I supposed to do?" Nawa mumbled to herself. "Where can I spend the night?"

"I am so sorry. Please give us one more month," he pleaded.

"Okay, that's a deal!" Nawa sighed. "I hope you will find a new home as soon as possible. In any case, I need my home back in thirty days, whether you have found your new home or not."

159

"Of course, I promise. We will vacate the home for you when we find our new place. Thank you!" He sounded quite sincere. Nawa accepted a month's waiting, though she was disappointed.

Nawa was a compassionate, well-educated professional who did not want to intrude into their privacy, so she did not ask to inspect her townhouse, though she was really eager to. After all, she hadn't been inside since she rented it to this family. Many possibilities flashed across her mind. If they really had difficulty finding a new place, she could even allow them to stay in the basement.

Reluctantly Nawa left her house, worried that she might not get back her home even the next month. Indeed, no landlord could be sure until they received the keys from the tenant.

If they were honest people, they should have moved out already. Gosh! She sighed. She wondered why a homeowner could not move back into their own home after giving their tenants seventy-five days' notice.

She called her mother about the unexpected delay, and was invited to stay with her if she had nowhere to go. Then, she called a friend, also living in the capital city, who also offered to put her up, but she hated to bother a busy friend who was working full-time. Her mother was also working and had her own routine.

Should I go to the homeless shelter instead? she asked herself, shivering at the thought. Her mind began to spin with fears. *Oh, no! I don't belong there. It's a place for real homeless people, including drug addicts and mentally ill people. I could be attacked and robbed. Even raped or killed. Drug addicts can become extremely violent if they have to assuage a craving.*

Everything I have now is in this suitcase. I can't carry it like a wallet. If it's stolen, I will have no clothes to change into. Then, just think of their filthy toilets. Can you even take a shower there? I could be bitten by bedbugs. Maybe I could even catch AIDS there.

Her brain froze and she stopped thinking, but she was a tough woman. She bravely faced her reality. She owned a home and she could and should have it back.

It was getting dark and, feeling insecure, she realized her lack of a home had become an emergency. Finally, she decided to accept help from her friend and mother. That marked the beginning of her new life.

As she put it after her ordeal was over, "I lived out of my suitcase: a few days with my mother and a few days with my good friend, sleeping on their sofas for the night and wandering the streets in the daytime."

On September 30, Nawa returned to her townhome to get her keys, but the tenants had still not found a new place. They had not moved and they had stopped paying rent and their gas, water, and electricity bills altogether.

In desperation, Nawa threatened to file for an eviction order to force the family out, but the man was not intimidated. He occupied the house, so he had the upper hand.

"With the same budget, I cannot find a place to live anywhere in this city," said the tenant, watching her reaction. "There are several ways you can help us. If you have another rental home to rent to us, we can move. Or if you can find another townhome for us for the same rent of $1500 a month in this same neighborhood, we will move there. Or, if you want to pay us a lump sum, say $50,000, to help us cover the rent increase, we'll move somewhere else." He paused, but immediately added, "Or if you can give us a piece of land for us to build our own home, we will be happy to move too."

Nawa could not believe her ears. *How dare you! Who do you think you are? I have been renting my house to you for forty percent off the current market rent. You don't appreciate it, and instead you are trying to blackmail me! Are you a man or a beast? You want me to pay you $50,000 to move? You want me to give you a lot to build a house? I wish I could! But even if I could, I would never give it to you! You ungrateful tyrant, I despise you!* But she dared not utter these words. Hostile words could be used against her in court, or at a hearing of the Ontario Human Rights Commission.

Nawa became truly homeless now, knowing that she had a tough battle ahead. Living out of a suitcase, she felt poorer than her tenant and even homeless people living on the street, who often carried two or more bulging bags.

To ensure success as soon as possible, she hired Stancer, a well-regarded lawyer, to file an eviction application with the Landlord and Tenant Board on her behalf. She felt relieved after that; the application gave her a sense of security and protection. *You bastard, you will regret it when you go to court. Wait and see how the law will punish you to its fullest extent!* She gritted her teeth. *It's my house. I don't want to rent it anymore. I want to live in it. That is my right. You dare to demand a ransom from me! God damn you, ungrateful beast! You will taste the brutality of the law!*

But the spirited Nawa's hopes were dashed when she got the court hearing date—May 29. That would guarantee her homelessness for another eight months.

"My home?" she choked out. "So I just cannot move into my own home? Something isn't right!" She asked her lawyer to speed up the eviction process, but he said, "The legal procedure has started and we have to follow it through. There's no shortcut."

For eight months, Nawa did not eat well or sleep well, and she found work difficult. Every day was a nightmare. After seven months of this, she began to feel more positive about the upcoming hearing. But three days before the hearing date, the tenant requested that it be conducted in French because he was French-speaking. The court agreed and postponed the hearing for four months so that an interpreter could be present. It took three more months after the hearing to receive an eviction order, then another three to secure an execution order. Throughout the process, the tenants tried to delay their eviction by hook or by crook, so as to live in her house for free for as long as they could. It was easy, convenient and free of consequences—free of punishment, so why not?

On April 11, 2022, after a 20-month battle, Nawa finally got her home back. The tenant refused to pay the $30,000 rent in arrears (which might have been $75,000 at a fair market rate). Nawa had spent more than $10,000 on legal fees. Then, the damage caused by the tenant cost a further $50,000 to repair.

In Canada, it appeared to Nawa, a tenant could live in your house for twenty months for free. They could damage your property without penalty. Yes, as it appeared, tyrant tenants were protected and could delay hearings by lying to the court, which didn't fully investigate most cases. They not only could cover up their own wrongdoing but also smear landlords. The judges in the LTB knew this but didn't hand them over to the police for criminal investigation. While landlords might lose thousands of dollars of rent and would have to pay for expensive repairs and court-endorsed blackmail—"cash for keys," abusive tyrants could just march away triumphantly in the end.

"I find it inconceivable that tax dollars pay for a government body that has zero accountability and that thinks it is okay for someone to own a home and be homeless," a frustrated Nawa said. "How is it possible that someone can rent a place, stop paying rent, and live in it for twenty months? Why doesn't the court seize their stolen money to pay the rent in arrears back to the landlord?"

The answer is that the law does not allow this to happen. To Nawa, it seemed a mockery of justice, or perhaps an excuse used to cover up official incompetence. If the law was victimizing innocent, law-abiding citizens, it ought to be amended. It should have been done long ago. Everyone seemed to agree that the system that supposedly protected landlords as well as tenants was broken. It worked for some lawbreakers at the expense of law-abiding people. The taxpayers knew it, the police knew it, the judges knew it, but the lawmakers ignored the issue.

Hoping for change, Nawa began to write letters to members of the provincial parliament and Premier Doug Ford. To strengthen her case, she included the following news stories.

On December 1, 2021, Kailer Wolf, representing BNU Center, signed a lease with the owner of a residential property in North York. The occupancy date was February 1, 2022, and rent was due on this day. Wolf asked the landlord if he could have permission to enter the house to ready it for possession. The latter agreed and gave Wolf the keys. It was understood that Wolf was permitted to enter the property without additional rent and would only start paying rent on the official first day of occupancy.

However, as soon as Wolf got the keys, he replaced the locks on the front door without the landlord's permission. The landlord was kept out, and when they went to the house to inspect it in the same month, Wolf hired a lawyer to warn the landlord that it was illegal for him to enter or try to enter the property. When the landlord appeared again in January, before the tenancy had officially started, Wolf's lawyer escalated the tenant's accusation that the landlord had been harassing his client and would take legal action if such illegal activities persisted.

Then came February 1, when the rent was due and the postdated check was cashable. The landlord cashed the first rent check in the amount of $9,500, but a week later, the bank returned it to him due to the renter's stop-payment notice. More than two months later, Wolf still had not paid a cent of rent. Then, on the 28th of the month, he sent the landlord another check. It was again returned due to insufficient funds.

Realizing they had fallen into the trap set by a tyrant renter, the next month the landlord issued notice of termination of the lease due to nonpayment and filed it with the Landlord and Tenant Board. That was exactly what Wolf had hoped for. Many small landlords had accused the LTB of being the tyrant renters' protector. True or not, it had given the appearance of tolerating or at least being manipulated skillfully by unscrupulous tyrant renters. In multiple cases, it had given the impression of serving as a private court for abusive tyrant renters.

As summarized by Nawa, Wolf welcomed the eviction hearings, where he knew how to counter the landlord's arguments. When the landlord realized the lower court was not a place to get a fair judgment, they moved their case to the Ontario Superior Court, which was possible because the amount of money involved exceeded $35,000. Indeed, the landlord got better treatment in Superior Court. Yet, due to a notoriously dysfunctional system governed by outdated rules that tended to thwart not only complainants but also judges, the case lingered for months. Wolf claimed to have not received a notice from court to appear at the first hearing, followed by bold-faced lies at hearing after hearing, until the judge declared that he wouldn't listen to any more of his statements because he lacked credibility. The judge finally ruled in favor of the landlord, ordering Wolf to pay the landlord $304,000 rent in arrears, plus $100,000 in punitive damages. If the case had been dealt with by LTB, the last amount was unlikely to have been required, and the case could have dragged on for two more years.

The ruling judge represented justice in the system, giving hope to helpless victims like Nawa. Nawa was moved to tears by the judge's ruling, which showed sympathy to "the victim in the immediate case for the gaming of the administration of justice. The system was abused. ... That free ride must certainly end," the judge wrote. "I immediately grant the Plaintiffs a writ of possession and order Mr. W[...] and [...] Corporation to provide vacant possession forthwith." What Nawa did not understand was why Wolf and other tyrant tenants in other places were not thrown in jail. They had undeniably abused the administration of justice to get "that free ride."

"That is theft, and theft is a criminal offense that deserves imprisonment or at least a criminal record," Nawa told the politicians. "Clearly the law has to be amended to automatically upgrade such civil offenses to criminal offenses to deter brazen lawbreakers."

The second story Nawa included in her letter to the premier was titled "Landlady Forced to Jump to Her Death." It reported that the apartment owner had issues with her tenant, who had not paid rent for more than twenty months due to a complaint of mold in her apartment.

The rental apartment was a new property on the 16th floor without leakage from the roof, walls, windows, water pipes or faucets or anywhere else. To highlight the severity of problems tenants often complained about in court as their rationale to stop paying rent, Nawa included screenshots of students in a social media group exchanging ideas about how to blackmail landlords by repeatedly pouring water on the same spots in their rental properties until mold eventually started to grow. "Once mold is found, you can stop paying rent," a poster advised. One even told others that they could pour cement into the toilet bowl to block it. Whether or not any tenant really had done these things was unknown, but the deceased landlady had to hire a lawyer to evict her tenant. She had been threatened with a lawsuit accusing her of negligence that resulted in the growth of mold.

The immediate action she had to take was hiring a mold specialist to treat it. In Toronto, the cost of an urgent repair ranged from $10,000 to $15,000, depending on the size of the affected area and severity of the mold. Her inability to pay her mortgage and to sell the property due to the nonpaying tenant's refusal to move out and the unaffordable cost of removing the mysterious mold overwhelmed her, prompting her suicidal plunge from the balcony of her apartment. She died so quietly, so humbly, so mysteriously that no major newspapers or TV channels in Toronto, generally loath to report suicides, published an account. It was made known only when a community news website reported it one year after her death.

Nawa wept about this but was equally saddened by another tragic event in the same apartment building. A tenant who could not afford his rent, which had doubled since he moved into the rental apartment, had also plunged to his death, landing at roughly the same spot. His death was not reported in the major media either. "Why are there so many rental tragedies in Ontario?" Nawa wondered. "I never heard of such tragedies ten years ago."

Nawa proposed some changes at the provincial level in her letter to the premier:

"Dear Premier Ford, please eliminate the Landlord and Tenant Board and create a new system to handle rental disputes. A logical option is let the police fraud department deal with them. Honestly, paying a monthly rent to live in someone's property is just like buying something in the store. If you don't pay, you cannot take it out of the store. If someone does not pay rent but lives in another person's property without the landlord's permission, isn't it theft? Any theft is a criminal offense. What right does a nonpaying tenant have to dispute an eviction order? We already have the police and have the courts. Both could have been dealing with all the residential rental disputes far more effectively and efficiently than the LTB, which should not have been created in the first place. Needless to say, there are landlords who do not obey the law, but it is also easy for the police to arrest such lawbreakers and send them to court. Toughen the law and treat all rental disputes as fraud cases, as criminal offenses. Only when the law has sharp teeth can you deter bad landlords and bad tenants, especially tyrant tenants.

"It is high time to rewrite the [Residential Tenancies] Act and shift the responsibility from the LTB to landlords and tenants themselves. To repeat, treat landlords' abuse of tenants as a criminal offense and treat tenants' abuse of their rights as a criminal offense as well. Specify their rights and responsibilities so that neither will have any misunderstanding. Allocate sufficient funds for the police so that they can do their job properly, based on every lease a landlord and their tenant have signed. Arrest them, landlord or tenant, whoever has violated their own contractual duties set forth in their lease governed by the law, and fine them heavily. In the event a case warrants court time, a one-time two-hour hearing shall be the maximum, followed by a final court decision on the same day. Please be aware that the Landlords and Tenants Board has long made a mockery of the justice system, for it mostly appears to protect abusive landlords and tyrant renters, but not those who deserve justice. The sooner we eliminate it, the better."

Nawa felt much relieved when she finished her letter, but then she shook her head, sighing, *But will anyone listen to me? At the end of the day, will those abusive landlords, tyrant tenants, and the well-paid LTB employees want a single change in the system?"*

Unlikely.

Children under Protection

Perfect Candidate for a Bravery Medal

"It is twenty-four months since CAS (the Children's Aid Society) took away my daughter, Fionna. My life has been ruined. I cannot eat, I cannot sleep, I cannot work. I cannot live any longer," Sherlyn told me after she got to know me through a friend whose sad CAS story was published on a community news website in January last year. She felt the justice system had let her down and wanted me to write a story to tell my readers how her daughter was legally kidnapped, and how they both had been ruthlessly treated throughout the past two years. I told her that a story would not make a big difference, but she insisted, so I finally agreed. Here is the story based on what I heard from her.

On a brutal Monday in January 2022, Sherlyn, a Toronto single mother, was attacked by an acute pain in the chest at 8:00 a.m. She clung to the breakfast table while gasping for breath but managed to call 911.

"I feel terrible pain in the chest, I'm dying, I need help," she cried to the operator, who asked for her name, address, and details of her pain. "I have a girl. She's twelve. She cannot take care of herself. My old mother's living with me. She's seventy-two. She doesn't speak English. She cannot take care of herself either," she sobbed. "I don't know what to do." Then, there was silence on the phone line.

When she woke up, she found herself in a strange hospital bed surrounded by a group of people: a doctor, two nurses, and a police officer. The doctor told her that she was very lucky to have survived. She had a hole in her heart and was losing blood rapidly. Ten minutes longer and she would have lost her life.

Knowing that she was worried about her daughter while hospitalized, the police officer told her that there was a very good program for children in Toronto. It was offered by a government-sponsored organization—the name was too long for her to remember—which offered food and lodging for needy children during the special Covid-19 period. Her daughter could also play with other children there. If Sherlyn agreed, she could

167

send her there. Her daughter could return home whenever Sherlyn was discharged from the hospital.

The doctor told her the surgery had been successful and she could go home within days. Hearing that her daughter would be properly taken care of, Sherlyn agreed and signed all the papers, permitting CAS to take her to the program.

"How grateful I am!" She heaved a sigh of relief. "How lucky we are to be Canadians!" Sherlyn had been enjoying full disability benefits since her back injury five years ago. She lived in a government-assisted two-bedroom apartment, for which she paid thirty percent of whatever income she had. Every month, the child allowance and other government funds were deposited directly into her bank account. She lived an easy life. "And now the government is going to take care of my daughter!" Grateful tears welled up in her eyes.

When she thought about the top-grade doctor and nurses who had saved her life, tears began gushing down her cheeks. "How lucky I am to enjoy all the great benefits here in Toronto! Free education through high school, free medical care, and even free child care and food for my daughter! Just free everything! "

Two days later, she was discharged from the hospital. She rested at home, worry-free, for a week, but she missed Fionna every day. The next week, she wanted to take her back, and so did her ex-husband, who had, in fact, complained that she had not consulted him before sending her to CAS.

She contacted CAS and told them she had been discharged from the hospital and was healthy now. She asked them to bring her daughter back home.

The CAS representative assured her that they would act accordingly, but they did not bring back Fionna that day. Sherlyn called them again the next day, then the day after. On her last call, Sherlyn was told that they did not know where her daughter was. The CAS worker also said that her daughter had complained about her parenting, and that they would visit her the following day.

The next morning, two CAS workers came to Sherlyn's home. They asked if she had any relatives in Toronto other than her mother and daughter, and she said no. They asked if she had any friends in Canada, and she said no, though she had a few in Toronto. They asked if she was born in Canada, and she also said no. They knew that without asking, since her English was extremely limited, like that of many newcomers.

Then, they asked her to sign two forms. Sherlyn did not know what the forms were but assumed they must be what she needed to sign for the return of her daughter. She cooperated with them politely, though she had a sense of unease. Somehow, something didn't feel right, but she did not know what.

"I thank you from the bottom of my heart for taking care of my daughter while I was in hospital," she said before they left.

"It's our job," they answered.

Sherlyn waited for another day without hearing anything from CAS. Then, she called them again the next morning, impatient because of her longing for her child's return.

"You should go and see a psychiatrist," the CAS representative said to her. Sherlyn was stupefied. She felt not only offended but really worried now. When she called again in the afternoon, they told her that Fionna was sick and had been hospitalized.

"That's easy," Sherlyn thought. "Since she is in the hospital, I can go see her there, and when she is well, I can bring her home directly." She called her ex-husband, and both of them went to the nearby hospital. She gave Fionna's health card number to the receptionist, but the hospital could not locate her. She wasn't there.

Three days later, two CAS workers came to Sherlyn's home again. This time, they brought a letter from her daughter, in which she accused Sherlyn of abusing her physically and emotionally. Sherlyn read it and nearly had another heart attack. It accused her of forcing Fionna to study all day long and not taking her to after-school fun activities such as ball games. It also said Sherlyn did not allow her to date or have sex with boys she loved and disallowed her eating food and snacks she loved, such as french fries, chips, and cookies. Worst of all, it said Sherlyn had scolded and hit her every day.

"Lies! All lies!" Sherlyn screamed. "Who wrote this letter?" Her blood was boiling. She knew her daughter well—she was kind-hearted, honest, and respectful. She would never lie about her own mother. "Did you write this letter and force her to sign it?" she demanded.

"Are you all right?" they said. "Do you want to see a doctor?"

"Why do I need to see a doctor? It's you who need to see a doctor!" The CAS workers looked at each other, whispering something into each other's ears. Then they left.

The following day, eight police cruisers, an ambulance and a fire truck arrived at the same time outside the apartment building where

169

Sherlyn lived. Hearing the noises outside, she lifted her curtain and saw the scary scene. She wondered whether they were about to arrest her.

Her daughter's teacher had told her that two other children from her class had been taken away by CAS. She said that if the police knocked on the door gently, that meant they did not have an arrest warrant, and so she did not need to open the door. If they had an arrest warrant, they would bang loudly and might even break through her door. The teacher had also told her not to speak to them in her home but to talk with them outside, with friends and neighbors around. In that way she could protect herself from any kind of abuse. She felt scared. It was something she had never experienced in Canada.

Before she could calm herself, she heard a gentle knock on her door. When the police identified themselves, Sherlyn asked them to wait for her outside the apartment building. Then, she called some neighbors and friends to go out and witness her talking with the officers. Neighbors came with her as she left the building, joining others already gathered there to support her.

"We'd like you to come with us," one of the officers said.

"Why?" Sherlyn said. "I haven't done anything wrong."

"We've been told that you want to end your life. We want to help."

"I want to end my life? Me? Who said such a thing?" she protested.

"The Children's Aid Society."

"It's a lie!" she said. "I have never intended to commit suicide and I will never do it. If I wanted to commit suicide, why did I go to the hospital for treatment? I've just seen my doctor for more medications. CAS has stolen my daughter. I just want my daughter back."

"This has nothing to do with your daughter. We have come here because they were worried that you were thinking about taking your life. Come with us and we can find you someone to talk with."

"No. I won't go with you. I don't know what you are talking about. I would never commit suicide." Sherlyn was firm.

The police could not insist, not with so many neighbors and friends watching them. An older officer went up to Sherlyn and said in a kind, caring voice, "As police, we deal with many patients and doctors. We know the best doctors in the city. I know you have not fully recovered from your surgery yet. We'll find a great specialist for you, if you trust us and come with us."

"Thank you for your kindness," said Sherlyn. "I don't need any other doctors or specialists. But thank you again." Sherlyn was afraid that the police could take her away, put her in a mental hospital and force her to take medications that could harm her permanently.

Something like that had happened to a close friend. When she refused to take prescribed psychiatric medications, they threatened that she might get locked up forever and would never again see the child CAS had taken away. In the end she gave in and began to take them. The medications made her so weak that when she was released two weeks later, she could hardly walk. When she got home, she threw the medications into the garbage. As far as Sherlyn could see, she was a healthy mother who had no mental problems except anxiety, and anger caused by CAS's kidnapping of her child.

Finally, the police and ambulance left her at the apartment building. She had won a small victory.

Sherlyn shivered, thinking she should buy her daughter's teacher a big box of chocolate to thank her for her advice. Without it, she might have been forced into a psychiatric ward. Fearing that wasn't the end of it, she didn't want to return home. A good friend offered her refuge for the next five months, letting her sleep on her sofa at night. But homelessness wasn't her only struggle.

Five days after the police visit, she was standing in court in the prisoner's dock, accused by CAS of abusing her daughter, which she flatly denied.

"I love my daughter more than myself," she told the court. "She is a great daughter. I am so grateful for being her mother. She loves me and I love her. She has nutritious food, wears good clothing, perhaps better than the average schoolgirl's. She never lacks any necessities. I have also opened a bank account for her, and her savings for university education are now over $90,000. My ex-husband and I are older parents, and we want to make sure she will have enough money for her university education, should one of us or both of us die before she goes to university. That's why I let her keep all the child allowance money throughout the past years."

Surprised by the size of her daughter's savings, the CAS lawyers immediately bombarded Sherlyn with questions about why she and her daughter appeared to be well-off but had applied for the government-assisted apartment, typically reserved for the needy. They succeeded in depicting her as an untrustworthy citizen, a potential tax evader, and overall an unfit mother.

"CAS had a team of lawyers who lied professionally," Sherlyn said with contempt. "They knew how to discredit their victims. They attacked me in all aspects, discrediting me in every way they could. I admit that my answers to the judge's questions regarding my permission to let CAS take away my daughter were not consistent enough. I initially agreed to send my daughter to them, but only under the condition that she would come back as soon as I was discharged from the hospital. But when I later said that I did not agree to let them take away my daughter, I meant that I never agreed that they could keep my daughter after I returned home from the hospital. But I could only answer yes or no to the judge's questions. It was unfair. I did not have a chance to explain myself.

"By exaggerating my inconsistency, they succeeded in impugning my character. When I helplessly cried in court, they again accused me of having mental illness. Finally they made me look like a dishonest mother with severe mental problems, unfit for parenting. Their lawyers are the most shameless liars in court."

Next came the ruling. The judge decided that it was not illegal for CAS to take away Fionna. Thus, Sherlyn had lost the first battle in court. CAS's next move was to prove in court that Sherlyn had abused her daughter physically and mentally and therefore must give up custody of her daughter forever.

In desperation, Sherlyn tried to publicize her case by contacting CTV, CBC, and the major English newspapers, but as soon as they heard her accusations about the CAS, they all politely declined to follow up. She also contacted some lesser known community newspapers, but also in vain. The only thing she could do was send letters to MPPs, city councilors, social workers, and anyone who could make her voice heard. She protested loudly against CAS's cruel treatment, but her agony lingered on, day after day. From the ruling against another mother, she had learned that a child could be taken away from the parents only if one or more of these scenarios occur: "(1) both parents fail to provide the necessities, (2) both parents give up custody rights, and (3) the child becomes violent, and the parents are incapable of raising him/her." Sherlyn told everyone that CAS had broken the law by taking away her daughter.

To arm herself with more legal knowledge, she started to read and research until she had become a competent fighter against CAS. In her course of learning, she learned that CAS was paid by the provincial government based on the number of children in their care. Specifically, its employees had annual salaries somewhere between $70,000 and $150,000. The agency's revenue was based on the headcount of children in their custody. Their lawyers were paid somewhere around $600 an hour. A foster family was paid around $1400 per child per month.

"Everyone involved in any CAS case is making good money at the expense of the victims," she said. "They continue to press charges against me, hoping to steal my daughter for good. They kept accusing me of child abuse, but they couldn't provide any proof. On the other hand, I have evidence to prove they have been abusing my daughter and me."

Throughout the twenty-four months, her life was dark. What CAS had done to her daughter and how she had been living remained a mystery to her. With no other information available, I decided to end her story here, praying for their prompt reunion.

To my disbelief, on a sunny spring day in May—four months after our initial contact, or now twenty-eight months after her daughter was taken away—Fionna called her mother and said she was coming to visit her at home. Sherlyn was so excited that she was shaking.

The next morning, Sherlyn got up early to prepare for Fionna's visit. She had bought her favorite fruit and cookies, and she started cooking her favorite dishes as soon as she finished breakfast. At 11:30 a.m., she heard gentle knocks on the door. Three in a row. It was Fionna.

"Oh, Mom!" cried Fionna as she threw herself into her mother's arms.

"Oh, my child!" sobbed Sherlyn. "Let me look at you. I missed you day and night, my child."

"I missed you too, Mom."

"How have you been doing, my child?" Sherlyn said, raising Fionna's head with both hands. "You look very weak."

"I am sick, Mom." Fionna coughed. She went over to the sofa, and then to her bedroom, then to the bathroom. Tears streamed down her cheeks.

"Fionna, you look very sick," said Sherlyn. "You're not even walking steadily."

Fionna coughed again, this time spitting up blood.

"Oh, dear!" cried Sherlyn. "We must go to Emergency in the hospital immediately."

"Okay, Mom."

Ten minutes later, the doctor in the emergency room was talking with them.

"Why didn't you come earlier?" he asked, seeming to blame both mother and daughter. Fionna coughed non-stop. Then she coughed out blood again. "I must let you know that not getting prompt medical care can be considered child abuse. By law, I am supposed to report it to the police," said the doctor.

"Please don't, Doctor," begged Sherlyn. "It is not my fault. It is the Children's Aid Society that has made my daughter so sick. They have kept her for twenty-eight months. Today is the first day I saw her. She just came to see me an hour ago, and I brought her here immediately. Please help us. Please."

"CAS, again!" The doctor seemed to murmur something to himself. He ordered tests for Fionna immediately and sent her to the ICU.

The lab report showed that thirteen factors were abnormal, with a TSH level (a measurement of thyroid activity) of 0.01. Fionna had suffered health problems many times over the past two years due to malnutrition, cold, anxiety, and depression. She could easily have lost her life if she hadn't received proper treatment in a timely fashion. The hospital staff did their best and with meticulous care, Fionna was rescued. She stayed in the hospital for a month, and when she was able to walk, she was discharged.

For unknown reasons, the CAS workers had taken away Fionna's health card. Had she not been with her mother when she was so sick, she might not have been able to see a doctor without her health card. Sherlyn was prepared to pay for her treatment out of her own pocket if necessary, but luckily, by entering Fionna's name, birthday, address and other information, the hospital was able to find her on the system. Therefore, they did not have to pay the six-digit bill.

Sherlyn and Fionna felt they could not return home, worried that CAS and the police might show up to take Fionna away and arrest Sherlyn for kidnapping her. So they planned to flee Toronto. With the help of many kind-hearted people, including friends and other CAS victims, Sherlyn rented a temporary home, a small bungalow, in a small town where no one knew who they were.

While Fionna was in hospital, Sherlyn managed to find time to send letters to MPPs, including the premier of the province and his ministers, to expose CAS's wrongdoing and call for rescue. Surprisingly, those letters seemed to have caught their attention. The following fall, the Ontario government finally launched an overdue investigation into their case, among others.

Now safe in their newly rented home far from Toronto, mother and child started crying again. This time they cried out of happiness, and for their overdue reunion. They knew they would never leave each other again. They vowed to live together and die together. With Fionna in her arms, Sherlyn asked, "Tell, me, my dear child, who wrote the letter that accused Mom of abusing you physically and mentally? I know you did not do it. I know you would not do it."

"Mom—" Fionna cried hysterically, "Mom, they forced me to do it."

"You are safe here, my child," Sherlyn comforted her. "Stop crying and tell me what happened. We are safe here. Mom won't let you leave me again."

"Mom, after they took me away from home, they threw me into a mental hospital and forced me to take medications."

"What?" Sherlyn could not believe her ears.

"There were mentally ill people and drug addicts there. I was scared. I couldn't sleep at night. I was afraid of being hit or bitten by somebody. I thought they could hurt me as well."

"That was a crime!" said Sherlyn.

"I asked them why they put me in the mental hospital."

"And what did they say?" asked Sherlyn.

"'You want to kill yourself,'" they said. I told them it was a lie. I never wanted to commit suicide, but they did not care and just forced me to take their medications. Maybe they put other kids they take away from their parents in the same mental hospital so they won't cause trouble, or something. I don't know." She looked at Sherlyn, whose face reddened. "Mom, after taking their medications for two weeks, I felt really weak. I could only take slow, tiny steps, because my strength was all gone."

"God damn them! Why did they do this to you?" The indignant mother gritted her teeth.

"I really don't know," said Fionna.

"Then they moved me to a temporary home. There were two ladies living together there. They slept in the same bed and they behaved like a husband and wife. They were nice to me. They talked a lot about same-sex relationships and all that. I felt kind of disgusted sometimes. After three months, they knew we weren't getting along, so they gave me back to CAS. Then they put me in another foster home, this one with two adult sons living in the basement. They gave me a room on the second floor, but these two men often came to my room at night. They said they came to protect me, but they did not protect me. They would sit on my bed, and then ..." Fionna burst into tears. "I was alone. I was scared. Just heartbroken, Mom. If you don't mind, I would rather not talk about this. They have ruined my life, the whole family. I have nightmares every day." Fionna kept sobbing.

"Be brave, my child," Sherlyn comforted her. "Mom's with you. I am always with you."

"Mom, when I was in the mental hospital, they forced me to write a report to them. They wanted me to tell them that you were a bad mother," cried Fionna, looking guilty. "I refused to do it in the beginning, but they threatened me. They said if I did not do it, they would not give my cellphone back to me. They would not allow me to use their Wi-Fi, and they would not give me food. They also told me, "Everything you tell us is confidential, and your mom won't know it." I didn't know how to say bad things about you, so they showed me some paragraphs and sentences and words they had prepared for me. I still didn't know how to put them together, so they just did everything for me and then told me to sign at the bottom. That is how I wrote the letter. I am really sorry, Mom. I didn't know what I was doing, and I didn't really want to do it." Fionna broke down again.

"Never mind, my child. It was not your fault. You were always a great child," said Sherlyn. "I knew the letter was not written by you the moment they showed it to me. I was absolutely sure about it. I asked them who wrote it, but they dared not answer."

"The day after I wrote the letter, they told me they couldn't even send it to you, because you had died in the hospital. They told me the doctor couldn't save you."

"Goddamned liars!" Sherlyn felt her face burning, worried that she could have a second heart attack, so she tried to calm down. *No*, she said to herself. *For my child, I must calm down and stay healthy.*

In Sherlyn's eyes, CAS had kidnapped her daughter as soon as they seized control of her. Fionna was twelve then and about to turn thirteen. To Sherlyn, she was worth more than her weight in gold. On the internet Sherlyn had read conspiracy theories about how kidnapped teenage girls were sold as sex slaves or tortured to death somewhere in America, but before they breathed their last, their organs would be removed and sold to the super rich or most powerful dying men who needed organ transplants. Every kidnapped teenager was said to have signed organ donation forms, which would legalize the predators' organ transplants. Most horrific of all, so the story went, some victims were brutally tortured and slowly starved to death for organs that sold for hundreds of thousands of dollars each.

Sherlyn shivered to think that her daughter once had ten tubes of blood taken from her for a blood test. It was an amount she had never heard of, and now she wondered what the blood was used for. She dared not think about it; just the suspicion was too much for her to stand. "I would rather believe that such things do not happen in a democracy like Canada and America," she said under her breath.

Mother and daughter continued talking until daybreak. More details unfolded to support Sherlyn's theory of a plot. As she saw it, the predators first tortured Fionna in the mental hospital for two weeks to subdue her spiritually. Then, to keep their criminal actions from her, they told her that her mother had died, so that she would have nobody to miss and would logically become more obedient and cooperative. Perhaps she would even be grateful for whatever life she would have to live. Somehow Fionna found out that her mother had survived her heart attack and bought her a gold necklace that she'd asked be given to her, but she never received it. With these actions, Sherlyn theorized, they had reduced the possibility of losing the prey now in their possession. Similarly, all the letters her daughter had written for her mother were destroyed without reaching her. Her mother's calls had been blocked in hopes that Fionna would forget her gradually. These people were, in Sherlyn's view, kidnappers, liars, and thieves—three-in-one—whose ultimate purpose was to enslave Fionna and turn her into profit.

Fionna continued to shock her mother with other details. She claimed she'd been fed moldy bread, and when she showed them they would just pick out the moldy spots and give it back to her to eat. She complained that her room had been kept below 15 degrees Celsius in winter and she was shivering all the time, but they only gave her a thin blanket. As a result, she fell ill. When she was sick, they did not allow her to see a doctor. They had taken away her health card, so she could not go to see the doctor herself. She had fallen seriously ill several times. Sherlyn began to connect the conspiracy theory to Fionna's plight: were they trying to make her die so they could sell her organs? No other explanation justified what they were doing to her daughter. They could have bought a used blanket for Fionna for two dollars at a thrift store, and healthcare is free in Canada, and with a card she could go to see a doctor herself. Sherlyn did not want to tell her daughter what she was

177

thinking. She did not want to hurt her. She was just grateful she had returned alive.

Three months later, while the provincial government was launching an investigation into deaths of children in CAS care, CAS passed a message to Sherlyn through her friend, threatening to have her arrested if she did not return her daughter. When she refused, they proposed to her that she sign a declaration that her daughter had become sick while under her care, in exchange for Fionna's release from CAS. Sherlyn flatly rejected their offer. She did it for justice, fairness, and dignity. Mother and daughter continued to hide, readying for arrest.

The following week, under unknown pressure, CAS closed Fionna's case without requiring Sherlyn to confess to negligence. They just humbly asked Sherlyn to keep the story to herself, but she continued to expose their actions wherever she could.

"It is not for personal reasons," Sherlyn said. "I just want to make sure that no other parents suffer in the same way I did."

What a heroic mother Sherlyn is! She makes a perfect candidate for a Governor General's commendation for bravery.

Foster Parents at Work

Drug abuse took a toll on Roy and his wife, an Indigenous couple who ultimately became incapable of caring for their own children. In October 2019, MCFD (the Ministry of Child and Family Development, B.C.) came to their rescue and removed their three children from the mother's care and placed them with an Indigenous family Roy trusted. Two of the rescued children were ten-year-old Rel and his seven-year-old sister Nirl.

"We will take good care of your children," three MCFD social workers assured the father, who was touched that they had taken over the parenting for him and his wife. *The government has lots of professionals and never runs out of money. How lucky I am!* he thought. *I can just concentrate on battling my addiction and regain my normal life within the shortest time possible. Then I can bring back my children.*

On the Sunday before Christmas, the father was given permission to visit Rel. He took him out for shopping and they had a meal together. Then, following the rules, he took Rel back to his foster parents.

"I don't want to go back to them, Dad!" Rel burst out crying outside the foster parents' home, throwing himself into his arms. But Roy was not allowed to take him back, even if Rel really wanted to go home. If Roy did so, he would be arrested for kidnapping. He kindly comforted his son and finally persuaded him to go back into the house. He just thought that Rel was missing him badly because they had not seen each other for quite a while, but the son's crying seemed filled with fear and desperation.

No one knew what had happened to Rel and what would happen later, but then, after Christmas, came a surprise from his foster mother.

"I can't cope," she told the MCFD office on the phone. It was an Indigenous family caring for Indigenous children. Wasn't it a perfect arrangement? At least, it appeared to be politically correct. To some politicians and government officials, being politically correct is more important than doing something right. The foster mother had applied for the job, accepted it, and had been paid over $4,000 for what she was doing. The MCFD office had no intention of taking back the children.

"Call us if you have any problems," they told her, persuading her not to quit.

It's my own fault! she told herself. *Why did I apply for the job in the first place?* Dejected, she did not call again. She continued to look after

Rel and his sister anyway. After all, the government paid her and her husband more than $4,000 every month.

Rel's grandmother, who had heard about the foster mother's frustration, contacted MCFD on the same day.

"Can my husband and I look after our grandchildren? I love them, and I miss them. Please return them to us and let us take care of them, please," she begged the MCFD official on the phone.

The answer was a no.

"Every child matters" is a slogan published everywhere in the province. A person cannot just offer herself and bring a foster child home.

The grandmother wept, remembering those children in the notorious residential schools forcibly stolen from their parents in the past. Now children were being taken away by MCFD! History repeats itself. The grandmother could only hope for the best for her grandchildren.

The MCFD social workers in charge of supervising the children's foster care told the media that they last saw Rel and his sister on July 27, 2020, and found nothing abnormal. By law they should have been visited at least once every three months, but staff were too busy to do this and never saw them until seven months later, when Rel was taken unconscious to a hospital emergency room.

The doctors and nurses were scrambling to save the boy's life. He was placed in the ICU on life support for five days, after which the doctors gave up. He died at the age of eleven, never having regained consciousness.

Rel had become a sack of bones, weighing twenty-nine kilograms instead the average fifty of a boy of his age. More mysterious and horrific still, he showed signs of trauma and torture. His foster parents were immediately arrested, followed by an investigation.

On June 16, 2023, news reporters from all over Canada and elsewhere crowded into the provincial court in Chilliwack, B.C., to hear the ruling on the case.

Here is what happened, as summarized by Chilliwack Provincial Court Judge Peter La Prairie and CTV Vancouver journalist Michele Brunoro, among others.

Rel and his sister were inhumanly abused at their foster home until the day Rel was taken to the hospital. The 16,000 hours of video recordings from surveillance cameras inside the home showed 400 hours of horrific abuse by the foster parents: slapping, kicking, throwing and confining the children repeatedly and for prolonged periods of time.

More specifically, among other abuses, the children were
- forced to wear diapers,
- locked in a closet,
- struck with a 2-by-4-inch block of wood and a broom handle by the foster father, who had also taught his son to strike Rel in the same way, among other routine assaults

Rel and his sister were forced to drink urine, eat feces and vomit. Food was restricted as a form of punishment, which reduced Rel to his skeletal form.

On the last day, as the boy lay on the ground, the foster mother kicked him and grabbed him around the neck. He struggled while he was on the floor to put on his shirt. Meanwhile, she kicked him and then grabbed his wrists to make him stand up. He was unsteady on his feet and she slapped him in the face. The boy fell back to the floor. She picked him up and threw him back down. The boy's head bounced off the wood floor. He was unable to brace himself, as his hands were stuck in his shirt. She kicked him while he was on the ground until he became unresponsive. Finally he was taken to the hospital.

The foster mother pleaded guilty in exchange for a lighter sentence. Both foster parents were found guilty of manslaughter, each handed a life sentence without the possibility of parole for ten years. Rel's biological mother died after the shocking news of her son's death. His sister also suffered physical and emotional wounds that will never heal.

A self-destructive couple blindly trusted their government to place their innocent children with a caring foster family. The foster parents brutally tortured them, killing one and inflicting horrific injury on another. They finally ended up in jail for life! A story sadder than a Shakespearean tragedy.

Fleeing Father

Dave and I are not just good friends, we are like brothers. We grew up together in our subtropical hometown in Asia. We went to the same high school and then the same university, though we were separated after graduation. After working in an IT company near the university for three years, I immigrated to Toronto. Two years ago, Dave immigrated as well and bought a large $2 million house on an upscale street in Markham. He lives happily with his wife, Susie, and his son, Nort. We each cherish our friendship dearly.

Dave is proud of Nort, who does well at school and even happily goes to evening and weekend tutorials. Unsurprisingly, Nort is a top achiever in his class. Since they moved to Markham, I have invited them to come and visit with my family from time to time. My son and Nort like each other and enjoy every game they play together.

Unexpectedly, Dave called me last Monday, asking if he could stay in my home for a few days.

"Of course, buddy!" I said. "Stay as long as you want to. I always want you and your family to come and stay with us."

Though I welcomed him sincerely, I was puzzled why Dave, who had never come to my home without a second invitation, had asked to stay with us. That evening, he came carrying a suitcase full of clothes. He looked tired and worn out. I thought he must be working too hard.

The next day, I asked if he wanted to go grocery shopping with me, hoping that he could pick his own favorite food. He was not very enthusiastic but still went with me.

We arrived at the T&T at Warden and Steeles in less than ten minutes. This supermarket serves Markham and northeastern Toronto, but Dave had never shopped here. Once we were inside, I began telling him about the special products it was selling, including traditional nut candies, pastry, and hot food, but he was not really interested in anything. We first went to the seafood section, where I picked out the best salmon, shrimps, and a lobster. Then, I took him to the produce department. I was about to take him to the hot food stands when he suddenly tugged my sleeve and started to run, shouting, "I need to leave the store."

He was panicking. Near the cashier, he snatched the shopping basket from my hand, dropped it on the floor, and continued to drag me out of the store.

"What's happened?" I asked, wondering if he had a mental disorder.

"I'll tell you soon," he said, running westward. He was my guest, so I had to follow him, no matter what. We were out of breath when we reached Ferrier Street. Then we went over to the window of the Dumpling Restaurant. He tried to hide his face from passersby.

"Am I five hundred meters away from the grocery store?" he asked nervously.

"Why? I think you are at least a thousand meters away from it," I said.

He uttered a sigh of relief. "Brother, this is really embarrassing. I have got into trouble with the law. I saw my son in the grocery store!"

"You saw your son in the store, and then you started to run? Why? What happened?" I asked. "But you've been a law-abiding man all your life. What trouble did you get into?"

"I hit my son last week before he went to school," he said sadly.

"Why?"

"Lately, he's stopped studying and plays computer games from morning till night. He doesn't do his homework. He used to be a top student, but his grades are dropping. I'm worried he may even become the last one in his class this semester. I cannot sleep well at night."

"Take it easy," I comforted him.

"Last Monday, I was waiting for him at the door to drive him to school, and we were already late, but he just kept playing. Finally, I scolded him, but do you know what he said? 'It's Canada. I can do whatever I want.' he said. 'I have my own life to live!'"

"Oh, boy!' I said, surprised too.

"I couldn't stand it, and I slapped him in the face," Dave said. "When he got to school, his teacher saw red finger marks on his face and asked him what had happened. He told her I had hit him. The teacher immediately reported it to the principal. When I got back home from work in the evening, two police officers were waiting for me. I was arrested. In fact, I was jailed overnight and was released only after I appeared in court and signed a lot of papers. One of the conditions is that I cannot be close to Nort. Now I cannot even live with him or my wife. That is the reason why I asked to stay in your home. I must stay at least five hundred meters away from him. If I violate this rule, I will be arrested again, and that will be considered a re-offense. The punishment would be much harsher. As you know, I have nowhere to go. I must stay in Canada. I have yet to apply for Canadian citizenship."

"Oh, my poor friend," I said. "I am so sorry to hear about the incident. Just relax. Everything will be fine. Until I come back from T&T, just stay right here with your face against the wall. This way, even if your wife and son happen to come by, they won't see you. And even if they really see you, just look away. It is not your fault, even if your son bumps into you. I'll go back to the grocery store and pay for the food. Then I'll come to pick you up and we will go back home together."

On my way back to T&T, I kept wondering, "What rights does a man or father really have in Canada?"

Christmas Gift for Chalway

Chalway's blood was boiling while he was driving home from the parent-teacher interview. His daughter Janice had become a stranger. When she was twelve, she was very cooperative. She would go to school on time, attended every class, and do all her assignments, but her last report card told a different story. Janice had missed thirty-six classes and was late for fifty. Chalway did not scold her in front of her teacher, intending to lecture her at home. If he'd had a heart condition, this could have triggered a heart attack. The veins on his temples were bulging out. Janice could see them rising and falling. It was a sign of extreme agitation, but he still tried to remain calm. Then, all of a sudden, he shouted, "Why did you skip thirty-six classes and were late for fifty?"

"The classes were boring," Janice said.

"Boring? But why did your grades drop to the 60s? They used to be in the 90s or at least high 80s?"

"High school courses are more difficult," she explained.

"You said they were boring, and then you said they were difficult? If they were difficult, why didn't you work a little harder? If you didn't miss so many classes and arrive late so many times, don't you think you could have done a little better?" Chalway scolded her.

"I don't think so," she said carelessly.

"I drove you to school every morning, and we were always on time. How could you have missed so many classes and been late so many times?" He raised his voice.

"It's none of your business!" she said arrogantly.

Chalway could not tolerate her talking back this way. He freed his right hand from the wheel and tried to slap her face, but he missed it. Instead, he hit her nose. Instantly blood started gushing from it, so he pulled the car over and tried to stop her bleeding. He pulled several tissues from the box, gave them to her, and told her to press her nose tightly. Then, he wiped the blood off her school uniform and the seat. Finally, the bleeding stopped. It was quite a scare for both father and daughter, so neither said anything more.

"Go and wash your face," Chalway told Janice when they got home, and so she did.

It was already 9:45 p.m., so they went to bed without further quarreling. When they woke up the next morning, Chalway took a look at

Janice's nose. There was no more blood, but the stains were still visible. He thought of cleaning it for her, but if he poked it, it might start bleeding again, so he didn't touch it.

At 8:30 he drove Janice to school as usual, dropped her at the school gate, and then came home. He was still massaging the chest area around his heart when he heard loud knocking on the door. He opened the door only to see two police officers and two other official-looking people standing behind them.

"Are you are Janice's father?" asked the officer facing him.

"Yes?" He had no idea why they were here. They wrote down his name, birthday, address, and his driver's license number.

"You are under arrest, under suspicion of child abuse," announced the officer. The two officers handcuffed him.

"What have I done wrong?" Chalway protested.

"Your daughter told her teacher that you struck her nose last night after the school interview. Her teacher noticed dried blood around her nose and asked what had happened. She told her what you did. The teacher reported it to the principal, as is required in these situations, and the school principal called us. Did you hit her yesterday?"

"She skipped thirty-six classes and was late for another fifty," he explained.

"I am asking you: did you hit her and cause her nose to bleed? Yes or no!"

"Yes," said Chalway, lowering his head.

"Thank you! Let's go." The officers took him away. Chalway's wife was dumbfounded at seeing her husband in handcuffs and taken away by the police officers. "Oh, my God! What's happened?" she screamed, not knowing what to do.

"Janice will be taken to a safe place for the night," one of the Children's Aid Society officials said to her.

Chalway's wife burst out howling, but it made no difference.

At the police station, a standard procedure started immediately. Chalway had his photo taken and an identity number created, but he was not afraid. He answered all the questions asked. He admitted to overreacting to Janice's report card but insisted that he loved his daughter and had just over-disciplined her and that he had the right to correct his child's misbehavior. The interrogating officers were very professional. They wrote down what he said and made no comments. As

186

for whether or not Chalway should be found guilty, it was up to the court to decide. He was locked in a cell in the police station overnight.

He appeared in court the following morning. When the judge asked if he was pleading guilty to child abuse, he denied it and said, "You can lock me up. You can throw me in jail, but I can tell you. It is your education that has ruined my child. If we had not immigrated to Canada, she would not have changed into such a careless student."

Having heard arguments by the prosecutor and the defendant, the judge announced, "Mr. Chalway, I'm finding you not guilty of child abuse. Accordingly, you are free to go. But you are ordered to cooperate with the Children's Aid Society until the case is closed."

Chalway was released on the spot. He returned home at 2:30 p.m. Then he got his car key and drove to Janice's school to pick her up. While he was waiting for the school bell to ring, he saw a van belonging to the Children's Aid Society in the parking lot, its doors open. Four people from the vehicle went into the school and came out with Janice.

"Janice," shouted Chalway, "I'm here."

"Daddy," she cried. But the government officials walked her straight into their vehicle. Tears started streaming down his cheeks. He sighed, "This system!"

In the Children's Aid Society office, designed like a large playroom, Janice was given cookies, ice cream, and fruit juice. She was asked to relax, make herself at home, and fear nothing. She had all their support and the protection guaranteed by law.

All the workers treated her like a darling. Then came the caseworker who would make the most important decision regarding the fate of this girl.

"Janice, I am sorry that your father hit you," said the motherly caseworker. "Are you still hurt?"

Janice shook her head.

"Don't be afraid of anyone. Don't be afraid of your father or your mother or your brother. We are here to help you."

Janice did not say anything.

"If you feel threatened, you don't have to go home. We will find a safe home for you," the caseworker continued. "Come on, say something."

"I don't know why I'm here," Janice finally said.

"You are here because your father hit you. It is against the law for him to hurt you. You are here because you deserve our protection. We want to make sure you are safe, safe from abuse, safe from new harm."

"But I don't think my father really wanted to hurt me," said Janice.

"The fact is, your nose was bleeding. You can still see blood stains in your nostrils, can't you?"

"I think my father loves me very much," Janice said.

"Well, dear, you think about it carefully and let me know. You don't have to go back home. If you go home, and if your father hits you again, you will be in more trouble. But if you really want to go back home, we won't stop you." The caseworker looked disappointed that she could not convince Janice to stay.

"I really want to go back home," Janice insisted.

"You decide for yourself," the caseworker repeated. "Do you want to stay with us or go home?"

"I want to go home." Janice became more insistent. Seeing there was no chance of keeping her, the caseworker said, "Okay, Janice, we will send you home this evening."

At about 6:00 p.m., Janice arrived home, running into her father's arms tearfully. "I am so sorry, Daddy!"

"It's all right, my child," said Chalway. "I love you."

What followed was a pack of legal documents Chalway was required to sign by law. If he ever abused his daughter again, he would be considered a repeat offender, and his punishment would be harsher. For the sake of having his daughter back, he signed everything and promised to do everything stated in the legal documents. Both father and daughter were only conditionally released. Their case kept people in the Children's Aid Society busy for two years. When the observation period was finally over, they told Janice, "You have loving parents. You can stay home with your parents."

On a Friday two years after Chalway's arrest, CAS finally closed their case. They said it was a Christmas gift for Chalway and his whole family.

But Chalway wasn't sure whether he should be celebrating or condemning,

A Fight Between Father and Son

Frank Chime and his wife, Dora, immigrated to Canada with their 11-year-old son Errol four years ago. Frank has been anxious about Errol's schoolwork ever since. He always wants him to read books in print and do extra homework. He becomes restless whenever he sees him using the computer.

"Errol, don't play on the computer all the time," he will say.

"But I'm not playing, Dad. I'm doing my homework," Errol will tell him.

Frank will look at his monitor, but the English words all look like bean sprouts to him. He cannot understand a single word, so he is never sure whether it is homework or a game. Frank shares his concern with some other parents on the interview night and soon discovers he is not alone. Other newcomers have the same issue. A few parents whose English is better than his say that some children take advantage of their parents' poor English proficiency and claim to be doing their homework while playing games. Two of them are Errol's friends, Jim and Ted. Frank becomes even more worried after hearing this.

"No wonder his grades are dropping," he says to Dora. She is also worried, though not as anxious about it.

"Son, we need to talk. You need to get off your computer and do some real work. I know you are lying to me. You are not studying, but you play on the computer all the time," he says to Errol after returning home from the parents' interview.

"This is a group project I'm doing," explains Errol. "We have four students in the group. Two of my group members do not contribute anything. They really play on the computer without doing work, but I'm doing my share. In fact, I also have to do their work for them."

"You sound like a hardworking student, but why would you bother to help them? Why not just do your own share and get off the computer?" Frank does not really believe what Errol says.

"If I don't finish the whole project, all of us will fail," explains Errol.

"Who are your group members?"

"Jim and Ted and another student you don't know."

"Jim and Ted?" Frank yells. "But why did you pick them for your group members?"

"I didn't pick them. The teacher put us together into the group."

"No matter what I say, you always have a good reason for being on the computer!" Frank raises his voice, which surprises his son.

189

"But everything I said is true," Errol insists.

"I don't believe it. You have been lying to me all the time!" Frank's face reddens and he sounds furious.

"Dad!" Errol is shocked at his father's accusation.

"No matter what, you must stop playing and get off your computer at this very moment," Frank orders.

"Dad, our homework is due at ten o'clock tonight. If we don't submit it, we'll lose marks," he begs Frank.

"No more of that. I have had enough!" Frank seizes the keyboard, threatening to smash it. "If you don't listen to me this time, I am going to smash your computer right away."

"But why?" Errol raises his voice, too. He feels desperate, not knowing what to do.

"You don't study. You play every day. You lie to me. That's why your grades have dropped to 60s and 70s now," Frank's accusations go on and on, most of which are groundless.

"Dad, I don't know what you are talking about. I study all the time," protests Errol.

"You think I don't know what you have been doing? Don't take me for a fool! I know everything," Frank shouts, seizing Errol's computer.

"No. Please don't!" Errol wants to resave his homework, but Frank thinks he is trying to take back the computer. In their struggle, Errol's group project is lost. He is furious now. "Look what you've done!"

"You can't live without the computer for just one minute. You are addicted to the computer, just like a drug addict!" Frank uses the harshest words he can find in his vocabulary.

Errol can't stand it any longer. "What f--king nonsense are you talking about!" he shouts at his father, giving up the computer to him.

Frank can't swallow that, no matter what. He drops the computer back on the desk, raises his hand, and slaps Errol hard in the face. "How dare you!" Frank grits his teeth, meaning that, no matter how badly he has wronged him, Errol cannot talk back that way.

Errol soon realizes what he has said is not the best either, but he does not fight back. He bursts into tears, goes back into his bedroom, and locks the door.

Father and son know something terrible has happened, but neither knows how to correct the wrong. Errol turns off his light and goes to bed, but he cannot sleep a wink the whole night. At school, he is well respected by all his teachers and classmates, including many pretty girls. This is the first time he has been humiliated for no reason. He is strong and could have hit back, but he restrained himself. Yet, he feels he has to teach his father a lesson, so that he will remember to respect him.

At about four o'clock, he gets up quietly, goes to the shoe shelf, picks up the black shoe polish on the floor, and then spreads some over the front of each of his father's dress shirts. The shoe polish runs out quickly, so he goes to the washroom, takes the toothpaste and spreads it over the front of his father's two suits. "Let's see how you go to work tomorrow. You ruined my group project, so I will ruin your day's work tomorrow."

Errol gets up as usual the following morning, waiting to see how his father will react to his ruined clothes. His father is about to go to work after breakfast when he finds his suits are covered with white toothpaste, and the dress shirts with oily black shoe polish.

Frank cannot wear these clothes, but if he doesn't go to work, he could lose his job. He roars with rage, "You son of a bitch! How dare you!" Frank decides to teach his unruly son a lesson and begins punching and kicking Errol with all his might, until his hands are bruised and sore. This boy, once a little emperor at home, is today his number one enemy. Heavy, painful blows rain on Errol, sending him rolling and screaming on the floor.

Errol finally escapes to his bedroom, where he calls 911 for assistance. Frank hears him talking in English but does not know what he is doing. Within five minutes, two police officers arrive, followed shortly by two Children's Aid Society workers. The police go into Errol's room and speak with him in private. In no time they come out, handcuff Frank, and walk him into the police cruiser. The two CAS workers take away Errol, leaving behind a terrified woman screaming for help, not knowing what will happen to her husband and son.

CAS determines that Frank used excessive force on his son and broke the law. He has thus disqualified himself as a care provider for his son. Accordingly, he is locked up. He is scheduled to appear in court the following day. Errol, on the other hand, is placed in a temporary home until the court makes a decision as to how he should be protected.

The next morning, Errol's desperate mother thinks of his ESL teacher, who can speak her language. So she runs all the way to the school to beg her help. She tells the teacher that in their culture, "Beating a child shows the parents' intimacy, and scolding a child means loving them." The teacher passes her message on to the authorities, but it is flatly rejected. In Canada, beating a child is physical abuse and scolding a child may be verbal abuse. Both could be illegal if they are proven to be severe, and there is no shortcut; the case has to go through its process.

191

Appearing in court, Frank apologizes for his action to the judge and, with the help of his lawyer, he is bailed out, pending another hearing. Until then he may not live with his family and must keep a standard distance of at least five hundred meters from Errol. If he gets caught within that distance, he is liable to be arrested, with the error to be treated as a re-offense, with harsher penalties to follow. Frank, who had never been handcuffed or put behind bars, truly appreciates freedom, so he accepts every condition imposed by the court.

His wife goes home at four o'clock in the afternoon, but Errol is nowhere to be found. Neither parent knows where he is, what has happened to him, or what he is doing. The ESL teacher does not know where he is, either.

The next day, CAS informs them that Errol has been kept away from his home because it is not safe for him. Frank has yet to convince the court that his home is a safe place for his son. The process will take longer than a year.

Like his father, Errol finally realizes he has made the wrong decision, that is, to leave home. He realizes he should have stayed with his parents. Comparing them with others, he realizes his parents are undeniably the best in the world, who love him unconditionally. He has received the best care any parents could provide. He regrets soiling his father's clothes, which provoked the corporal punishment that put his father behind bars. He tells the CAS caseworker that he wants to return home, but they do not allow him to go right away.

"Everything takes time. Everything has its process," they tell him.

Being with a strange family is just not the same, and he finds life much worse than before. It affects his health and also his schoolwork. Back home, his parents would cook the best food for him and even find a tutor for him if he had trouble with schoolwork. He starts to lose weight and his grades drop significantly while he is cared for and protected by the foster family. Down in his heart, he knows his father loves him, even though the punishment went too far. In any case, he is sure that his father did not really mean to hurt him. Nor will he be likely to punish him that way again.

It is not until two years later, when Errol has lost thirty pounds and been taken to the emergency room five times, that the family of three is finally reunited.

What a nightmare!

Harvard University Boy

Ms. Woo is a heartbroken mother living in Toronto. She breaks down whenever she mentions CAS (Children's Aid Society). Last January, she complained to the media that Toronto's CAS took away her then 10-year-old son by deceit and, as she told the story, while he was under its custody he was beaten and starved to the point of becoming skeletal. His two upper front teeth are now missing, and his lips bear permanent scars. All of this can be traced back to the "kidnapping" of her child twelve years ago.

Three days after Ms. Woo went public, I interviewed her for two hours, clarifying several important details underreported in the news. Following is a summary of her news story, the interview, and additional information provided by one of her close friends.

1.

"CAS, its lawyers, and the court are like organized gangs," Ms. Woo said, bursting out crying involuntarily. "They worked together to kidnap my son."

"What happened?" I asked. "Why did they take away your son in the first place?"

"They are robbers and bandits," she cried. "My son used to be a great student. I have a good friend. Her son went to Harvard University. My son also wanted to go to Harvard University. He talked about going to Harvard every day. He studied day and night, reading from the time he got up until he went to bed. He kept talking about going to Harvard at school too. He was such a brilliant boy!" The mention of her son and Harvard University triggered a tsunami of proud, sad tears spilling down her cheeks. "My son was an ambitious boy. He could have gone to Harvard University," she repeated in a choked voice.

I wanted to comfort her, but she was too emotional to listen to me. I felt helpless and thought, *When a baby is born, almost every parent thinks their child is a genius and can do wonders. You have a great kid, who talked about going to Harvard University at home and at school every day! You are proud of him, and your friends and relatives probably admire you for raising a young child who started dreaming of going to Harvard in his early childhood. And he even took action and studied hard, hoping to achieve his goal, but his peers and even his teachers in*

193

Canada might consider him an abnormal child. They might even suspect he had a mental problem. What's so great about Harvard? Is Harvard University the only thing in his life? Why does he have to go to Harvard? As a parent, you don't seem to know that, like other universities, probably only ten percent of Harvard graduates may be worthy of its name. Most of the world's top talents are not from Harvard, but you are Harvard-obsessed and you seem to have brainwashed your son and ruined his childhood and his life!

"The reason I let my son join CAS activities was because he didn't have a father. He needed a role model." She continued to pour out her bitterness, including how she had naively believed another parent who told her about the fun activities CAS offered to children.

"My friends all said that 'Canada is a paradise for children, a battlefield for young workers, and a graveyard for seniors.' I really thought Canada was a paradise for my son. That is why I sent him to the CAS summer camp. I thought I could then give myself a break, but it was a trap."

"What fun activities did he have there?" I asked.

"It was a cult. They brainwashed my son. They taught him to write a letter accusing me of abusing him," she said regretfully. "They lied that they would camp in a provincial park, but he never went camping. That is how they kidnapped my son. He was such a great child!"

She kept sobbing uncontrollably.

"Calm down," I said. "You need to calm down. You want me to write a story about your pain and suffering, but if I cannot hear you, I can't help you."

"I'm so sorry. I am just heartbroken." She squeezed out her words. "I haven't seen my son for more than ten years. He is part of my body. He is my life. They never allowed him to meet me. They took him away by force and put him with a group of teenage troublemakers—13 to 17 years old."

"But how did—" I wanted to find out how a common CAS activity could have turned into a kidnapping, as she had claimed, but she immediately cut me short.

"They did not give him food and clothes. They did not buy him shoes. The family received more than $1000 from CAS, but they treated him like shit.

"The big boys in the group home beat him in the kitchen. My son lost two front teeth. His face and body were covered with blood. He was

194

taken to emergency in the hospital, but they did not even let me know. I had to find him myself. When I finally located him in the hospital, they did not allow me to see him.

"It was a carefully planned kidnapping. They first lied to me to take away my son. Then they forced him to write an accusation against me. They taught him how to write it, sentence by sentence and paragraph by paragraph, by showing him prewritten sentences and paragraphs, accusing me of abusing him physically and mentally, like taking him to after-school activities such as music and art lessons on the weekends. If my son did not cooperate, they would not give back his cellphone and would not allow him to play games on the computer. They taught him to play computer games in less than a week, which he soon became addicted to, just like a drug addict who has become addicted to drug substances.

"My son was too young to know their malicious plot. He indulged in gaming all day and all night and stopped reading and studying. He never did his homework again. They had turned him into a brainless boy they could easily control and manipulate. Meanwhile, they continued to brainwash him, portraying me as the worst mother in the world. They told him to stay away from me, if he wanted to continue playing computer games. They completed their brainwashing in a period of two years, until he turned twelve.

"When he turned twelve, by law he was old enough to make his own decision whether to return home or to stay with the foster family. They coaxed him into refusing to return home. The case workers had friends or other unknown individuals who loved my son and wanted to adopt him. Their last step was to complete the legal procedures in the kidnapping of my son. After his birthday, they took me to court.

"The CAS lawyers and the judge were all liars. They lied that I was an irresponsible, abusive and mentally ill mother—because I cried whenever I talked about my son. They said I was unfit for being my son's mother. As they had planned, the judge concluded that I was a bad mother who had no right to raise my child and that I must give him up to someone else. The armed sheriffs simply walked him away from the courthouse. They did not give a damn about me when I collapsed onto the floor. I have never seen him, ever since that day.

"They have ruined my life, legally! I have been living in hell since. I cannot sleep. I cannot eat. I cannot work."

Ms. Woo burst into howls, unable to utter another meaningful sentence. Again, I was helpless, not knowing how to comfort her.

"Well, Ms. Woo," I finally said, "we may as well stop here today. We can continue to talk about your story on another day." She agreed and we said goodbye to each other.

I was still in disbelief that a summer camp activity had turned into such a shocking event. Could Ms. Woo have exaggerated the story? Could she have hidden any important facts? Regardless of the answers, it was an undeniable fact that she had lost her son and that her life had been ruined.

2.

The next week, I emailed Ms. Woo asking if she would like to continue talking with me about her ordeal. I was expecting a quick reply, but it did not come until five days later. 'Yes' was her answer. To my surprise, Ms. Woo did not cry when we resumed our interview.

"Ms. Woo," I said. "I just want the plain truth. Could you tell me the real reason why the court had decided to take away your 12-year-old son?"

"Well," she said hesitantly, "in fact, there was one thing I did not tell the news website. I thought it wasn't very good for my son."

"What was it, then?"

"He had a fight with his classmate at school when he was eleven," she said. "One morning, one of his classmates tripped him in the playground, and he fell. In the afternoon, he took revenge in the classroom. Something pretty bad happened, and the principal said that his classmate was taken to emergency in the hospital."

"Oh!" I uttered in shock.

"A chunk of flesh came off the boy's arm, leaving a deep hole there," she continued. "He was bleeding badly, and I was told his arm was broken."

"Oh, my!" I shuddered. It surely sounded more serious than most school fights.

Her son was eleven years old then. By law he was exempt from legal responsibility. I did not need to confirm it with her, but he would have been arrested by the police briefly and, once his age was verified, he would be released immediately.

While I was still trying to link this event with his CAS kidnapping, Ms. Woo continued to blast the justice system, accusing the CAS workers, the police, the CAS lawyers, and the judge of ganging up against her for the purpose of stealing her son.

"He used to be such a good boy. The only problem he had was that he was holding a book in his hand all day long. He read while eating breakfast, he read while eating lunch, he read while eating dinner. He even read under his duvet in bed with a flashlight after he had turned off the light in his bedroom. Before he got into trouble, he was determined to go to Harvard University.

"By now, after he had been taken away by CAS many times, he had changed. As I told you last time, he had become addicted to gaming. The case workers had told me that if he played computer games he would have more conversation topics with peers. They had even sent him to the public library and let him play computer games there for as long as he wanted, without signing in. The library workers gave him all the privileges. They were spying on him for the school.

"The CAS workers tricked him into writing another report against me, saying I had physically and verbally abused him and mentally tortured him, and so he did not want to come back home. Since he was twelve years old now, as I said last time, he could make his own decision whether to come home or stay with a foster family.

"Then one day—I was just dumbfounded, and I don't even remember which date it was—I was told to appear in court, where the judge ruled that I could not have my son back. Perhaps it was the damn kidnappers' strategy to tame my son. He was first put in the group home, as I said last time. Ever since then, I have never seen him again. It was only recently that, through the arrangements of one of his friends, I had a chance to talk with him on the phone."

To my disappointment, she started sobbing again, "He was such a nice boy. He is now twenty-one. After he was put with the bigger boys in the group home, they taught him to steal and do other bad things. He got into trouble with the police many times. It is CAS that has ruined my child."

"I still don't know the exact reason why they took away your son," I said.

"They simply told me that my son was a violent person and he might hurt me, and so he had to be taken away," she said. "That was a lie. He was such a nice child. He would never hurt me. CAS was paid according to the number of children under its care. The more children they kidnap, the more money they receive from the provincial government. Then they

197

put the children with families that want to make money—they often give the stolen kids to their friends. As everyone knows, the family gets more than $1000 per month for each child. I hear many childless couples, including same-sex couples, are all eager to adopt children from good families. They can only steal these children through CAS."

"Could you show me the ruling from the court?" I asked instead of commenting on her claims. I still did not know the exact reason why the judge ruled against her. Also, the incident in the classroom remained a mystery to me.

Ms. Woo complained about many other things, but she still did not indicate whether she would show me the ruling. It was 2:00 a.m.by now, and I had missed two hours of sleep already. Therefore, I said, "If you feel your constitutional rights have been violated, you can sue them. And, since you have told me you have contact with more than a hundred families who have been cruelly treated by CAS, you should form a coalition of CAS victims and take them to court. You can fight all the way to the Supreme Court of Canada." Then, we ended our long conversation for the second time.

3.

Another week later, Ms. Woo called me and asked, "Are you familiar with the justice system in Hong Kong?"

"Why are you asking?" I said, surprised

"What's the maximum jail time for assaulting someone there?" she asked.

"It's hard to guess," I said. "I am not a lawyer, and I am not a judge. It all depends on the nature of the assault, I guess." I was really baffled. "Why are you asking such questions?"

"Well." She hesitated. "It's my son. He hit his girlfriend's father in Hong Kong."

Your son again! I said to myself. "How bad was it?"

"He fell onto the floor and was taken to hospital. He was hospitalized for about twenty days," she said. "I have been sending money to him, and he has been released on bail. A lot of money already. Do you know if there are rental rooms in Hong Kong that cost less than $50 a night? I want to go there and help him."

"Are you sure your son really has got into trouble in Hong Kong?" I asked. "Could it be a scam? Could you have been sending money to a scammer?"

"It can't be a scam," she said. "He has given me his address in Toronto and asked me to move out his stuff and also his friend's, so that he could terminate his lease. He also asked me to remove his food from the fridge."

"Do you have his address?" I asked.

"Yes," she said.

"Did he give you the keys?"

"No. He just gave me his address," she said. "It's on Don Mills near Seneca College."

"Has he given you his landlord's phone number?" I said.

"No."

"Then how are you going to enter his place to take his food out of the fridge and move out his belongings?"

She remained silent.

"Since you have his address and it is so close to your home," said I, "Why not go over to make sure if he really has been living there?"

"There's no need. I think it's true," she said. "Could you find a friend or relative in Hong Kong to help me find a lawyer for him to get him back to Canada? Please, I beg you. If his sentence is more than two years, he cannot come back to Canada after he serves his time there. He can't go back to Asia, either. He has nowhere to live there. He came to Canada when he was six. He has no home there and doesn't know anyone there."

Oh, my Lord! I thought to myself. *If he really has broken the law in Hong Kong, he shall receive his fair judgment. If he has to go to jail, then he should do his time.* At this moment, I realized that her son must have become quite a different person. He was no longer the boy she knew.

She kept repeating that she would go to Hong Kong to rescue him. It was then that I started wondering: Maybe the Canadian court made the right decision. It may have saved her life. I had read three cases in the news about two sons and a daughter killing their own parents in Metro Toronto and Vancouver.

"My son said he wants to make up a story that someone else assaulted the father," Ms. Woo said. "He is confident that his girlfriend will side with him in court. She was the only witness, and there was no one else on the scene. Another plan he has is to escape from the Hong Kong authorities."

On hearing this, I decided she needed no help or advice from me. She would not listen to me anyway. Thus, I ended our conversation. I

199

was disappointed that I wasn't able to write a good story despite three interviews.

4.

Last Sunday, another CAS victim called me and asked me to forward Ms. Woo's document to her. I seized the opportunity to ask her about Ms. Woo's son.

"She has brought him back to Toronto," she said.

"How wonderful," I exclaimed. "But he can't be the same ten-year-old boy, and Ms. Woo shouldn't be surprised."

"You are right," she said.

"Is he working?" I asked, eager to know more.

"No. He isn't," she said.

"How does he make his living, then?" I asked.

"He told his mother he has plenty of money, and he doesn't need to work."

"Where does he get his money?"

"He told his mother if he needs money, he'll just break into someone's home or pry open someone's car, drive it off, and then sell it. In a good month, he can make half a million dollars," she said. "He is way richer than his mother."

I was lost in silence. A once naïve, lovely ten-year-old boy who could have become a Harvard scholar apparently attracted multiple predators. In the most legal manner they took custody of him, each trying to change him—physically, mentally, and morally—for their respective reasons, possibly malicious purposes that they would never admit or let the outside world know about. In the end, every predator found their prey too difficult to swallow. He has thus became a parasite that has come back to live on a system that created him.

Paradise gained, paradise lost. Hell in paradise, paradise in Hell. The only thing that remains unchanged is Ms. Woo's unwavering love for her brilliant boy.

Never Came Back

"I hate you, I hate this house, and I'm leaving for good!" Teenage Jed was furious that his father had destroyed his computer. He began flinging clothing into a reusable shopping bag.

"Go and don't ever come back," Mr. Brave shouted back, as furious as his son. Jed had left home once after a similar heated dispute, but having nowhere to go, he eventually came back home.

Mr. Brave regretted having bought the computer for him and allowing him to keep it in his bedroom. His original intention was to arm him with the tools to keep pace with rapidly developing information technology, enjoy some fun activities, and improve his grades at school. But two years later, everything had gone wrong.

Jed had become addicted to gaming, just like a gambling or drug addict. He couldn't sit or stand still, or sleep at night if he did not play on the computer for an hour or two, as though suffering withdrawal. If he had access to the computer, he would indulge in endless games and other content irrelevant to his study and life. Recently he had also taken to finding pornography online, with photographs of naked women in bright colors. His parents couldn't enumerate all his unhealthy activities. All they knew was that Jed was not the same boy they used to know.

They had tried to negotiate, hoping they could reduce his hours on the computer so he would have some left for schoolwork, or at least, go to the park once a day, or just out to the backyard. They had asked his teachers, school counselors, and school friends for assistance, but none of them could help. His father had imposed a rule that the power cord be plugged into a timer locked in a metal box, to keep him off it from midnight until 7:30 a.m., but Jed managed to pry it open and damaged the timer within a week. He was growing into an adult and his parents could not do much more.

On June 25, the parents received his final report card, showing he had failed five of his seven subjects, except physical education and home study, which everyone would pass as long as they attended half of the classes.

His father was so furious he simply took away the power cord. When Jed could not find it he left home, threatening to never come back to his hateful family, but when he could not find food and a place to stay, he returned, remorseful only that he had failed to make good on his pledge. His parents were relieved he came back but found no change in his behavior.

On December 19, a new report card triggered another quarrel. Jed not only had failed all seven subjects this term but had skipped half of his classes and was late on every one of the days he had attended.

"You've got to change, Jed," said his father. "You need to study. You need to go to school. You are in high school now, and soon you will be wanting to go to college or university. Your grades have to improve."

"I'm not interested in going to college or university. I don't see any point in going to college or university," Jed said.

"But what are you going to do after you finish high school, then?"

"Don't you worry about me," Jed said, his eyes still fixed on the monitor. "I will do better than you and Mom. You both finished university, but look how poor you are! You're still driving the old Honda that should have been dumped in the car graveyard long ago."

"Jed!" Mr. Brave shouted.

"What?" Jed said. "Leave me alone, and go away!"

"How dare you!" Mr. Brave seized the monitor and flung it to the floor with all his might.

It broke into pieces. "Go on, keep playing!" Mr. Brave said, feeling his blood pressure shooting up. He felt he might faint, or even have a heart attack. He stormed out of Jed's room only to bump into his surprised wife.

"That's the end of our relationship," shouted Jed, following his father out of the room.

Then came the conversation between father and son in the beginning.

As Jed threw his clothes into his bag, his father began helping, underscoring his happiness that Jed was leaving.

Later, as emotions cooled, the parents waited for Jed to return home. They waited up until midnight, but he did not show. Last time, he had come back before 11:00 p.m. They waited until 3:00 a.m., but he still did not appear. Then they began to worry. Where could he be? It was a cold December day, with the temperature dropping to minus 20 degrees Celsius.

They did not sleep a wink that night. When they turned on the morning news at 7:00 a.m. they were stunned to hear the first headline: Teenage boy found frozen to death under a maple tree in Owen Park. They did not need verification. The description of his clothes and bag matched those of their son.

Mrs. Brave fainted instantly, and Mr. Brave, who had never cried in his adult life, burst into uncontrollable sobs.

A Child in Pain

Bang! Bang! Bang!

Shaw was surprised by the thunderous knocking. Quickly he rose from the sofa and went to the front door, lifting up the curtain on the window.

My God, it's the police! He felt intimidated by the presence of two officers accompanied by two other people dressed in ordinary clothes.

"Police. Open the door," one of the officers said.

"Why are you here?" he said, opening the door cautiously. "I haven't broken any laws, nor have my wife and kids. May I see some ID?" Shaw said to the officer, who immediately presented his ID card to him.

"We're from the Children's Aid Society," said the woman in plain clothes. She showed her ID card to Shaw as well.

Shaw wondered briefly if they might be forged, not that he knew what they should look like. Not knowing what else to do, he opened the door wider to let them in.

"What's going on here?" the younger officer asked.

"What's going on?" repeated Shaw, baffled. "I don't know what's going on."

"Do you have any children?" the officer asked.

"Yes, I have two."

"Are they home?" He stared at Shaw.

"Yes," said Shaw, blinking.

"Is your wife home too?" The officer peered past him, into the living room and dining room.

"Yes," said Shaw, wondering why he was asking all these questions.

"Where are they?" the officer asked sternly.

"My daughter is drawing in the kitchen," said Shaw, pointing toward the kitchen door at the end of the hallway.

"Can we see her?" he said.

"Of course," said Shaw. The two CAS officials walked into the kitchen, where they surprised the seven-year-old girl, who immediately stopped drawing and fixed her eyes on them. Then they returned to Shaw.

"Where is your other child?" the woman asked.

"He's in the washroom, I think," said Shaw.

"And your wife?"

"She's in the washroom, too."

204

"Could you ask her to come here? We want to talk to her," she said.

Shaw shouted, "May, could you come out? The police and Children's Aid Society officials are here. They want to talk to you."

The officers heard groaning when May opened the washroom door.

"What were you doing in there?" the senior official asked. "We'd like to talk to you in private."

"If you don't mind," the younger officer said to Shaw, "we'll speak with you in a separate room."

"I don't mind at all," said Shaw. Thus, the younger officer and the male official from the Children's Aid Society started questioning May, while the senior officer and the female CAS official continued to question Shaw.

"Why was your boy groaning just now?" asked the police officer.

"He has trouble pooping," Shaw said. "He hasn't emptied his bowels for three or four days."

Asked the same question separately, May gave the same answer.

The officers seemed convinced. They walked out the door, whispering. Then they returned and called the parents and the two government officials together to see if they had any other questions.

"Mr. and Mrs. Shaw, you know your son has such severe constipation. He has been groaning in pain. Why haven't you taken him to the doctor?"

"We did. He has also taken the medications the doctor prescribed for him, but it isn't working yet," said May.

"Can you show us the medications?" the female CAS official asked.

May ran back into the washroom and immediately returned with two bottles. The police officers and the CAS officials looked at the date on the bottles and said, "Thank you."

"Mr. and Mrs. Shaw," said the senior officer, "your neighbor called us and told us she had heard a boy groaning in your house. She was worried about child abuse. As a rule, if someone calls to report possible child abuse, we are required to investigate. If severe child abuse exists, the Children's Aid Society may take charge of the child and place them with a caring family. You both appear to be loving parents. We would like to thank you for your cooperation."

Then they walked out the door, leaving Shaw and May in shock. They blinked at each other as if they had just woken up from a dream.

"My Daddy Touches Me"

Rick's daughter Chelsy is in senior kindergarten this year. Ms. White, her teacher, who was abused by her parents and cousins during her childhood, is very sensitive to any form of child abuse. She hates child predators more than she does murderers. She considers it her sacred duty to protect every child in her class and create the safest and healthiest environment for them possible.

"Boys and girls," Ms. White says when their first January class starts, "today, I want to teach you about child abuse. If your father beats you, it's called child abuse. If your mother hits you, it is called child abuse. If anyone touches your private parts, that is sexual abuse. You must never let anyone touch you there. If something like that happens and you don't know what to do, just let me know and I will help you. I will protect you, so don't be afraid to tell if anyone abuses you."

The children listen to her attentively. They seem to understand her, but not quite yet.

"Do you have any questions?" she asks, smiling kindly at the innocent faces.

Chelsy suddenly thinks of something, and her face reddens.

"Chelsy," says Ms. White, noticing her discomfort. "Do you want to say something?"

"Well, I don't know," Chelsy says.

"Don't be afraid. Just speak up," Ms. White says.

"My daddy touches me every day," Chelsy says, looking ashamed.

Ms. White becomes alert.

"Class, we're going to take a short break. You can play any games you like, but just don't make any noise. I'll just be outside in the hall for a moment."

She beckons Chelsy outside into the hallway with her and closes the door, glancing back quickly through the window to keep an eye on the class.

"Where exactly does your father touch you?" she asks.

"Where the pee comes out," Chelsy says, and points toward her private parts.

"Are you kidding?" Ms. White can't believe her ears. "How long has he been touching you?"

"Since last week."

To Ms. White, no other form of child abuse is more serious than this. She returns to the classroom with Chelsy, and when the children go outside for recess, she checks in at the principal's office to tell him what she has heard. The principal immediately reports the father's suspected criminal activity to the police.

Shortly afterward, four police officers knock on the front door of Chelsy's home. There is no answer for some time, and the police, becoming impatient, kick it open. Rick has just come up from the basement, where he was doing laundry. Rick is home during the day because his company was recently sold to a foreign investor, which resulted in his layoff.

"What are you doing here?" Rick, in shock, steps back, wide-eyed. The police have their guns out, though he knows he has done nothing wrong.

"You are under arrest. Put your hands above your head and walk backwards toward us."

"What? Why am I under arrest? I haven't done anything wrong."

"You are being charged with sexual assault of a minor. Your daughter."

"Sexual assault?" shouts Rick. "What nonsense are you talking about? How dare you insult my character?" Frantic, he grabs a pair of scissors from the hall table and charges the officer who just spoke.

Bang! Bang! Bang! Merciless shots are fired at him. Blood gushes from Rick's chest. He dies instantly.

Rick's wife, who has just pulled up in the driveway, is horrified when she hears gunshots inside her home. She calls 911 at once, saying someone is in their home and she heard multiple gunshots.

Three more police cruisers arrive within minutes and take positions around the house, until they realize the so-called intruders are other police. Rick's wife enters the house and collapses beside her husband's body in horror.

When she regains consciousness, the police explain to her that her husband not only resisted arrest but had charged at them with a dangerous weapon. They tell her they had ordered him to surrender but he refused. They opened fire in self-defense. The unfortunate result was a death no one wanted to see.

"But why did you come to our house in the first place?" she asks.

"Your daughter reported to the school that your husband had been touching her private parts. That qualifies as possible sexual assault."

207

"Chelsy? But how could you take a five-year-old's words seriously? Why didn't you call me before you came or when you arrived? I know what was going on. I know it better than any one of you! Oh, God!" She starts howling, but it is too late. "Give me back my husband. He is the best man in the world. He is the best father in the world, you murderers! You have killed an innocent man. May God punish all of you who have abused your power!"

"Be careful. We don't want to have to arrest you," they warn her.

She keeps howling as detectives arrive. She gives them her daughter's pediatrician's name. "Call her. She'll tell you what my husband was doing to my daughter."

The detective steps out of the house and places the call.

"Yes, I certainly know Chelsy's father," said the pediatrician. "Rick is a very good dad. She caught an infection in her pubic area, probably from swimming classes in school. He brought her to me and I saw her last week. I prescribed medications for her. She takes antibiotics four times a day and her father was asked to apply the medicinal cream on her privates—anywhere that is red and itchy, inside or outside. In an ideal world, the mother is the best person to do it, but Chelsy's mother has a full-time job, as far as I know. So I asked the father do it for the young daughter. Is there any issue?"

"Thank you for sharing the information with us," said the detective. "We will just end our conversation here."

Back in the classroom, Ms. White smiles with satisfaction when she thinks of what she has done for Chelsy.

A Daughter That Is Not

Carol, an immigrant from Asia, is a petrochemical engineer registered in Ontario, Alberta, and British Columbia in Canada. Competitive and competent, she re-established herself in the new country much faster than most of her peers. In the first year she secured a permanent job with a six-figure salary. In her second year, she bought her first home in Toronto. In the third, at the age of thirty-seven, she became a mother. With a good car and a house in her possession, she fulfilled the North American dream in less than half of the time it takes other newcomers. Her baby girl, Joy, immediately became the most important person in her life. Giggling and laughter resounded in her home from morning till night.

"Your daughter looks just like you. She's so beautiful." Every friend who visited her would flatter her with the same praise. Carol would smile from ear to ear.

From kindergarten through Grade 7, Joy was a top achiever in every subject she took. Carol was so proud of her academic success, grinning at her when she gazed at her sitting on the sofa, at the table, and in bed. She was affectionate, hugging and kissing her daughter as often as appropriate. She thought her daughter was a darling, until her fifteenth birthday, when she suddenly became a stranger.

"Mom, I need to tell you something important. I've felt for a long time, deep inside, that I'm really a boy. I know you think of me as your little girl, but I really want to live as a boy, as a man eventually. That's just who I am. I'd appreciate it if you could call me Jay instead of Joy, that is, if you want to. At school, they all call me Jay now," Joy said after breakfast on her birthday.

"What?" Carol was shocked. "What do you mean?"

"It's all right. The doctor has been helping me for the past couple of years, along with the psychologist he referred me to. You must have noticed that I haven't been developing breasts like the girls. That's because I've been taking a hormone medication for a while, a puberty blocker." Carol's gaze went to her daughter's chest and arms, and she suddenly realized her strong muscles looked more like those of a young man.

"I still don't understand." Carol frowned. "You said you want to be a man? How is it possible? You've been taking hormone medications? But why didn't you tell me earlier?"

209

"I knew you wouldn't let me do this. But you can't stop me, not legally," Joy said.

"What are you talking about?" said Carol, in shock. "I have no right to know?"

"That's the law," Joy said. "The school counselor told me the doctors and teachers have no right to tell you if I don't want them to."

"What kind of law is that? Why don't parents have the right to know?" said Carol.

"I don't know," said Joy. "They said I don't need to let you know, but I love you and I decided I wanted to tell you now, myself."

"How exactly can you change into a man?" said Carol.

"Something like, the doctor will flatten my breasts, and build a penis for me," she said. "But that won't happen for a while. The hormone blocker was a way of giving me time to think about it."

"It's such an important decision. You should have let me know before you started taking medications," said Carol.

"Sorry, Mom. I didn't know you would want to know I was transgender," Joy said. "It's exciting, Mom. I'm going to be the person I want to be. I was miserable trying to fit in with the girls, when I just never felt like I was one, deep inside."

"I am ignorant, and I am curious. Will this mean you can never have a baby?"

"No, mom, not if I go through with the full surgery. It means taking out my original reproductive system. Sorry."

Carol's face dropped. The beautiful daughter she had been proud of was becoming a man. As a mother, she did not even have the right to know, and her underage daughter did not need her approval.

Carol was wondering who was behind all this. She looked as if had been struck by a thunderbolt. Fifteen years ago, she had been full of the joy of motherhood. Now she felt like she had lost half of her body and soul.

Misfortunes seldom come alone. The following month, she and her husband finalized their divorce. She found comfort after meeting a man at a mutual friend's Christmas party, a man who fell in love with her and seemed compatible. At least, he seemed more understanding and considerate than her ex-husband. The next year, they married. Her new husband, who owned his own home, moved into her house after the marriage.

Unfortunately, Joy resented the new stepfather. She openly showed him a lack of respect, putting Carol in the middle of their conflict. They managed to get along somehow, often like strangers, but sometimes like neighbors and colleagues. Nothing out of the ordinary happened until nearly three years later, when Carol fell while shopping in the Scarborough Town Centre mall.

Her pain was acute, but she thought it was temporary and that she would recover after some rest and good treatment. But her injury turned out to be much worse than she had thought. Eventually she became bedridden, unable even to look after herself, let alone Joy.

Throughout these difficult days, her Canadian-born husband had to cook, help her with her bath, carry her to the toilet and change her diapers. He also had to drive Joy to school and do all the other household chores. How grateful Carol felt for all his meticulous care.

Strong painkillers and other medications failed to improve Carol's condition while producing unpleasant side effects. One day in May, she felt overwhelmed by stress and called 911 for an ambulance. Hospital care saved her life, and after her discharge her husband continued to look after her. Three weeks later, to ensure she would receive the best care possible, he took her to his own home instead.

As Joy was not quite eighteen, Carol asked her ex-husband to come to her home to stay with her overnight, which he happily did.

Joy began talking in earnest about surgery after Carol moved to her new husband's home. Carol, anxious and worried about this, advised Joy to wait, because she had read about girls who had changed their gender only to regret it later.

"It's not only a long and painful surgical procedure, but it is dangerous," she said, but Joy would not listen. She had already made plans for the surgery, and the cost, probably around $150,000, would be covered by OHIP. Once she was eighteen, she could have it whenever Joy and the doctors thought they were ready.

The Children's Aid Society had played an important role in legally protecting Joy from potential harm and harassment by her parents. Carol felt CAS ignored her rights and unfairly sided with her daughter.

"If you want to take your mom's calls, you can. If you don't want to, you don't need to," a CAS worker told Joy. "If she ever threatens you, just let us know. We will call the police and have her arrested right away."

Shortly after Carol's injury, Joy continued going to school, but after her stepfather took her mother into his home, she dropped out. She used to do chores around the house and even cooked sometimes, but now she did nothing. Her bed, her room, the entire house was a mess, and she did not care. Nor did she seem to care much for the mother who was unable to walk or work

Loathing her stepfather, she lied to CAS that he had sexually harassed her and had him arrested. He had to spend $40,000 hiring a lawyer to prove his innocence. Nonetheless, Carol continued to love her. She was just frustrated and furious that she had lost her once lovely daughter who brought her joy and laughter every day.

"Why is life so cruel to me!" she wailed.

She had ended up losing her good health, her professional job, and her beloved daughter.

Parents' Meeting on LGBTQ2+ Issues

"Harri, don't we have more important things to talk about than LG-whatever-you-call-it issues?" said an agitated Joe, whose daughter was in Grade 11. "I am sick of this. Our kids spend all their time talking about tolerance, respect, equality, political correctness every day, instead of studying. Canada is becoming a transgender country under the current Prime Minister's leadership. He calls himself a proud feminist, but can't he do better than that? We all respect the homosexuals, but honestly, many parents and I don't care about their issues. I am worried about my children's schoolwork. I just don't care about homosexual issues and politics."

"You don't care about them, but they care about you!" answered Harri, chair of the school council. "That is exactly the reason why we have this topic on the agenda. I hope you will find tonight's information useful."

"I hope so, too," said Joe ironically, looking unconvinced.

It was another school council meeting at McDowald High School. Parents who cared about their children's education and were able to attend were sitting around an 8-by-4-foot table, chatting about inflation, home invasions, car thefts, and the Prime Minister's latest attack on the premier of Alberta. At 7:05 p.m. the presiding secretary declared the start of their meeting. She announced their agenda, surprising every parent when she read out loud the most important activity of the evening: "LGBTQ2+ issues parents must know." Then, she gave the floor to the school council chair, Harrilo, whom they called Harri, triggering the response from Joe at the beginning of this story.

"Good evening, everyone," Harri said. "I will begin with the most important and most sensitive issue in Canada today. I am not an expert on the topic. I may have read a little bit more than some of you have, but whatever I say at this meeting must not be taken as anti- or pro-LGBTQ2+. I'm elected by you, the parents, so I just want to act in the best interest of the parents and the students. To begin with, the LGBTQ2+ people are like any other community in our country. They are just like you and me. They could be your husband, wife, boyfriend, girlfriend, son, daughter, colleague, or your neighbor. They work, pay taxes, and live their own life, just like you and me. Personally, I respect them in the same way I do all other Canadians. What I want to stress is that I am not promoting the LGBTQ2+ mission or their relevant issues. Neither am I anti-LGBTQ2+."

The tight muscles on Joe's face loosened, as he nodded indifferently.

"Why do parents need to know about some basic LGBTQ2+ issues?" Harri swept his eyes across the parents' faces. "If you don't know what is going on, you may end up breaking the law. You may end up having a son deciding he is really a girl or a nonbinary child, or a girl turning into a boy or a nonbinary person. All this may happen without your knowledge, and whatever your children decide to do is protected by government policies. You may have no say in it. Don't misunderstand me. Don't think that I am attacking the present policies or the children's rights. I am not. I'm just sharing with you what I have read recently about these important issues."

Joe raised his hand and said, "Could you be a bit more specific and come straight to the point, Harri? It sounds very disturbing. I am really worried. How could my daughter suddenly become a boy or something neither a boy nor a girl? And could a girl all of a sudden become a boy, or someone who is neither a boy nor a girl? Sounds like magic!"

"Joe, it's not magic, and it does not happen suddenly. According to my limited knowledge, in most cases, it happens gradually, step by step. I know parents may be concerned. Maybe you could allow me to finish a brief intro to the topic first, so that you will have a basic idea what it's all about, but of course, do feel free to interrupt me and ask questions." He paused. Joe and the other parents nodded in agreement.

"Do you know what is at issue between the Prime Minister and the premier of Alberta?" continued Harri, looking from left to right. "More than half of you are shaking your heads. Let me brief you on what they're fighting about. First, there was this headline last Friday: Prime Minister of Canada blasting premier of Alberta, denouncing her 'most anti-LGBT policies of anywhere in the country.' He attacks her for misplacing her energy and fighting 'against vulnerable LGBT youth.' The news flooded the media on February 2. The powerful, united LGBTQ2+ community immediately joined the Prime Minister and many newspapers and TV channels in condemning the premier. They are also threatening to take her government to court if she goes ahead with her agenda."

"What did she do exactly?" asked Kate, whose son was in Grade 10.

"I will soon come to that," said Harri. "They are outraged that the premier and her government claim that when it comes to sex education and gender identification of the students, schoolteachers have more

214

rights than parents do. She believes that innocent schoolchildren would be better protected if parents are involved in any life-altering decision making.

"Therefore, her government has proposed new policies that will ban sex reassignment surgery for minors and forbid the use of puberty blockers and cross-sex hormones on children aged fifteen or younger. Older youth who wish to take hormones and blockers can still do so but will need the support of their parents, doctor, and psychologist, with exceptions to be made for youth who have already commenced treatment. School officials will need to obtain parental consent before recognizing any new names or pronouns for students under the age of sixteen.

"Older students will not need this consent to officially change their names or pronouns, but parents still need to be notified should such changes occur. In fact, her proposed new policies are not new. *National Post* reports that Norway, Sweden, and Finland have recently restricted access to hormones and surgery and adopted a cautious approach to other important transgender issues until the phenomenon can be better understood.

"The Alberta government believes these are not games that children can afford to play and lose without knowing what they are doing and what will happen to them before adulthood. As it appears, Alberta is just clamping down on pediatric transition. It would continue to provide gender-affirming care for transgender adults.

"In this regard, Alberta is firm: any help for children wanting to transition behind their parents' backs will no longer be permitted in the province. Of the 1,500 comments left after the *National Post* news article that reports her proposed policies, the overwhelming majority fully support the premier."

"Her proposed policies don't sound unreasonable to me," said Kate, "but what right does the Prime Minister have to intervene in Alberta's policies?"

"Perhaps he thinks Alberta is sabotaging what he has been doing for a fragile group. The federal government created a law to protect LGBTQ2+ people in 2016. Since then, their life has changed. True or not, some people even complain that they have more rights than other Canadians now."

"Harri, do you happen to know how many people in Canada belong to the LGBTQ2+ group?" Kate asked.

"The number of people who identify as LGBTQ2+ has increased rapidly since 2016," said Harri. "According to Statistics Canada, 'In May 2021, there were 59,460 people in Canada aged fifteen and older living in a private household who were transgender (0.19%) and 41,355 who were nonbinary (0.14%).' The two groups combined would be over 100,000. In 2024, logically the number could have increased, and the other unconfirmed groups are not included yet. Though unknown, a significant number of schoolchildren may have grown up to join the LGBTQ2+ group, so we should not be surprised if the number is doubled today. By the way, research shows that the suicide rate of transgender people is forty percent higher than that of the general population."

"I really hate to ask," said Kate, "but when a person decides to change his or her sex, do they change their private parts?"

"Many of them do, eventually, usually as adults," said Harri.

"How do they do it?" she said, looking shamefaced.

"It depends. These are complex procedures," said Harri. "This may sound graphic. If you feel uncomfortable, please just ignore my answer. Since you have asked, I will share with you what I know about the procedures. For a female to change to a male, the most thorough procedure involves flattening her breasts and removing her entire uterus and both ovaries, which by the way will result in many changes in her body. After that, she will have a neopenis made from her own skin, among other surgical issues. The neopenis is built on her clitoris. All these surgeries are irreversible. If she regrets this change some day, she would not be able to restore all the lost organs. For a male, full transition means having his genitalia removed and having a fake vagina made from his own private parts. The procedure has similar consequences. My humble opinion is that leaving this important decision to be made by people aged eighteen or older seems reasonable and appropriate. The premier has not gone too far. When the Prime Minister attacked her on this issue, she said the Prime Minister was being hypocritical, because surgeries and other treatment for transgender people eighteen or older is covered by the health system to the tune of $75,000, but that money isn't allocated to children under eighteen. Indirectly, she claims, the Prime Minister also believes this important decision should be made by adults."

"It's all disgusting!" said a new voice, drawing Harri's attention.

"Please don't use that word," said Harri. "It could be misunderstood and misinterpreted. Some people have lost their jobs because they have

216

shared a personal opinion on a group chat that was not even supposed to be public."

"Can transgender people give birth to children?" Joe asked.

"Not usually, but I have read two news stories about trans couples giving birth to babies," said Harri.

"How does it happen?" Joe asked.

"Couples who have not removed their original reproductive systems have that opportunity, I suppose," Harri said.

"As parents, how can we ensure that our children will grow up in the normal way?" asked Kate. "And could there be predators trying to harm our children? I'm scared because I have two smaller children, a seven-year-old boy and a nine-year-old girl."

"Good question. I am not able to answer your question, but I can tell you what I read in a *New York Post* news article. It's a report that said pharmaceutical businesses, which are among the biggest and richest companies in America, rake in hundreds of millions of dollars from selling hormone treatments. Once a young person starts hormone treatment, they become a very stable consumer of their products—often lifetime. These companies can set their prices at a high level just to benefit themselves at the expense of the young consumers.

"Another point you may want to be reminded of is that a growing number of children's books promote LGBTQ2+ thinking. It's okay for small children to read books about how normal a two-father and two-mother family is. It is the book's hidden message that may matter more. There's no problem telling others how kind and how great any community is, but parents just need to be aware of what their children are reading and learning.

"Some parents don't even want teachers and schools to teach sex and gender topics in the classroom. They consider it as an ideological, religious, or cultural issue that should not be taught to children before they can make the best choices for themselves. And that is another area where parents, teachers, and the government often get into fights. I don't know how to comment on these issues, and I honestly don't know if there is any right or wrong answer."

"Harri," said Joe, "I am truly grateful to you for bringing our attention to these important issues. Are there any other important things you want us to know about? I mean things that are a threat to our kids."

"There's the same old drug issue parents should also be aware of. It has not gotten better. In fact, it has gotten worse, because the government has been too helpful, in a way. Again, this is my personal opinion, and I may be wrong."

"That also worries me, Harri, even if it is just as bad as before," said Joe.

"As you all know," said Harri, "the federal government has legalized marijuana and decriminalized the personal use of hard drugs. The intention was good, but this has indirectly encouraged more teenagers to try drugs and created more addicts since his law came into effect. As you all know, some provinces have set up supervised injection centers to keep drug addicts from dying of overdoses. But, as recently reported, there are more overdoses and more addicts than ever before."

"What is becoming of this country?" Kate sighed.

"The world is changing. Canada is changing. Are we changing for the better or worse? I don't know," said Harri. "Do you have any other questions?"

"Could you tell us what that long acronym stands for?" said Kate. "I am really embarrassed that I don't know."

"Don't worry, you're not alone," said Harri. "Me, too. I used to have trouble even with the previous form, without the '2.' Originally I only knew the two words *lesbian* and *gay*, so I only knew for sure what LG referred to. But the longer the acronym became, the harder it was for me to remember. Wouldn't it be a joke that a so-called scholar with a so-called PhD in linguistics can't even tell you what LGBTQ2+ refers to? But that's life, my dear friends. Luckily, I am retired, so no one could force me to resign from my job for that reason. Now, putting all that aside, LGBTQ2+ stands for "lesbians, gay, bisexual, transgender, queer or questioning, two-spirited people, and more. I quote that from a government document. Also, I know the words, but I may not know their exact meanings, especially *questioning* and *two-spirited*. Please don't laugh at me. If anyone of you can explain those more fully, I am ready to learn."

"Thank you, Harri," said a new voice. "I have one more confusing point. Could tell us what pronouns we should be using for ourselves?"

"Good question! I had the same question until not too long ago. Honestly, I had never thought I would live to see the day when I did not know what pronouns stood for me. I guess it depends on who you think you are. Generally speaking, if you think you are a woman, then *she/her/hers*. If you think you are a traditional male, then *he/him/his*."

"What if we don't indicate our pronouns in the forms that we have to fill out?" said Kate. "Isn't it clear we are what we are and who we are?"

"Well," said Harri, "it could be misinterpreted as some form of disrespect or exclusion or resistance against the LGBTQ2+ people. I don't know, but it could be something negative. They have created a social atmosphere where everyone must be acting in conformity with the trend."

"How do you identify yourself?" said Joe. "What pronouns do you use for yourself?"

"*Shit*," said Harri.

Everyone looked at him with wide eyes.

"You are all surprised, aren't you?" said Harri. "I really mean it, but I dare not use it officially. I'm just worried they may have the same reaction as you do if I call myself *shit* openly. Since you are all surprised, I may as well tell you how this *shit* has come about."

Everyone frowned, though they knew he was not joking.

"In this case, I am also a trendy person. I have heard that everyone in Canada can call themselves a female or male at will. If I am not mistaken, if you think you are female, you can go to the women's washroom. If you think you are male, you can go to the men's. Probably, you can call yourself a male in the morning and a female in the afternoon and something else at night. Then, I thought, 'Why can't I also call myself a thing on the third day?' So thinking, I am *she/he/it*. To make it easier for others to refer to me, I thought I might as well combine the three pronouns into one and use it as a subjective, possessive and objective pronoun—three in one. Therefore, I have this compound pronoun for myself, *shit*. Though it does not sound as good as *sweet*, *love*, and *sex*, it is an identifier for me. But, please, it is not a noun. It is Harri's 3-in-1 pronoun. Do you like my *shit*?"

Laughter roared in the meeting room.

www.ingramcontent.com/pod-product-compliance
Lightning Source LLC
Chambersburg PA
CBHW060358030726
47497CB00003B/771